# SHATTERED

## Marti Jones

## *Shattered*

Copyright © 2024 by Marti Jones.

All rights reserved. No part of this publication may be reproduced, distributed, or transmitted in any form or by any means, including photocopying, recording, or other electronic or mechanical methods, without the written consent of the publisher. The only exceptions are for brief quotations included in critical reviews and other noncommercial uses permitted by copyright law.

**MILTON & HUGO L.L.C.**
4407 Park Ave., Suite 5
Union City, NJ 07087, USA

**Website:** *www. miltonandhugo.com*
**Hotline:** *1- 888-778-0033*
**Email:** *info@miltonandhugo.com*

Ordering Information:
Quantity sales. Special discounts are granted to corporations, associations, and other organizations. For more information on these discounts, please reach out to the publisher using the contact information provided above.

| Library of Congress Control Number: | 2024911208 |
|---|---|
| ISBN-13: 979-8-89285-119-0 | [Paperback Edition] |
| 979-8-89285-120-6 | [Hardback Edition] |
| 979-8-89285-118-3 | [Digital Edition] |

Rev. date: 06/04/2024

# ACKNOWLEDGEMENTS

I would like to express my sincere appreciation to my husband, Sam, for being so supportive and patient with me throughout the entire process of this book. Thank you for the many nights you endured microwave dinners and spending lonely evenings without complaining, while I hibernated in the den writing into the wee hours of the morning.

I feel indebted to my daughter, Jenifer, for her tireless effort in proofreading and editing that involved many long hours. Thank you for your ability in sentence structure, missed punctuation, and keeping me using the right tense throughout. Also, for helping me in researching the culture of that era. I don't want to forget the contribution that your husband Kirk made. Thanks, Kirk, first and foremost, for the many hours you allowed Jenifer to work on this project with me and secondly for your appreciated two cents worth from time to time.

I am so grateful to my extremely artistic grandchild, Kieran, who designed my book cover. Thank you for working so diligently in delivering my concept of the cover and for capturing the essence of the story so perfectly.

A shout out to my publisher Milton and Hugo. Thank you for your patience and for taking me step by step from start to finish.

Thanks, also to my friends and family for their encouragement, support, and patience. It's been a long time coming.

Last but not least, thank you God for giving me the inspiration, the motivation and tenacity to see this project completed.

*Sounds of one writhing in pain were heard by neighbors who ran to help. Only to find someone on the floor screaming, "I've been poisoned! I've been poisoned!" while another looked on laughing like a banshee...*

# Chapter 1

February 1911

It was a cold and blustery Sunday afternoon. The sun peeked ever so slightly through the low-hanging clouds that promised snow before the day ended. The bare, skeleton-like branches of the trees were slowly dripping water onto the ground. The accumulation of ice that had formed on them from the previous damp, cold night was beginning to melt. Many of the town's people were heading home from attending the little community church that sat in the middle of town. Whether they walked or rode in horse-drawn buggies, they were all hurrying to their warm homes to enjoy a typical Sunday afternoon with family. It would be no different this afternoon at Lily and James Miller's home.

Lily had risen early that morning to prepare for the noon meal as she always did on Sunday mornings before getting ready for church. She stoked the fire in the old cook stove and put on a pot of coffee. James would be up shortly. She wanted to make sure his coffee was ready, and breakfast was nearly done when he lumbered out of the bedroom to the kitchen table. It was about the only time she and James had together to talk when he was sober, and she took advantage of that time.

James provided well for the family through his farrier business. With the many farms that were scattered throughout the countryside, there were a lot of farm animals whose hooves needed cleaning and trimming, and horses that needed shoeing on a regular basis. He worked in conjunction with the town's veterinary clinic and the blacksmith, Clyde, who smithed the shoes for the horses. Clyde and James became good buddies and spent many nights in James' barn playing cards and drinking around the old wood stove that James had placed in the center of the barn. Lily rarely saw James because he was always up before the crack of dawn and would not get home until after dark. He would sometimes come home famished, demanding to be fed before heading out to the barn where he would meet up with Clyde. Other times, he would not go to the house at all but would just go straight to the barn, start a fire, grab a drink, and kick back. She never knew if he would be home expecting to be fed, or even know what kind of mood he would be in, but she always needed to be prepared. Whenever she complained about never knowing what to expect each evening, he would be quick to remind her that he was supplying the family with what they needed, and the case would be closed. She knew money wasn't everything. She longed for his companionship and for him to spend time with the family. It was for their beloved family that Lily would rise early each Sunday morning to begin preparing Sunday dinner. The girls had grown up, married, and moved on with their lives, except for Emily.

There was Amanda, their oldest, who married Jake after his wife died during childbirth, leaving him with a precious baby boy. Jake's wife's name was Charlotte, so Jake thought it appropriate to name the baby Charlie. Jake had an established dairy farm about a mile down the road, where Amanda's family got their milk. After Jake's wife died, Amanda babysat Charlie numerous times and fell in love with the little fellow. Charlie wasn't the only one Amanda fell in love with.

Amanda would always ask her mama, "Do we need more milk?" And then she made sure she was the one who fetched it. She would tell her that she wanted to go play with the baby, but Lily knew there was more to it than just seeing the baby. So, it didn't surprise anyone when they started courting each other and eventually got married. She became a great stand-in mother for little Charlie and then to their own little one, Willie.

Then there was Sarah, their middle child, married at a young age to a young man with whom she attended school. Harry was the only boy in his family and was a big help to his father running their farm. Lily never quite understood how James was convinced to let Sarah marry so young. Sarah and Harry must have caught him in a vulnerable frame of mind, or perhaps he just wanted her out of the house, since they didn't get along. For whatever reason, James gave his permission. They had lived with Harry's family until he built a small cabin on the family property for himself and Sarah.

Lastly, there was Emily, Mama's baby girl. She was their youngest, who was fifteen and blossoming into a young lady, but it seemed James didn't even notice.

Lily would tell Emily, "You will always be my baby no matter how old you are."

When Emily became the only one at home, Lily spent a lot of one-on-one time with her, teaching her how to cook, sew, garden, and keep a clean house. She was her mama's girl.

Something was different about this Sunday morning. Lily was not feeling quite right. She had not slept well the night before so attributed her tiredness to lack of sleep. James, with hair askew came out of the bedroom, which was just off the kitchen, pulled out a kitchen chair and noisily dragged it across the wooden floor before plopping down in it. Lily placed a cup of hot coffee in front of him and fixed him a plate of scrambled eggs and ham. He gruffly thanked her and then buried his nose in his cup of coffee.

As Lily busied herself around the kitchen preparing the noon meal, she would always start the conversation by asking James, "Going to church with me this morning?" even though she knew what the answer would be.

Although he would never attend church with her, fortunately, he never gave her or any of the girl's grief about going. She poured herself a cup of coffee and sat down at the table across from him.

"You know," she said, "today being Sunday, the family will be here for dinner, and I would really like for you to please make time to be here and eat with everyone and spend some time with the grandchildren." He just grunted and plopped his empty coffee cup in front of her.

Most of the time he would comply but would never stay long. *I have things to do*, he would always say.

Lily put the finishing touches on her Sunday dinner, carefully put the pan with the roast and vegetables in the oven and went up to the loft to wake Emily. To her surprise, she was already up and getting dressed. Emily noticed that her mother was breathing heavily.

"Mama, why are you so out of breath?" she asked.

"Oh," Lily replied, "I think I came up the stairs too quickly. We need to hurry now because we are a little behind schedule. Papa has the buggy ready for us."

James meandered around doing his usual Sunday routine of cleaning and sharpening his farrier tools, getting his schedule of appointments worked out for the week, and visiting some of his neighboring friends.

Lily and Emily met Amanda, Sarah, and their families at church and afterward made their way to Mama's house for dinner, as usual. The aroma of the roast filled their nostrils as soon as they entered the cabin.

"Oh yum," Sarah said, "that smells wonderful and I'm so hungry."

The girls began pitching in by setting the table, all the while chattering over one another about what was going on in each of their lives. Emily and the boys went to the sitting room where Emily pulled out the toy box filled with wooden blocks and trucks for Willie, who was three, and a stack of board games for Charlie, who was seven. Charlie pulled the checkerboard from the stack of games, and he and Emily played a game of checkers, his favorite, while Willie played with the wooden blocks and trucks. Jake and Harry went out on the back porch to be able to hear themselves think over the girl's chatter and talked about the farming business.

The house was filled with chatter and Lily loved it. She loved the warm feeling she got when all her girls were around her and she enjoyed presenting them with a good homemade dinner. The house was small and seemed even smaller when everyone gathered there, but it just made for a sweet closeness. The cabin was mainly a large room known as the kitchen. It served not only as a kitchen but also as a dining room, family room, and meeting room. Lily and James' bedroom was off the kitchen, nestled beneath the loft, as well as a room known as the sitting room, which became the toy room when the children were there. There were two bedrooms in the loft, and now that Amanda and Sarah had moved out, one was used for a sewing room, and one was Emily's bedroom.

Just as they were ready to sit down for dinner, to everyone's amazement, James came through the door. For once, he was in a good mood too, which was an even more welcoming site.

"Papa, so good to see you," Amanda said, "I was afraid we wouldn't get to see you today."—she pulled out a chair between Harry and Jake—"Sit here Papa, and you fellows can catch up on things."

"Fat chance of that. How do you think we will be able to hear one another over you four hens chattering away?" Harry teased.

They all laughed. Lily was so pleased that James had made it home in time to eat with everyone. She settled in her chair taking it all in.

After dinner, Harry and Jake went into the sitting room to play with the boys. James, of course, had things to do. He excused himself and disappeared.

The girls stayed around the table to talk and enjoy Mama's company.

"Mama," Sarah began, "I don't know how you put up with the way Papa treats you. He shows you no respect. He never takes part in anything with the family. He never helps you around here. He only makes demands, and only thinks about himself. Oh, Mama, I just hate him."

"Now, now Sarah, you're not to hate anyone. You can hate what they do, but not the person. He's a good man, he really is. He hasn't always been like this. There was a time when he didn't drink so much. Life has taken its toll on him, and he has turned to the bottle."

"But I still don't know how you put up with him," Sarah continued. "He's running you ragged. You look so tired these days."

"I'm just fine," Mama said and gently patted Sarah's hand. "Yes, he may do all those things you said, but God helps me see the good in him. I love him and I know deep down, he loves me too. I pray for him every day. I pray that he will find his peace in God like I do instead of trying to find it at the bottom of a bottle. Until then, I will trust God to take care of me. I pray for all of you every day."

"I know Mama and we pray for you too." Sarah sighed.

"Enough of this, let's get this kitchen cleaned up," Mama said and smiled lovingly at her girls.

The girls began cleaning up the kitchen and as they were doing the dishes, they noticed that Mama was sitting at the table watching them work. This was very unusual because she was usually the one orchestrating the cleanup. They asked her if she was alright.

"Yes, I'm just tired from not getting a good night's sleep last night," she explained. "I just need to sit for a spell."

The girls continued with the dishes and when they were finished, they decided it was time to go.

"Mama," Amanda said, "we're going to go now so you can get to bed early and get a good night's sleep. Hopefully you will feel better in the morning."

Mama did not argue with them because she really didn't feel well. Amanda went into the sitting room to find that Harry and Jake had both fallen asleep on the floor while the boys played with the scattered toys.

She nudged them with her toe. "Hey, wake up. And you little fellows, put up the toys and get your coats. It's time to go."

"You need to bundle up good, it looks like the wind is picking up and the temperature is dropping," Mama said. "But first, come here boys and give me a hug and a kiss before you leave."

She gave them butterfly kisses. They squirmed and giggled and ran off to pick up toys and get their coats.

Both Sarah and Amanda kissed Mama goodbye and reminded her to get to bed early.

"Make sure she does, Emily," Sarah said.

"I will," replied Emily as she skipped across the floor to give them hugs and kisses goodbye.

After they left, Emily went up to her room to read while Lily prepared for bed. "Thank you, Lord, for giving us such a wonderful day," Lily prayed, as she drifted off to sleep.

## Chapter

# 2

Two men, James and the town doctor, dismounted their horses and quickly tethered them to a nearby tree. It was the wee hours of a very cold Monday morning in February. The moon, still high in the sky, shone on a new skiff of snow that brightened the area. A dim light from an oil lamp shone from the window of the small log cabin. They wasted no time, ran to the cabin, and entered, not bothering to kick off the snow from their boots.

"She's in here," James said. He grabbed the lamp from the table and ushered the doctor into the cozy little bedroom where his wife lay. The doctor quickly checked for a pulse but found none. Even though James headed out to fetch the doctor as soon as he realized there was a problem, they were too late. James knelt by the bed in disbelief. She lay there just as if she were asleep, yet cold and lifeless. He got up and stumbled to the kitchen, slumped into a chair, and sobbed.

Emily was snuggled in her bed, sound asleep, when she was awakened by strange noises coming from the kitchen. Startled, she pulled the covers away from her chin and stretched her neck to listen. A chair scraped across the floor, floorboards squeaked from someone's heavy steps, and she heard muffled sounds as though someone was crying. She looked around the room. Through the lace curtains that hung at her little window, she could see the pink hue across the sky as the sun was beginning to rise. She then heard the front door close and a horse whinny and gallop away. *Mama must be up super early, this morning,* she thought, *but why, and who would be visiting at this time of day?* She sat up, trying to see if she felt the warmth of the fire from the cook stove or smelled the coffee that Mama always made, but nothing.

She threw off the covers, swung her legs over the side of the bed, and her feet searched for her warm slippers. When she found them, she very slowly stood up, went to the door, and very quietly cracked it open to listen. The only sounds she heard were shuffling of feet and muffled sobs. She opened the door further and cautiously moved to the railing of the loft that looked down over the kitchen, where she saw her papa pacing back and forth, running his hands through his hair and crying, "Why God, why?"

Frightened, she quickly moved down the stairs to the kitchen where she met her papa. "What's wrong Papa? Where's Mama?"

"Oh Emily, she's gone."

"Gone? Gone where?"

He moved to where she stood, took her in his arms, and said, "Emily, my sweet girl, she died during the night."

Pulling away from him, she said, "No! What?"

She broke free, ran to her mama's room in disbelief, and peered through the crack in the door. She very quietly pushed open the door, tiptoed in, and went over to the bed where her mama appeared to be sleeping. She stretched out her arm and gently shook her mama as she softly said, "Mama, it's me, Emily. Wake up."

But she lay still, cold, and lifeless. Emily ran from the room, screaming, "No! No!"

She escaped her papa's grip as he tried to console her and ran up to her room sobbing and crying out, "No! No!" repeatedly.

She grabbed the quilt her mama had made for her off of the bed, wrapped herself in it like a cocoon, and huddled in the corner of her room. It was not long before the downstairs was bustling with people.

The doctor had gone to fetch the constable and the coroner. On his way, he stopped at the homes of Emily's sisters, Amanda, and Sarah, to inform them about their mother. As Amanda gathered their two little boys from their beds, Jake went to harness the horse to the buggy and brought it around for the family. They all quickly crawled up into the buggy and hurried to Mama and Papa's house. The boys, still half asleep not understanding what was going on, snuggled up together beside their mama. Amanda and her family arrived about the same time as Sarah and Harry did. They all gathered as they tethered the horses. They talked among themselves about what had just happened and went inside. They found Papa roaming around in a daze. They quickly asked him for details, and he told them how he woke up to Mama groaning and complaining that her chest hurt. She was having a hard time breathing and he knew he needed to go get help. He set out to get the doctor but by the time they got back, it was too late. In disbelief, Amanda and Sarah carefully pushed the door open and tiptoed into the bedroom where they saw their mama lying lifeless and cold. They stood together arms around each other crying in disbelief. Slowly, they bent over and gave their mama a kiss. With tears streaming down their cheeks, they whispered their love and goodbyes before walking out of the room and quietly closing the door.

In a fog, they moved about the kitchen, ramped up the fire in the cook stove, and put on a pot of coffee. It was now daylight, and they could see the horse-drawn wagon coming down the road to pick up their mama.

"Where is Emily?" Amanda asked Papa.

"She's up in her room. She came down to see what was going on and when I explained that Mama was gone, she didn't believe me. She went into the bedroom and saw that she was dead, screamed and ran up the stairs. Please go check on her."

Together, Amanda and Sarah ran up the stairs. They found her nestled in the corner wrapped in her quilt sobbing.

"Come here, sweetie," Amanda said, but Emily scrunched even closer to the corner and tightened the quilt around her.

Sarah, bending over her whispered, "Emily dear, we are here for you. It's going to be ok. We are here for each other. Come here to us. We need to feel your hugs."

After a little more coaxing, she slowly and very cautiously unwrapped herself, then grabbed onto her sisters, sobbing, and fell into their arms.

"What am I going to do without Mama?" she sobbed.

Emily, at fifteen, did need a mother at this vulnerable stage in her life. The girls knew they were going to have to step up to the challenge.

Sarah moved back down the stairs to tend to her nephews while Amanda continued to console Emily. She moved the boys into the sitting room area as the constable knocked on the door, and Harry went to let him in. The doctor and the coroner were right behind. They entered the bedroom where Lily lay. After doing the necessary examination, the doctor and the constable sat down at the kitchen table to talk with James while the coroner prepared Lily to be moved.

Upstairs, Emily quietly tiptoed out of her room to the railing and peered down to where the men were sitting talking to Papa.

The doctor explained to the constable that Lily had been seeing him over the past few months complaining of chest pains and that he had prescribed medicine for her.

"Wait, just a minute," James said. "You say she has been seeing you for months?"

"Yes, James, she has."

"I knew nothing about that. I didn't even know she was having any problems," James explained.

Emily's hands tightened on the railings until her knuckles turned white. *If you would've been home in the evenings where you were supposed to be instead of out with your buddies drinking, you might have known about Mama having problems,* she thought.

After the constable finished talking with the doctor and James, he completed his paperwork and instructed them to move the table out of the way to make a clearing for them to bring Lily to the wagon that was waiting outside.

Amanda suggested that Emily move away from the railing and come back with her to her room until Mama had been moved, but Emily sat frozen on the floor looking through the railing and refused. She heard the men talking to one another, and then heard a shuffling of feet as they emerged from the bedroom, took her mama wrapped in a sheet across the room to the door, and to the wagon. Emily's little body went limp, and she melted into the floor, too weak to move. Sounds such as that of a mewing kitten enveloped her.

*Chapter*

# 3

By noon the news of Lily's death spread around the town. The neighbors brought baskets of bread, casseroles, and sweets to the house.

Later that day, the family met with the minister and made plans for the funeral to take place at the little community church where the family regularly attended, except for James. He had no time for church. He held the idea, and was quick to express, that he thought the church was filled with hypocritical Christians and wanted no part of it. Lily had reminded him over and over that he should not put everyone in that category just because of a few, who were probably just that, hypocrites.

"You shouldn't allow people to lead you astray by their hypocrisy," she would tell him.

The community knew who those few were that James was referring to and his run-ins with them from time to time fueled his beliefs. But since he knew how much Lily loved going to church and had so many friends there, he agreed to the family's wishes. With the minister's approval, it was decided that both the viewing on Wednesday evening and the funeral on Thursday morning would be held at the community church. After which, Mama would then be taken to the church cemetery for the internment.

Against her father's wishes, Amanda insisted that Emily come stay with her, Jake, and the boys until things settled down. Emily did not want to be alone and clung closely to Amanda. She remained quiet, tossing thoughts around in her head, mostly keeping them to herself. She only allowed her emotions to surface when Amanda sat with her and held her close.

She missed her mama so much and felt so abandoned. Amanda became a soft place for her to land.

Amanda kept Emily busy by having her work alongside her as she did the house chores, such as cleaning and preparing meals. Emily also spent time helping to entertain Charlie and Willie. The boys were a good distraction and provided an avenue for her to escape from her thoughts for a short time.

Late Monday evening, with Lily gone and Emily at Amanda's, James became restless, and the weight of being alone came crashing down on him. Realizing there was no longer a need for him to confine his drinking to the barn, he went out, fetched his bottle of whiskey, and went back to the house where he tried to drink his sorrows away.

"I've been abandoned!" he yelled out, as he walked the floor with his fists clenched. "I have nothing without you, Lily, nothing," he wailed. "It's so cold and empty here without you. Oh Lily, I miss you so much already."

Lily, he now admitted to himself, was the one who made his house a "home" and made it feel warm and inviting. Seeing her apron hanging by the stove, he took it from the hook and pressed his face against it. "Oh Lily, I love you. Why didn't I tell you or show you how much?"

He sat down at the kitchen table holding onto her apron, as memories flooded his mind. He imagined Lily moving around the kitchen with a sense of calmness and grace and could almost smell her homemade bread baking in the oven. He was reminded of how tender and patient Lily remained as she taught the girls how to sew and bake. Also, of times when he watched her and the girls laugh together and talk about their sewing projects or the recipes they wanted to bake.

Suddenly, jolted from his thoughts, he sat straight up in his chair and yelled, "Emily!" Putting the apron down, he got up and again yelled, "Emily! Yes Emily, you belong here! You need to be here doing the things Mama taught you and you need to be here to help me."

His emotions were all over the place, moving in and out of loneliness, anger, and melancholy. He headed into the bedroom to try and get some sleep. *Tomorrow*, he thought, *I will see to it that you, my Emily girl, will be home where you belong.*

The bedroom brought him no solace, and sleep evaded him. The thought of Lily not lying beside him haunted him even more. He tossed and turned until he finally realized that he wouldn't be able to sleep. He got up and went out to the barn to make a wooden coffin for Lily to be buried in. He chose the best boards that he could find from his stash of lumber, gathered his hammer and nails, and went to work. He lost track of the time, and before he knew it, the sun was creeping up.

It was a cold and dreary day. The storm clouds hovered overhead threatening snow or sleet. Ironically, it was a picture of his feelings and attitude. As he hammered away at the nails in the coffin, his mind swirled with many different emotions. He asked himself over and over, "What am I going to do without her?" He felt so alone. His grief took him through bouts of self-pity. *Why me?* he thought. *What have I done to deserve this? It's not fair.* Becoming angry, he swung his hammer faster and harder as he thought about how she left him so abruptly.

"Lily," he screamed, as though she could hear him, "why did you just leave me like that? You left me with a young girl to raise, left me to manage the house by myself, left me without any warning!" He thought about the night she passed and what the doctor said about treating her for some heart problems that he knew nothing about. "Why didn't you tell me you were not well and seeing the doctor?" he ranted.

In a moment of anger, he threw the hammer in the corner, walked over to his little closet of spirits, and grabbed a bottle of bourbon. Feeling the need to be sheltered with his own thoughts, he moved to a more secluded little room off the main barn area and sat down in the corner on fresh hay that had been scattered from a broken bale. He leaned back against the wall, pulled his cap down over his eyes and romanced his bottle of bourbon. With each swallow, he became more and more melancholy, and tears began rolling down his cheeks.

"Oh Lily, I miss you so much," he cried. "I need you here with me. I want to feel your arms around me and smell your sweet perfume. I'm sorry for all those nights I left you alone while I was out with the fellas. If only I had you back, I would be more attentive, more loving, and more helpful."

Eventually, his arms went limp allowing the bottle to fall across his lap, his head dropped, and he fell asleep. Only a few minutes had passed when he was startled and awakened by a thud above him in the loft. He raised his head and shook it, trying to remember where he was. He sat there quietly and listened for what it was that woke him.

The room he was in contained the ladder leading up to the loft. Thinking that some animal was up there, he threw his empty bottle into the loft and groggily yelled, "Get out of here you scoundrel!"

Listening again, he heard nothing except for the wind blowing and settled back down into his alcohol-induced fog.

The rays of daylight shone through the cracks in the barn door, and this time James awoke from hunger. He sat up, rubbed his eyes trying to remember where he was and why he was sitting on the floor of the barn. He tried to remember whether he just had a bad dream or was Lily's passing a reality. Slowly and carefully, he raised himself off the floor and stumbled outside to relieve himself. Running his fingers through his hair and scratching his overgrown beard, he realized it was no bad dream. His stomach gave a loud rumble which made him remember that no one was there to make him breakfast. He needed to go and bring Emily back home where she belonged right away. Ignoring his dirty, slept-in clothes and disheveled appearance, he hitched his mare to the wagon and hurried to Amanda's house.

It was James, in this frame of mind, who ordered Amanda to gather Emily's things because he had come to take her home with him.

"Emily needs to be with me, at the house," he barked at Amanda, "taking care of the chores and fixing meals for me."

Amanda wanted nothing to do with his idea. "She's a child, Papa. She's hurting and needs to be taken care of herself," Amanda argued. "She is dealing with a lot of emotions and is very vulnerable right now. By the looks of you, with pieces of hay in your hair and your clothes a mess, you spent the night in the barn. You need a good sleep, and you will see things differently."

But he kept insisting that he needed help and Emily was the one to do that. Amanda sat him down at the table, fixed him a cup of coffee, and prepared him a breakfast of ham and eggs, his favorite. Amanda realized that since Papa had no idea how to run a house, and could barely make coffee for himself, that he really did need some help. After much deliberation, he very reluctantly agreed to having Amanda and

Sarah take turns bringing him meals and checking on things that needed to be done at the house until after the funeral. Then they would talk about making proper arrangements for Emily.

Amanda was just biding time because she knew that there would be another big disagreement when it was time to discuss Emily moving back home after the funeral. She thought it would, at least, give her some time to come up with another plan that would allow Emily to stay with her and have the comfort of the family. She knew Emily was not ready to be moved back into the home where all the memories of Mama would surface. She knew that Emily, having to be in the house with all of Mama's things, using the pots and pans and dishes that Mama had used while teaching her to cook, and going into the bedroom where she last saw her mama would just be too much for her to handle. Let alone, Papa barking orders at her to do this and that. She knew it would send Emily into a downward tailspin of despair. *I must come up with something*, she thought.

After eating the breakfast that Amanda prepared for him, James left for home. Suddenly, it struck James that it was Tuesday. Tomorrow was the viewing, and the coffin was not yet finished. He knew he needed to spend the rest of the day and night, if needed, finishing the coffin. He clicked the reigns to his old mare and hurried her on home.

Entering the barn, he became aware of a presence. He stopped for a minute and looked around. It was cold, dim, and dank. He moved to the old wood-burning stove in the middle of the barn and threw in some kindling to start a fire. Still having an eerie feeling that something or someone was possibly lurking around, he grabbed a shovel and slowly and quietly crept into the hay room off to the right of the main barn area, where he remembered he had spent the night. He started up the ladder to the loft. Halfway up, he heard a scuffling noise.

He yelled, "Who's there?" But there was no response.

Thinking now that it was just some animal that had come into the barn for some warmth and protection from the cold, he moved on up the ladder. He saw a pile of hay where he thought the animal had tried to cover himself, but to his surprise, he saw the sole of a shoe. At this moment, he realized it was not an animal but a person.

He called out, "Come out and show yourself."

Slowly, the lump started to move, and a dirty, young-looking face with scraggly hair peered out from the hay.

"Who are you and what are you doing in my loft?" he demanded.

From the looks of things, he couldn't tell if it was a boy or a girl, but assumed it was a boy and said, "Get yourself up from there boy and tell me why you're here."

Slowly the figure pushed the hay away and stood up. James then realized it appeared to be a young girl.

"I'm cold and I ain't got no place to live, but don't get all sorry for me Mister, 'cause I don't need nobody takin' care of me."

"Don't go and get your feathers ruffled there little Missy," James spouted back.

"Don't call me that. I ain't no Missy."

James took pity on her even though he wouldn't let her know. She appeared to be near Emily's age and that raised a sense of concern. He told her to come down, sit by the fire, get warm, and they would talk. James moved down the ladder assuming she would follow.

Reluctantly, she moved toward the ladder. Stopping at the top, she said, "You know Mister, I don't need your fire to stay warm. I can start my own fire in the woods don't ya know. I don't need nobody to start me a fire."

"Well, then, how about coming down and keeping me company while I work on my project?"

"Don't call it a project, just say it like it is. It's a coffin for your dead wife."

James turned with a jerk and looked up at her and said, "How did you know that? How long have you been staying in the loft?"

"Well, let me just say, long enough to hear your whiny, drunken, *feel sorry for me* speech."

Feeling the hair on the back of his neck start to rise in anger, but at the same time feeling embarrassed, James said, "Well get yourself down here and let's talk. What's your name anyway?"

Climbing halfway down the ladder, then jumping the rest of the way, making a thud as her oversized boots hit the wooden floor, she said, "Well I'll let you call me Marge if you give me a drink of what ya got in that there box over there."

James knew she was not old enough to have anything in "that there box," but figured, with her *I'll do it myself* attitude, if he insinuated she was too young, she would probably be sure to let him know she was no child. Instead, he said, "Oh, if you are thirsty, I'll run to the house and bring some water," and then sheepishly added, "or milk."

"Are you kidding me man? I know what ya got in that there box and that's what I'm thirsty for."

James, giving in, said, "Well only if you tell me who you are, where you came from, and what you are doing in my barn."

"Oh, all right," she said, and grabbed the bottle of liquor out of James' hand and took a swig before he changed his mind.

James had a lot of questions and told her to start talking.

"Well," she said, "I ain't got no parents."

"What do you mean?" James questioned. "Everyone has parents. Where are they? What happened to them?"

"Do you remember hearing 'bout that clan of gypsies that were camping in the woods and were run off by the police?"

"Yeah, I remember something about that, but that's been some time ago."

"Yeah, well I was part of that clan. I was hiding in a tree when the police came through routing out the camp. I was tired of police running the clan from place to place and decided to leave them and stay put. I'm old enough to make my own way and I am tired of moving from place to place. I stayed up there in the woods until it got so freezin' cold."

"How did you get food?"

"I would come down out of the mountains at night and go through the garbage. I even got some of your leftovers that you left in the barn from time to time. Did you think it was animals that cleaned your plate when you left food?"

"Honestly, I never really thought about it," James said.

"Let me tell ya man, that was some darn good eatin'."

"What are you planning on doing?" James continued probing.

"Ah, well I don't rightly know. That might just depend on you," she piped back. She swung her leg over the sawhorse that James was getting ready to use for cutting his lumber for the coffin.

"Excuse me? What do I have to do with what you are going to do?" James said. Annoyed, he continued, "Get off my sawhorse and get over here and hold the end of this board and make yourself useful."

She jumped off the sawhorse, stood at attention, saluted, and said flippantly, "Yes sir, right away sir." She held one board after another and then gathered the hammer and nails for him to begin the assembling of the coffin. Handing him nail after nail was a big help to James and he told her she was quite the helper.

"Got anything else I can help you with around here?" she asked.

"Well, I don't know, I might," he said. "But my main concern is getting this box finished for the viewing tomorrow."

"Yeah," she said, "I do feel sorry for ya. It's a shame that you don't have no wife now to take care of ya. I could do some of that sort of stuff for ya." Slapping him on the back she added, "You know what I mean?"

"Now don't you go and get any ideas," he snapped. "I have three girls that have promised to look after me and bring me meals. And besides, I have a young'un that will still be living at home and her mama taught her right. She can do the cleaning and stuff like that. How old are you anyway?"

"What does that matter?"

"Just wondering, that's all," he said and shrugged.

It was getting to be evening and Amanda would be bringing his supper soon. He knew that she would not approve of him harboring this gypsy girl, whom he really knew nothing about. *Who knows*, he thought, *she may be a crook for all I know. But I can't in good conscience turn her out in this freezing weather.* He continued working on the coffin in silence when, just as he figured, he heard Amanda's buggy coming up the lane.

"That's my daughter bringing my dinner. You've got to get out of here, and now. Go back up in the loft and when she's gone, I'll share some food with you."

"I'll be as quiet as a mouse," Marge said. Wiggling her nose, she scampered up the ladder and out of sight.

# Chapter

# 4

Amanda pulled the buggy next to the house, gathered her basket of food, and went inside. She was surprised that it was so cold in the house. The fire in the cook stove was out and there were no signs of anyone being in the house all day. James came through the door.

Amanda gasped, "Papa, you look the same as you did this morning when you came to my house. Why haven't you cleaned yourself up and put on fresh clothes?"

"Been out in the barn all day working on the coffin," he said.

"Well, have you finished it?"

"Yep, all except for some last-minute sanding and polishing."

"That's good," Amanda said. "It's obviously warmer in the barn than in here because I saw the smoke coming from the chimney when I drove up. Why don't you get a fire going in the cook stove, and while it's heating up the place, we can take the basket of food out to the barn where it is warm. Then you can show me the coffin."

James, stammering said, "Oh, ah, well, I'll get a fire going and then I can eat in here. It won't take long for it to warm up. As far as the coffin goes, you can see it tomorrow before the viewing. I want it to be a surprise."

"No," Amanda insisted, "It is way too cold for you to eat in here. Go ahead and build a fire so it will be warm when you come in to go to bed but eat in the barn where it's warm."

James reluctantly agreed, hoping all along that Marge would stay hidden. He definitely did not want Amanda to find out that he was allowing a strange young girl to stay in the barn.

While James was building the fire, he started talking to Amanda about the viewing that was taking place. "Tell me again Amanda, what are the plans now for tomorrow?" he asked.

"Well, you must get the coffin to the funeral home in the morning so that they can get Mama ready for the viewing tomorrow evening. Remember, we discussed this with the Minister on Monday afternoon?"

"Oh, Amanda I've been so distraught and so busy with making the coffin that I don't know what I'm doing."

Amanda knew that her papa had not spent all his time working on the coffin. By the looks and smell of him, he had found time to drown his grief in his bourbon. "Papa, now listen to me. You must promise me that you won't go to drinking tonight and be drunk tomorrow."

"Oh, come on Amanda. You know I wouldn't do that."

"No Papa, I don't know that. I'll never forget that special Mother's Day celebration that the family had planned for Mama. You showed up drunk, embarrassed her and made her cry."

"Oh, I remember that, trust me, Sarah would never let me forget it. She wouldn't give me the time of day for months after that, but of course that's nothing new for her."

"Well, I don't want a repeat of that tomorrow. I am warning you, if you are drunk tomorrow, you will not go to the viewing. I will have Jake stay with you and keep you away. And furthermore, if you are drunk the day of the funeral, the same thing applies."

"Now, now, that's not going to be necessary. I promise."

"I'm serious, Papa," Amanda said sternly.

"I know you are, Amanda. What time is the viewing?"

"It's from four o'clock until six o'clock. The ladies of the church are bringing food here to the house for the family after the viewing. I'm sure some of our close friends will want to come to the house as well."

James turned to look at Amanda, "Are you telling me that people will be coming to the house tomorrow evening?"

"Yes Papa, but just our family and close friends. Clyde and some of your buddies may want to come for a while as well."

James started to object.

"What's wrong with that Papa?"

James got all beside himself thinking about people coming to the house. *How am I going to keep people out of the barn? I know the men will probably meander out to the barn to get away from the lady folks.* He got himself all worked up, and Amanda could tell he was bothered about something, because of the way he started pacing around the kitchen, running his hands through his hair.

"What's wrong Papa, what has you so fussed?"

"Well, I was thinking, just thinking, about all the things that need to be done around here if people are coming to the house. We got to get this house cleaned up. How are we going to do that Amanda? And I have to take the coffin first thing in the morning to the funeral home, right? And, oh, I almost forgot, we are to take clothes for them to put on Mama. Amanda this is all too much," he fumed. He continued, "That's why Emily should have been here. I told you I needed her here." But the thing that was really bothering him was how he was going to keep Marge from being seen.

Amanda, taking hold of his shoulders said, "Whoa Papa, slow down. Sarah and I will take care of everything. We will be here before you take the coffin to the funeral home and she and I will decide what clothes you should take with you for Mama. We will make sure the house is clean. And, by the way, what clothes are you planning on wearing to the funeral Papa?"

"I don't know Amanda. I haven't even thought about that. All my clothes are dirty. See, if you would have listened to me and let Emily come back home, we wouldn't be in such a mess."

"No, now Papa, stop it. Just let me gather your things and I will wash them this evening and bring fresh clothes for you in the morning."

It was noticeably getting warmer in the kitchen, so Amanda pulled out a chair and said, "Here Papa, sit down and eat your dinner while I go get the dirty clothes gathered up."

Amanda went into Mama and Papa's bedroom. It was the first time she had entered since Mama had passed. She gathered a big armful of dirty clothes and sat down on the bed. Memories swept over her and every one of her senses was filled with Mama. Tears streamed down her face as she dropped the clothes on the bed beside her. She tenderly touched Mama's pillow, pulled up the sheet from the unmade bed to her face, and smelled her mama's perfume. She felt emptiness. Emptiness in the bedroom and emptiness in her heart without Mama.

*What is Amanda doing in there that's taking so long?* James wondered. He laid his fork on his plate and went to find her.

She was jolted from her thoughts when James came through the door and gruffly asked, "Whatcha doing in here girlie?" Seeing the tear in Amanda's eye he put his hand on her shoulder and said, "There's no time for that now. Come on I've got things to do."

Amanda just sat there for a moment, thinking, *Yeah Papa, that's what you always say when you don't want to face reality. 'I've got things to do'. How many times have I heard that excuse when refusing to eat Sunday dinner with the family or getting up abruptly before dinner was over?* She dropped the sheet and gathered up the dirty clothes she had dumped on the bed beside her. Wrapping her arms around the bundle, she spotted a dress that would be perfect to bury Mama in. It was the one they all had seen her in the last time they were all together. She included it in the bundle of clothes that needed to be washed and pulled the bundle even closer to her heart.

"Oh, how can I do this?" she said to no one in particular. She knew, as the oldest, it was going to be her responsibility to get the whole family through this rough time. Standing up to leave the room, she paused for just a second to take one last look around the room. She spotted her mama's Bible lying on the bureau and a moment of melancholy flowed over her as she remembered the many nights gathered around Mama as she rocked and read to them from it. "You taught us well Mama," she whispered to herself. She heard Papa call to her from the kitchen, so she quickly placed the Bible among the clothes, took a deep breath, and walked out of the bedroom. She stuffed the dirty clothes into the basket that she had brought his food in and laid the Bible on top. She then neatly folded Mama's dress and placed it gently on top of the Bible and set the basket by the door.

Turning her attention back to Papa she said, "That's a nice fire you got going there. That should make it nice and warm in here for when you come in to go to bed. How long do you think it will take you to put the finishing touches on the coffin?"

"Not long."

"Good, then you can come in and go to bed early so you will be fresh in the morning to do all the things we need to do."

Amanda thought if she could get him to go to bed early that he wouldn't be so tempted to sit with his bourbon bottle feeling sorry for himself. She knew that would not make for a good day tomorrow. "Are you sure I can't take a peek at the coffin?"

"No," James said emphatically, "I said it's a surprise."

"Okay, then, Sarah and I will be here early in the morning, so don't worry about anything but finishing the coffin and getting to bed early. Will you do that for me, Papa?"

"Yeah, okay."

"Do you Promise?"

Somewhat aggravated he said, "Yes Amanda, I said OKAY!"

"Sarah and I will make sure you have a good breakfast in the morning."—she gave him a kiss on the cheek— "I'm anxious to see the coffin, Papa. I know it will be beautiful."

She picked up the basket of clothes, said goodbye, and headed out the door. As she rode home, she felt a lump well up in the middle of her stomach, thinking about all the things that could go wrong if Papa got drunk and did not get his rest. She wanted to believe him when he said he would go to bed early, but from past experiences, she knew that he was probably just agreeing with her to get her to go away and leave him alone. She was realizing what Mama had to put up with all these years trying to keep him in line and constantly trying to cover for him.

James watched Amanda leave and when he saw her turn and head down the road, he quickly filled his plate with food and hurried to the barn.

"About time you bring food," Marge said impatiently, "I'm starvin'."

Pulling the plate toward his chest away from Marge's grubby hands, he said, "Well you just hold on. Amanda was telling me about what's happening the next few days. She wanted to come out here and see the coffin, but I stalled her by telling her I wanted it to be a surprise."

"Speaking of the coffin," Marge interjected, "there's some sanding and staining still to do."

"Yes, I know Marge, you don't have to remind me. As soon as I finish eating, I'm going to get right to it."

"Excuse me, I think that food is for me."

James looked at Marge with irritation, but then softened as he recognized her hunger and pushed the plate to her. "Here, eat what you want."

"Well, it's about time. Gimmie that plate," she said and started cramming food into her mouth, as though she hadn't eaten in days.

"Oh, my goodness Marge, you eat like a pig."

Marge ignored his comment and kept right on eating.

James went to work on the coffin and actually finished it in less time than he expected, which was a blessing because Marge was beginning to get on his nerves. Thinking he needed to get away from her, he thought about going to see Clyde, but then he remembered what Amanda made him promise. He struggled with deciding whether he would go see Clyde or go to the house and get ready for bed. He rationalized that he could just stay at Clyde's for a little while and then still get to bed early enough. However, just thinking about all the things he had to do tomorrow made him tired, and he decided he would go to the house and get a good night's sleep so he could take care of things properly, for Lily's sake.

As he was leaving, he turned to Marge and said, "You know Marge, tomorrow evening is the viewing and there will be a lot of people in and around the house and barn the next few days. Jake is coming in the morning to help move the coffin to the wagon. You will have to stay out of sight until we figure out what to do about some type of living arrangements for you."

"I don't need you to make no living arrangements for me," she yelled at him.

Ignoring her, he continued, "I have enough to worry about without having to worry about you."

Marge spit on the ground at him and said, "I ain't never had anyone worry about me and I don't need anyone worrying about me now."

Again, ignoring her as if he didn't hear her, he said, "I'd appreciate it if you would keep the fire going tonight so the coffin will be good and dry in the morning. So, do what I say, and good night."

"Wait, where are you going?"

As he was going out the door, he turned to look at her and said, "None of your business."

The house was toasty warm, and very inviting when James walked in. The only light that shone was the light from the fire in the cook stove. He sat down at the kitchen table and kicked off his boots. Feeling all alone, he went into the bedroom and crawled into bed. As he lay there his thoughts wafted back to when Lily and he would curl up together. Oh, how he wished he would have spent more evenings with her. *I'm sorry Lily, so sorry.* He pulled the covers up under his chin holding on to them with both hands and drifted off to sleep.

# Chapter 5

When Amanda got home, Sarah was there with Emily and the boys anxiously waiting to hear how she made out with Papa. Barely giving her time to get in the door, Sarah began questioning, "Well, tell us Amanda, how did it go? What frame of mind was Papa in?"

"He's very nervous Sarah. Nervous about everything that's going on over the next few days. He was in the barn when I got there, and when he came into the house it was clear by the looks and smell of him that's where he had been spending his time - drowning his grief for Mama in his liquor."

"Are you kidding me, Amanda? He's not grieving for Mama. He's only thinking of himself with his poor me attitude. I'm so glad that you are taking the initiative in dealing with him because you know I wouldn't have the patience with him that you have."

"Please, Sarah, I'm begging you to get along with Papa these next few days. We don't need any added drama."

"I know, that's why I'm keeping my distance as much as I can."

"Sarah," Amanda quickly added, "you're going to have to interact with him tomorrow because early in the morning, you and I need to go to the house, fix his breakfast, and help him get ready to take the coffin to the funeral home. To keep him from completely losing it, when I told him that people would be coming to the house after the viewing, I told him that you and I would be taking care of everything. I told him not to worry about anything except finishing the coffin."

"Oh, did you see the coffin?" Sarah asked. "Is it nice?"

"No, he wouldn't let me see it, said it was a surprise."

*Shattered*

"Oh Amanda, that makes me nervous, do you think he really has made one?"

"Yes, of course, Sarah, now stop thinking that way."

Before Amanda went to check on Papa and take him his dinner, she had left enough food for the family. "Has everyone eaten?" she asked.

Emily spoke up, "The boys and I ate, with Uncle Jake."

"Well, I haven't eaten yet," Amanda exclaimed, "and I'm starving. Sarah, have you had your dinner yet?"

"No, I haven't."

"Then get you some of my homemade biscuits and stew and sit and eat with me. We need to talk." Turning to Emily she said, "Emily, sweetie, would you mind seeing that the boys take their baths and get ready for bed?"

"Sure, and I'll get ready for bed too, but then I want you to tell me all about what's happening tomorrow. I'm not sure I understand everything."

"That's a deal. Thanks so much. Now go on boys, go with Emily."

Amanda knew that Sarah's attitude toward Papa needed to change, and she thought their time alone would be a great opportunity to talk with her about it.

Sarah helped herself to the stew and biscuits and sat down to eat. "I see you brought a basket of clothes from Papa's."

After fixing her plate Amanda sat down at the table with Sarah. "Yes, that's part of what we need to talk about. But first, we need to talk about your attitude toward him. Sarah, I know you have reasons to be upset at Papa. He's made a lot of mistakes and wasn't the father to us or the husband to Mama that he should have been."

"That's for sure Amanda. You know it and I know it. I don't understand why you aren't as upset with him as I am."

"I'm upset with him too, Sarah, but my relationship with Jesus helps me be more patient and forgiving towards him." At that, Amanda got up from the table and took the Bible from the basket of clothes.

"Oh, you brought Mama's Bible with you."

"Yes, I saw it lying on her bureau and I just had to have it. Don't you remember Mama reading it to us?"

"Yes, I do Amanda, and I know I have to work on my attitude. But for now, what about that basket of clothes?"

"It's Papa's dirty clothes. When I asked him what he was wearing to the viewing, he said he hadn't even thought about it, and that all of his clothes were dirty. So, I gathered his dirty things. We should at least wash a few of them tonight so he will have decent clothes to wear tomorrow. I think he's been in the same clothes ever since Mama passed."

"Oh, my goodness Amanda, how awful."

"Yes, trust me. He's pretty disgusting right now and I am very concerned about what condition he will be in tomorrow. However, he promised me that he would go to bed early tonight and get a good night's sleep."

Sarah throwing down her napkin in disgust said, "Promises from Papa mean nothing. Look how many times he promised Mama things that he didn't follow through with and how many times we saw Mama brought to tears. Amanda, he makes me so angry."

"I know Sarah, but you are going to have to find it in your heart to forgive him. You know what Mama taught us - *You must forgive to be forgiven by our Heavenly Father* - besides, it is not good for you to hold grudges. It only hurts you. It hurts you physically, mentally, and emotionally. Let us just pray and trust that this time he will keep his promise. Now back to Papa. While we were going over all that needs to be done tomorrow, he remembered that when he takes the coffin to the funeral home, he also needs to take clothes for Mama to be buried in."

"Well imagine that," Sarah said sarcastically. "He actually remembered something of importance."

"Now Sarah, be nice. Anyway, I brought a dress to iron that I thought might be a good one for her. It's the dress Mama wore the last time we were all together. I thought that it was so pretty and would look nice, what do you think?"

"I'm not sure that's a good choice," Sarah said.

"Why not, do you not like that dress?"

"Oh, it's not that, it's just the opposite. I love that dress and memories of Mama in that dress are happy memories. I just think it would be a nice dress to have around for a while."

"You know, you may be right. Let's wait until Emily comes down and we will ask her what she thinks about it. That will give her a chance to feel like she's a part of planning Mama's funeral."

"Good idea Amanda, I feel so sorry for Emily. I've noticed her sometimes just staring into space, lost in her thoughts. What is going to become of her, Amanda?"

Pushing her chair from the table Sarah said, "If there's nothing else, we need to discuss right now, I've got to get home."

"Okay, be sure and take a plate of stew for Harry. Also, would you be able to wash at least a set of clothes tonight for Papa so they will be ready for tomorrow?"

"Oh, I suppose I can do that. For you, not for him."

"Thanks Sarah. That will be a big help to me. And do me a favor, while you are washing them, say a prayer for him and for your attitude about him. Remember, we are family and doing this for Mama. We want her to be proud of us over the next few days."

"Oh, all right, I will, and you can tell me in the morning what Emily decides about the dress." As Sarah dug through the clothes basket finding decent clothes for Papa to wear to the viewing, she asked Amanda, "What time do you want me over here in the morning?"

"I think we should leave around six o'clock. I think Jake is taking care of things tonight so he can get away a couple of hours in the morning to help Papa load the coffin. I'm hoping to be finished with all we need to do at the house by noon so I can get home and make sure we are all dressed and ready for the viewing. You know it starts at four o'clock, right Sarah?"

"Yes, I remember."

Amanda continued, "Eunice from church is coming to watch the boys in the morning because I think it's important that Emily doesn't have that responsibility. When she comes down, I'll ask her if she wants to stay here, sleep in and have a relaxing morning, or if she would like to go with us to the house. I'm thinking she may want to be part of helping to get everything ready."

"That is a good idea. It's good for us to include her in the planning and give her a chance to feel a part of everything. I think it will give her a sense of closure." As Sarah was going out the door, she turned to Amanda and said, "Okay then, sounds good, I'll see you bright and early."

Amanda sat for a moment, drifted into her own thoughts, and paused to say a prayer that Papa would truly keep his promise to her, that the coffin would be finished, and all would go smoothly. She was feeling the pressure of being the one who kept everything going as it should. She let out a huge sigh as she got up and started to clean the kitchen. She was washing dishes when Emily and the boys came downstairs, and Charlie and Willie came running into the kitchen.

Amanda looked affectionately at her boys, "Here are my handsome boys."—drying her hands on the dish towel, she bent down and gave them a hug and a kiss— "My, you smell so fresh and look squeaky clean."

"Mama," Willie said giggling, "I don't squeak."

Emily piped up, "Well, you may not squeak but you squealed when I washed your hair." They all had a good laugh as the boys sat at the table to eat their bedtime snack.

"Emily, I want to get your opinion on a couple of things," Amanda said.

Surprised, Emily said, "You want my opinion?"

"Yes, I do."

Emily, feeling important, slid into the chair closest to Amanda. With one leg bent under her to make herself taller, she propped her elbows on the table, and said, "All righty then, let's hear it."

Amanda, laughing, said, "Sarah and I are going to the house extremely early in the morning to help Papa get the coffin that he made ready to take to the funeral home. And we also need to get the house looking presentable because there will be friends coming to the house in the evening. Since Eunice from church is coming to take care of the boys in the morning, would you like to go with Sarah and me to the house, or would you rather sleep in and have a leisurely morning? Sarah and I plan to be back here shortly after noon to get us all dressed and ready for the viewing at four o'clock."

"Oh Amanda, it would mean a lot to me to help get things ready. I think Mama would be proud of me."

"Yes Emily, I think she would too."

"Then that's settled," Emily said. "What was the other thing?"

"Well, do you see that dress of Mama's on the chair over there?"

"Yes, and I remember that's the dress she wore to church last Sunday."

"Yes, it is, and I was wondering what you thought about having Mama wear that dress to be buried in?"

Emily sat quietly for a few minutes. "Well," she said, "I don't know if I want Mama buried in the same dress that she wore the last time we had such a good time with her. I can't explain it, but I think I would like to keep that dress around to remind me of her.

"I understand, and Sarah thought the very same thing."

"But," Emily continued, "do you remember how pretty she looked in pink? What about that beautiful pink dress she made with the white lacy collar? I always thought she looked so pretty when she wore that dress."

"Oh, you know, you are exactly right Emily, I had forgotten about that dress, but I think that will be perfect. I'm glad that you remembered it. You've been a big help." Emily sat for a moment feeling pleased with herself that she had something to contribute.

"Okay, boys," Amanda said. "It's up to bed with you. Miss Eunice will be here to take care of you in the morning while Emily, Sarah, and I go to help your grandpa at his house. But I will be home to fix your lunch. Emily, since you will be getting up early, you better be heading up to bed too." She went over to Emily, and walking with her to the steps, she leaned down and said softly, "Thanks for being such a big girl and for helping with the decisions." Emily just smiled, pleased with herself, and headed up the stairs. "I'll get you up around five in the morning," Amanda yelled up the stairs to Emily.

# Chapter 6

The next morning, the three girls arrived at Papa's house early as promised, with clean clothes. Worried about what they would find inside, they jumped from the wagon and tethered the horse. This was the first time Emily had come to the house since her mama passed and she moved slowly up the path to the door as a sign of respect for her mama's memory. Amanda and Sarah walked alongside her, assuring her it was all right and moved her forward to the door. Amanda was trying to reassure herself as much as Emily that things were going to be all right. She could only imagine what they were going to find. She was worried that Papa would be a drunken mess, but she had prayed about the situation and had to have faith that God heard and answered her prayer.

Just as they got to the door, it opened, and there stood Papa. He had bathed, trimmed his beard, and combed his hair. Saying they were pleasantly surprised would be an understatement. Amanda and Sarah just looked at each other, in shock.

"Thank you, Lord," Amanda said under her breath. "Wow, Papa, look at you," Amanda said giving him a hug. "I guess you did keep your promise."

He took Amanda's face in his hands and looked her in the eyes as he said, "I told you I would," and kissed her on the cheek.

Amanda couldn't help but think that if he had kept the many promises that he made to Mama, how different things could have been. Looking at him standing there in the doorway made her realize how different he could have been if he hadn't taken to drinking.

Amanda was jolted from her thoughts when she heard him say, "Come in, yes come on in. I got the fire going so you can fix some breakfast. He was so glad to see the girls, but especially his little Emily. He pulled her to him, gave her a hug, and kissed her on the forehead. "Glad you are home Emily," he said. "I've missed you."

"And I've missed you too, Papa," she said, giving him an extra hug.

"Here, Papa, here are your clean clothes," Sarah said coldly as she plopped them in the chair beside him.

"Thanks, Sarah, I really needed those washed."

Papa moved to give her a hug, but Sarah just brushed him off. Amanda, seeing that moment of disconnect, gave Sarah a look of disappointment and said, "Sarah, why don't you start cleaning the sitting room while I get breakfast started? The sooner we get the cleaning done, the sooner we can get back home."

Amanda continued busying herself around the kitchen preparing breakfast while Sarah started cleaning. "Papa is the coffin finished and ready to go?" Amanda asked.

"Yes, and it's beautiful, if I do say so myself. I'm anxious for you to see it now that it's finally finished."

"I'm anxious to see it, as well. Jake will be here a little later to help you load the coffin onto the wagon."

Putting the biscuits in the oven, Amanda said, "We came to a decision on what clothes you should take with you this morning for Mama to wear. Emily thinks Mama's pretty pink dress, the one with the white lace color, would be a good choice for her to be buried in. What do you think about that?"

"I don't know what dress you're talking 'bout but that will be fine. Whatever you girls think will be all right with me."

"Emily, why don't you go to Mama's closet, get it, see if it needs ironed, and then you can come set the table."

Sarah, having finished dusting and picking up the sitting room, paused a moment and looked around the room. A sense of grief enveloped her, and she sat down on the floor crying.

"This just can't be happening," she sobbed into her apron.

Just then Amanda announced from the kitchen that breakfast was ready, and Sarah, not wanting anyone to see her crying, wiped her tears, composed herself, and joined them in the kitchen. As they sat eating breakfast together, the loss of Mama hit Emily extremely hard.

"It's not right that Mama's not here," Emily cried out. "I miss her so much."

"I know you do sweetie. We all do," Amanda said.

This being the first time Emily had been home since her Mama had passed, she was feeling the emptiness of Mama not being there. Amanda handed her a napkin and Emily buried her face in it and sobbed. They all sat silently, giving her a few minutes to compose herself.

After breakfast, Sarah cleaned the lamp chimneys and made sure there was sufficient oil for the long evening ahead. Emily cleaned the kitchen, and Amanda ironed Mama's dress. Amanda tenderly folded the dress and underclothes and arranged them neatly in a basket for Papa. She went over the activities for the rest of the day and night again with him.

"Jake should be here anytime now to help you load the coffin onto the wagon. Speaking of the coffin, I think it's time we all go to the barn and see it."

That caused James to squirm a bit, and he said, "Okay, sure. I hope you like it. You girls put the basket with Mama's clothes in the wagon out back, and I'll go open the barn."

Hoping to somehow warn Marge that he wasn't alone, upon opening the barn door, he yelled, "Hurry up, girls, it's really cold out here."

After placing the basket in the wagon, they followed Papa into the barn. Amanda thought the smell of the fresh hay and the warmth from the old potbelly stove was a pleasant moment, but only until she saw the box that Papa had prepared for Mama. She gasped as she realized she was not prepared for this moment. The box he had made was beautiful, but oh so harsh and crude, the opposite of Mama's petite, delicate, and tender body.

"Oh my, Papa," Amanda said, "you did a great job. But we will have to fetch pillows from the house and make a soft fluffy bed for Mama to lie on."

"It's beautiful Papa!" Emily exclaimed. "I didn't know you could make anything like this."

"Well, thank you, Emily. Anything for Mama."

Sarah almost choked, but remembering what Amanda had told her about trying to get along with Papa, she bit her tongue to keep from saying what she was thinking.

Amanda patted Sarah's hand as if to say, "I understand," and then told them, "I'll go fetch the pillows and coverlet. Emily, do you want to come with me?" Amanda hoped she hadn't made a mistake leaving Sarah and Papa alone, but she thought that since everything had been going well so far, surely Sarah wouldn't get into a fuss with him today. Going out the door, Amanda stopped and turned to Papa, "Why don't you find some fresh hay to put in the bottom of the coffin for a cushion?' *That should keep those two busy,* she thought.

Amanda and Emily went to the house, gathered Mama's pillow, a blanket for her to lay on, and a quilt that she had made to lay over her.

Before going back to the barn, Emily said, "Wait, I have something I want to put in the coffin with Mama." She went into her mama's room and took a picture from the bureau. It was a picture of Mama and her girls. She brought it out and gave it to Amanda. "I want Mama to have this to let her know we will always love her."

"That is so sweet of you, Emily. I am so proud of you. You know Emily, Mama went to be with Jesus, and she's at peace now."

"I know," Emily said, "and I know He will take good care of her."

"Yes, He will, Emily, and one day we can go to heaven too and see Mama. Now let's go fix her coffin up really nice for her."

They hurried back to the barn and tenderly laid the blanket over the hay that Sarah and Papa had gathered. They placed the pillow at the head of the coffin and the quilt over the blanket, turning the corner down at the pillow. It was a bed for Mama. The girls stood for a moment with their arms around each other, lost in their own thoughts. Finally, Emily laid the picture she brought from the house on top of the quilt.

Amanda broke the silence, "Look, Sarah, Emily wanted to put our picture with Mama in the coffin. Wasn't that a sweet idea?"

"It sure was. Thanks, Emily, for thinking of that."

While the girls were chatting, James heard a noise coming from the loft and started shuffling his boot across the floor to cover it up.

Amanda turned to him and said, "There now, that's a nice soft spot for Mama to lie, don't you think, Papa?"

He didn't answer. He was too concerned that Sarah might have heard the noise he heard because she was standing right beside him.

"Papa, what do you think?" Amanda said again. "Does this meet your approval?"

He stepped closer and just shook his head in agreement, thankful that they had not heard the noise. They all stood together for a moment looking into the coffin. James, leaning over, gently put his hand on the quilt. They saw a tear run down his cheek. It was the first time they had ever seen their Papa in such a vulnerable state. Amanda moved close to him and put her arm around his shoulders and held him.

"Papa," she finally said, "I know this is hard for you. It's hard on all of us and it will mean a lot of changes for us, but together, we will get through this and be a family that Mama would be proud of. We are going back to the house now. You spend as much time here as you want. We'll wait for you in the house."

The girls left the barn and headed to the house, leaving their papa alone with his thoughts.

James was lost in thought when suddenly, Marge, so rudely interrupting his tender moment, jumped down from the loft with a bang. "Boy, I thought they would never leave. Did you bring me any food?"

Totally disgusted, James told her, "No, I did not! And the way you ate last night you don't need anything for a while. Now get back up in the loft and stay until I tell you it's safe to come down."

"Oh, all right," she grumbled.

When James was sure she was out of sight, he went out to the stall where his old mare was and hitched her to the wagon. He drove the wagon out to the front of the house to wait for Jake.

It wasn't long until Jake showed up and he helped move the coffin to the wagon. "You did a really nice job on this box, James. It's very nicely done," he said.

"Thanks, Jake."

"Can you manage it from here?"

"Yeah, they will have someone at the funeral home help me unload it, I'm sure. Thanks for your help."

"You're welcome, James. I just wish this wasn't happening."

"You and me both, believe you me. It still seems like a bad dream."

Before they went their separate ways, James and Jake went into the house where the girls were making sandwiches for them, and enough for Amanda to take home for the boys' lunches. Jake went over to Amanda, who was busy putting the sandwiches together, put his arm around her, and asked if she was alright.

"Yeah, as good as can be expected. Thanks for helping Papa."

"No problem, I just wanted to let you know I'm heading home."

"Okay, Jake, thanks for your support. Here, take a sandwich with you."

"Don't mind if I do," he said, and gave her a kiss on the cheek before leaving.

James came into the kitchen. "Well, I'm ready to go to the funeral home," he announced. "Is there anything else I need to know?"

"No, the basket of clothes is in the wagon, and I think that's all you need. We probably won't be here when you get back. The house is clean, and there are sandwiches here for you. I laid the clean clothes that you should wear this evening on the bed. Just be dressed and ready by around three o'clock and we will all meet here and go together to the church. Are you okay Papa?"

"Yes, but this has been quite an ordeal. I'm just thankful for all the help you girls have been."

"Well, you are doing good, Papa, I'm proud of you. You be careful going into town now."

James left for town, and the girls checked the house and did the last little bit of tidying up before heading back home.

"Emily, before we head out, do you need to get a dress from your closet to wear tonight?"

"No, I know what I'm going to wear and it's at your house already."

They gathered the sandwiches for their lunch and headed home to eat with everyone before getting ready for the viewing.

James delivered the coffin. When he came back to the house, he made a couple of plates of sandwiches and went to the barn to share lunch with Marge. Entering the barn, he called Marge to come down.

"Oh, it's safe now, is it?"

"Get down here before I take these sandwiches back to the house. You are really making things difficult for me. You made that noise on purpose when the girls were in here fixing the coffin didn't you?"

"Now what would make you think a thing like that?"

"Here, just eat your sandwiches and hush. I'm warning you, if you mess anything up tonight, I'll have your hide."

"Oh, I'm so scared," she laughed.

"I don't know why I'm putting up with you Marge."

"Because you, like me, James, that's why."

"Oh, hush up that kind of talk and finish your sandwiches."

He stayed until she finished, then took the plates back to the house, washed them, and put them away so there would be no questions asked about the two plates being dirty.

# Chapter 7

As far as Amanda was concerned, everything was going as planned, and she was so happy about that. Jake helped get the boys ready. Emily had on the pretty green gingham dress that Mama had made for her. It made her green eyes sparkle. She had her hair fixed on top of her head making her look older than she really was.

"You look so pretty, Emily," Amanda said, giving her a hug. *She is really beginning to blossom*, Amanda thought to herself.

"Jake, are you and the boys ready to go?" Amanda yelled down the stairs.

"Yes, we are just waiting on you ladies."

Emily looked at Amanda, put her hand over her mouth, and giggled. She stood as tall as she could and patting her hair said, "Okay Amanda, this 'lady' is ready."

Amanda smiled and yelled down the stairs, "Ok, we are ready and will be right down." Arm in arm Amanda and Emily went downstairs.

Amanda got everyone into the buggy and sat quietly beside Jake as they drove to meet up with Papa, Harry, and Sarah.

It was hard on Amanda trying to take care of Papa, trying to keep peace, and making sure everyone was where they were supposed to be and when. She was so thankful that he was behaving himself and whispered a prayer of thanks. She was concerned about what he might do this evening after the viewing, but right now everything was good, and she was grateful.

When they arrived at the house, James was ready and waiting for them with his clean clothes on and looking quite dapper.

"You look nice Papa. Are you ready to go?" Amanda asked.

"Yeah, as ready as I'll ever be, I suppose."

"It will be all right. Come on and ride with us."

They got to the church early, and the funeral home was just bringing Mama up the drive toward the church.

They parked their buggies and watched as the horse-drawn carriage carrying Mama in the beautiful wooden box that Papa had so tenderly made came up to the front of the church. Following it was a long caravan of buggies. Their friends had followed the carriage through town and to the church. They all waited outside while the coffin was moved inside and placed in the prepared area. Emily's best friends from church, who also went to school with her, came up to her and gave her a hug. Emily was so happy to see them. Beth and Ruthie Ann both told her how sorry they were that her mama had passed away. They stood with her holding her hands until it was time for the family to go inside the church.

The coffin lid was opened, and the family members were invited in first. They were all grief-stricken when they saw Mama lying so still in the coffin that they had fixed for her earlier that day. They all clung to each other for a few minutes.

It was hard on the girls to see their Papa break down, if only for a brief moment. He composed himself, and said, "Okay, now that's enough, we've got things to do. Allow the visitors to come in. Be strong for Mama."

Friends of the family came and paid their respects. Eunice told Amanda not to worry about anything. She would take the food that was dropped off to the cabin and see that it was set out. Amanda was so grateful and told her so.

"Tell everyone to make themselves at home and thanks so much, Eunice."

"Do you want me to take the boys to the cabin?" Eunice asked.

"No, but thanks for the offer. They are actually being very good. We'll be along soon."

After the viewing, they left the church and went to the cabin. There were horses and buggies parked everywhere.

"Oh my, I never imagined this many people," James exclaimed nervously.

The visitors came in and out all evening, bringing food and goodies to share with everyone. They visited with the family, sharing memories of Mama, and extending their sympathy.

The sun was going down, and Emily sat on the wood box by the kitchen window, just staring out at the garden area and thinking about how she and her mama worked together planting vegetables. Out of the corner of her eye, she thought she saw a movement. Not sure what she saw, she scooted closer to the window and sorted through the shadows that were cast on the yard by the bare winter tree branches. Yes, there it was. It was a rugged-looking person sliding along the edge of the barn and darting to the edge of the wooded area out of sight. *Who can that be and what are they doing?* She ran to tell Papa what she had seen.

Papa was busy visiting the many people who were still there. So, she waited, but rather impatiently. Once he moved from the sitting room and into the kitchen, she quickly ran up to him and excitedly pulled on his arm to get closer to his ear and said, "Papa, I need to talk to you. I need to tell you what I saw out the kitchen window."

"Slow down, child. What is it?"

"I saw someone, I don't know if it was a man or woman. They were sliding along the side of the barn and when they got to the end, they darted towards the edge of the woods, and I couldn't see them anymore. Papa, I'm scared. Who do you think it could have been, and why do you think they are sneaking around our barn?"

James knew exactly who it was and, getting a little hot under the collar, he searched for something to say that would make sense to Emily and calm her fears.

Speaking softly, he said, "It's probably someone from town who saw all the buggies coming out here and wanted to come and see what was going on and then just tried to sneak away without being seen. I don't think there is any reason to be alarmed."

Just then, his friend Clyde strolled in the door, which gave him a good reason to slip away from Emily to greet him.

Clyde took off his hat and said, "Man, I'm so sorry to hear about your wife. What a shock. Didn't even know she was ill."

"Yeah, neither did I," James said. "We have a lot of catching up to do when everything settles down. I've got a lot to talk with you about. I should be here tomorrow evening with nothing to do after the funeral, so come on over and we'll do some catching up."

"That sounds good to me."

"Get some food man. Look at all this spread. Have you ever seen so much food?"

Finally, and not too soon for James, everyone started leaving. Eunice and several other ladies stayed to help Amanda and Sarah put up the leftovers and clean the kitchen.

"You ladies have been such a great help. I can't thank you enough," Amanda said.

Agreeing, Sarah said, "Yes, thanks so much."

"Well, there is plenty of food left over for you all after the funeral tomorrow," Eunice said.

"That's great. Thanks again," Amanda said, and gave her a hug.

---

Relieved when everyone had gone, James hurried to the barn. "Marge," he growled in a loud voice, "you better show your face and explain to me why you allowed yourself to be seen."

He waited for her to make an appearance, but there was no sound. He walked to the bottom of the opening to the loft and yelled, "Marge, you better get down here right now!" Still, no sound was heard.

He cautiously moved up the crude ladder attached to the wall and peered into the loft. It was empty and there were no signs of her. "Well good," he said to himself, and carefully climbed down the ladder. *Maybe she left and is gone for good.* After looking around the outside of the barn with no sign of her, he went back to the house and went to bed.

*Chapter*

# 8

The next day, after the funeral, the family was totally exhausted and ready to head home. However, Amanda knew she needed to face Papa regarding the arrangements for Emily but hoped that he would agree to wait until tomorrow, since everyone was tired and needed to regroup. As Amanda approached him about it, she expected him to insist that Emily go with him right then and she was prepared to insist otherwise. However, surprisingly, he agreed and even sounded relieved. Amanda thought it seemed strange but was happy she didn't have to deal with him right then. She asked him if he was going to be alright and he assured her that he would be fine. She reminded him of all the food that had been left over from the day before, told him she would see him tomorrow, and they went their separate ways.

---

When James got home, after changing his clothes, he remembered that Clyde was going to come spend the evening with him, so he meandered out to the barn. Stepping into the barn, he heard some scuffling from the loft above. *Oh no, is that scoundrel back again?*

"Marge, is that you? I thought you were gone. I don't need you hanging around here anymore. You've got to go."

Marge, hurrying down the ladder, missed a rung halfway down and fell on her backside with a thump on the floor. Neither could keep from laughing and James' attitude softened.

"Did you bring food?" she asked. "I'm starved."

James expected Clyde to show up any minute and needed to figure out what he was going to tell him about Marge. He knew he couldn't keep her hidden forever and was sure Clyde could help him come up with a plan. He really didn't want to send her packing because he was starting to get attached to her for some strange reason. About that time Clyde came lumbering into the barn.

"Well, well, well, what do we have here?" Clyde said, surprised.

Turning with a jerk, James said, "Yeah, partner, come on in, I need to talk to you about some things. This is Marge. I found her sleeping in the loft. Do you remember back a month or so ago when they ran a bunch of gypsies out of the woods up by Craig's Creek?"

"Yeah, I do remember something about that."

"Well, she refused to leave and hid up in a tree until everyone cleared out and was alone in the woods. When it got so freezing cold, she found our loft and has been up there for a while now and I'm not sure what to do about her."

Clyde looked at Marge as she was chunking wood into the stove and asked, "Where are you headed, and how long are you planning on staying around here?"

"Nosey ain't ya," she shot back.

James realized this was not going to go well and quickly asked Clyde to go with him to the house to get some of the leftover food. He thought it would give him some time alone with Clyde to fill him in on some of the details about Marge. Turning to Marge he said, "We'll bring food shortly, keep the fire going."

As they started for the house, James began explaining to Clyde how he found her up in the loft the night after Lily passed and how she eavesdropped on him during his time of grieving.

"She is a very feisty and crude person with street knowledge beyond her years, yet there is something about her that makes me feel sorry for her, and I find myself caring for her. I just can't turn her out."

"James, for goodness' sake, listen to yourself. She's probably not much older than Emily, and your wife just passed. Do you know how that will look and what people will say if you keep her around here? How will your girls react to her?"

"I know, I know, Clyde. That's why I need your help. I know you don't have a wife or children that rely on you, but please can you try and see my side for once? Marge, even though she's too young, sat and had a beer with me and was actually willing to work with me building the coffin I was making for Lily. I never had that kind of relationship with Lily. She never came out to the barn with me and let her hair down. She was always making me feel guilty for not being home and made me feel like I wasn't the father I needed to be."

"Well, I know you aren't going to like what I have to say James, but maybe your guilt wasn't coming from Lily, but from you knowing you shouldn't have spent so many nights out there in the barn away from her. You know you didn't spend the time with the girls that you should have. Guilt usually comes from within when someone knows in their heart of hearts that they are doing wrong. Lily is not to blame for the guilt you felt. That is something you caused, and you are the only one that can fix it.

"I hate to admit it, but I guess you're right. I have a lot of regrets now that Lily is gone."

"Well, I guess I shouldn't have come over so often and hung out either."

James gathered the food in a basket, headed out the door, and said, "But now, what am I going to do with Marge?"

"For starters, I would suggest that she gets cleaned up. She's probably never had a bath. She's one mess."

They entered the barn to see Marge sitting cross-legged in front of the fire with a beer in her hand. "It's 'bout time you came with the food. Grab a drink and bring that food over here. I'm past starving."

"Where did you get that beer?" Clyde asked.

"Oh, like you don't know where the beer is kept around here."

"Girly," Clyde continued, "you are too young to be drinking beer."

"What did you call me?" Marge snapped. "Don't you 'girly' me. My name is Marge. And now I see you're not only nosey, but bossy too."

James, trying to de-escalate the banter, said, "Now, now. Come on, let's eat and be more civil and enjoy these good sandwiches and cookies."

With her mouth half full of sandwich, Marge asked James, "Well, James what *are* you going to do with me?"

The night in the barn extended into the wee hours of the morning. The three discussed the pros and cons of the situation. James explained that Emily would be back home tomorrow and there were definitely some decisions that needed to be solidified before then.

"How in the world, James, will you explain to your girls why the likes of her is hanging around your barn?"

Given the fact that James remembered how well Marge worked with him on building the coffin, he said, "Well, what about this scenario? What if I tell them I hired Marge to work with me on my farrier appointments?"

Clyde, scratching his head, reluctantly agreed that might work since he realized that Marge was not going anywhere.

"Marge, what do you think about working every day with me?" James asked.

"I would love it, but what's in it for me?"

"For one thing, you won't have to hide all the time because I can explain to my girls that you are someone I've hired to help me with my business, and that I'm renting you a space in the barn to live. I can bring bedding out for you, put it in the loft, and make sure you have something to eat. How does that sound?"

"Bedding sure would be nice," she said to herself. She was so thrilled that he was considering keeping her that her heart was pounding. She got up and paced the floor so he wouldn't notice her excitement. Then took her time answering because she didn't want to seem too eager. Finally, she said, "Yeah, I guess that would work."

Clyde, who was so disgusted not only with this arrangement but mostly with Marge's attitude, said, "Given you don't have a place to live or food to eat, except scraps from garbage cans, you would be stupid to turn down that offer. But I'll tell you this, I wouldn't let you come onto my farm with you looking like you do."

"Yeah, about that," James said. "You do need to get yourself cleaned up if you are working for me and especially before my daughters see you. I'll get a bucket of water and put it on the stove to heat for washing up, and I'll bring some things from the house that I know you will need."

Clyde took this opportunity to explain that he needed to be going home and that he would see them tomorrow.

*Shattered*

James brought a metal watering trough for Marge to bathe in and wash her clothes. He also brought a towel, soap, one of Lily's hairbrushes, and one of his nightshirts, which he explained she could wear while her clothes dried by the fire till morning. He gave her a pillow and a couple of blankets from the sewing room, as well.

He was so thankful that Emily was not home while he was getting Marge taken care of and thankful that Clyde had helped in the decision-making process. He took a deep breath and, sighing a sigh of relief, he said to himself, "I think this will really work out".

After gathering up the food scraps, he told Marge to be ready for work in the morning. "We'll be heading out around noon tomorrow after I settle things with the girls about bringing Emily home. There is a lot of work to catch up on, having been off for the past several days."

"I'll be ready, you can count on me," Marge replied.

Leaving the barn, he said over his shoulder "I sure hope so."

## Chapter 9

It was late Thursday afternoon when everyone returned home from the funeral. Amanda and Jake's house was a large, yet quaint, farmhouse. Even though it had many spacious rooms, everyone always gathered in the big country kitchen with the big stone fireplace. Hooks where winter coats were hung lined the wall on one side of the fireplace, and a large open wood box that was stacked high with wood, on the other. In front of the fireplace was a huge oval rag rug where the children could play, but you would mostly see their lazy golden lab curled up. In the middle of the room was a long wood table and benches that Jake had made. It was plenty big enough when the whole family would gather for dinner. It was the place where games were played, plans and decisions were made, and discussions took place. And tonight was one of those nights when a discussion needed to take place between Amanda and Sarah. One that neither of the girls really wanted to have but was inevitable. Amanda hadn't had much time to talk with Sarah about what arrangements should be implemented regarding Emily. However, she knew Sarah was not in favor of Emily living alone with Papa. Since she knew that he was expecting her to bring Emily to him in the morning, she invited Sarah and Harry over for a later-than-usual dinner so they could discuss the plans.

After Emily and the boys were finished eating, they were excused. The boys scampered to the playroom and Emily went up to her room to read. Harry and Jake moved to the living room to relax, talk, and play with the boys for a bit. That left the girls alone to come up with a solution for Emily.

Sarah started the conversation by asking Amanda if Emily was going back to school on Monday.

"Yes, that's the plan if Papa will agree. Emily and I have talked, and she is excited to get back with her friends. I think seeing Beth and Ruthie Ann will be good for her. But she knows that Papa wants her to stay home to take care of the house, and that bothers her."

"Well, we need to just tell Papa our decision and tell him this is the way it's going to be and be done with it. Mama always gave in to him, and he thinks that he can continue to call all the shots. As far as I'm concerned, that's going to stop. He doesn't know what's best for a fifteen-year-old girl," Sarah said emphatically.

Amanda agreed that she and Sarah needed to come up with a healthy plan for Emily and stick to their guns. But she also knew they needed to handle Papa with respect, or he wouldn't agree to anything they had to say.

"As I promised, I'm supposed to take Emily to Papa in the morning. But I will go and see if he will agree to letting her stay with us until after church on Sunday. What do you think, Sarah? How about us taking dinner to Papa's and all of us eating there after church? Then Emily could stay and be ready to go back to school on Monday."

"You can take dinner to Papa's after church if you want, but I'm not going. I really don't want to see Papa right now. I don't think he treated Mama right, and if he had, Mama would still be with us. And I don't think Emily should go back there either. After going back and forth, Sarah reluctantly agreed that Emily could go back home on Sunday. Amanda would propose the idea to Papa tomorrow. Then on Sunday, Amanda and her family would take dinner over and spend the afternoon.

"I want to stay long enough to get Emily settled back in her room and get things ready for her to get back into the school routine," Amanda said.

Having reservations about everything, Sarah wanted to make one thing clear. "I want to make sure that both Papa and Emily know that she can come back here if she feels used or uncomfortable. That's the only way I'll feel comfortable with her staying with Papa long term."

Amanda agreed and said she would go talk with Papa in the morning and explain their decision. "Hopefully he will go along with our plan," she added.

Before clearing the table, they called Emily down and went over the plan they were going to propose to Papa. They wanted to see how she felt about their decision.

"Oh, that sounds like a great idea. I'm especially glad, Amanda, that you will be spending the afternoon with me. I hate the thought of staying there without Mama, but I am looking forward to sleeping in my own room."

"We'll see about you spending some weekends with us, and we'll pick you up for church on Sundays and have dinner together. How does that sound?" Amanda asked.

Emily went over to each of her sisters and gave them a big hug and said, "That sounds like a great plan. That way I'll get to see Beth and Ruthie Ann too."

"Some Sundays, if you want, you can invite them to come have dinner with you."

"That would be so much fun," Emily squealed.

The three girls cleared the table and started putting things away. Emily seemed relieved and had a little bounce in her step when she grabbed the drying towel and said she would help dry the dishes. Sarah and Amanda looked at each other and they knew they had made the right decision. All of them had a sense of relief and chit-chatted as they worked together.

"Sarah, can't I talk you into going with me tomorrow morning to talk with Papa for moral support?" Amanda asked.

"No, but I will come over and watch the boys for you and stay with Emily. I don't want you to take her with you in case he doesn't like the plan and insists that she stay."

"That's great. Then you will be here when I get back, and I can tell you what he said and how he took everything. I'm not looking forward to it at all."

## Chapter 10

James woke early as usual. It was still dark, and the room was deathly silent. He turned over, threw off the bed covers, and slid his legs over the side of the bed. He sat there for a while with his elbows on his knees and his head in his hands, trying to bring his thoughts in line with what day it was and what he needed to do today. He ran his fingers through his hair, remembered that it was Friday, and he was taking Marge to work with him today.

He stood up, put his hands on the middle of his back, stretched, and said, "Why is this happening to me?"

It had only been a few days since Lily passed, yet to him, it seemed much longer. As he was getting himself dressed, he realized how much he missed smelling the coffee brewing that Lily made for him each morning, and the sounds of her softly moving about the kitchen getting breakfast ready. It was the incentive he needed each morning to get up and get his day started. However, now he had to go stoke the fire, and put on the coffee himself. *I don't need to be doing this*, he thought to himself, as he placed the coffee pot on the stove much harder than necessary. "That is why I am insisting that Emily stay home where she belongs," he bellowed to himself.

Speaking Emily's name jogged his memory that Amanda was supposed to be bringing Emily home this morning. Realizing this, he quickly fixed his breakfast and made extra for Marge. She had promised to be ready this morning to go with him on his rounds, and surprisingly, she was up, dressed, and waiting for him when he entered the barn.

"Well, look at you. You are up early and looking right nice, if I do say so myself. I see you took care of getting your clothes washed and dried." Laughing, he continued, "And you smell better too."

"Oh, come on now. What ya got there in that pan?"

"I made you some eggs and scrapple. The eggs didn't turn out so good. I'm not used to cooking. That's why my Emily is needed here, and I'm going to make it clear to Amanda when she brings Emily home this morning that she stays here from now on. Marge, you be sure and stay out of sight while they are here. When I'm finished with Amanda, I'll be out to get you, and we will get to work."

James went back inside to wait for Amanda and Emily. He was happy to leave the kitchen for Emily to clean up.

"After all," he said convincing himself, "that will show her how much she's needed around here." He sat down to have another cup of coffee and wait.

When Amanda's horse and buggy came up the lane, James jumped up from the table and ran to the door excited to see the girls. Amanda stepped down and started toward the house.

"Where is Emily?"

"She's at the house with Sarah and the boys." Waving him back into the house, Amanda continued nervously, "Sarah and I had a discussion last night about Emily's wellbeing and—"

"There's no discussion needed," James interjected. "She's coming home and that's all there is to it."

"No, Papa! That's not all there is to it. She is a child, blossoming into a young lady, and since she doesn't have Mama, she needs her sisters to look out for her."

Oh, how she wished Sarah was there to back her up. But she pressed on. "What we have decided is, that since this is already Friday, she will stay with me until Sunday after church. Then Harry, the boys, and I will bring Sunday dinner for us to eat together. I want to stay awhile until I'm sure she is settled back in her room, and she has everything ready for school Monday morning."

James grunted, "I told you she is not going back to school. There is too much for her to do around here."

"Well, then she's not coming home, Papa," she said and headed for the door.

"Wait!" he yelled after her. "Where do you think you are going? We are not done here."

"Yes, we are, unless you consent to her continuing school. We talked with her last night, and she wants to come home to her own bedroom and familiar surroundings. But even more, she is excited about going back to school and being with her friends. You only think about yourself, Papa! That's the way you were with Mama. We saw it, and it hurt us watching it. And I'm not going to let you treat Emily that way."

Amanda surprised herself by speaking to him that way. She always tried to respect him even though his behavior was uncalled for and upsetting to her. That was where she and Sarah differed. Sarah was always quick to speak her mind and got into many spats with him. That's the reason for Sarah not wanting to be around Papa any more than she had to. James slumped down in his chair knowing she was right but sat there not saying a word.

"Well, Papa, what will it be?"

"You've got a point I guess," he said. "I'll see you Sunday then, right?"

"Yes, but know that if we find out you are putting too many demands on her, or if she isn't comfortable here, we will make other arrangements."

"Yeah, yeah, I hear you. Now go on, I've got work to do."

"All right, but I mean what I say."

Amanda was relieved that her message to Papa was over, but she didn't feel very confident that he was going to keep up his part of the bargain. When she got home, Amanda explained to Sarah that she had let Papa know how they felt and told Sarah how she had talked back to him.

"I sounded like you for a minute, Sarah." They both laughed and agreed they would keep a close watch on things.

## Chapter 11

James was chomping at the bit to get going on his rounds and was glad when Amanda left. He had a lot of catching up to do since he had been off work the last few days. Things had to get back on schedule. He went to the barn to harness up his old mare and load the wagon with his tools.

"Marge," he yelled, "come here. Let me show you how to do this because this is a job I will expect you to do each morning."

Marge stood up and put her hands on her hips. "Oh, you do, do you? So, you're ordering me around now? What's in all of this for me?"

"Marge, are you really saying that right now? I'm giving you a place to sleep and making sure you have food. Isn't that worth something to you?

"Well, yes, but it's hard for me to sleep up there on that hard floor when you are sleeping in a nice, warm, comfy bed all alone." Giving him a punch in the arm, she said, "But I guess, I'll have to wait until you think I deserve a *raise* before I get that privilege, huh?"

Hoisting himself up in the wagon, he said, "You know, Marge, you talk too much. Get on up here and let's get going."

She climbed up and scooted a little closer to him than necessary, but James really didn't seem to mind. He said, "I have to stop at Clyde's to pick up some things."

"Okay, but I don't think Clyde likes me so much," she said.

"Why would you say such a thing?"

"I think he thinks I am in the way of you and him being the buddies you used to be."

"Well, Marge, everything has changed since Lily passed, so I don't think it's about you. And besides, don't tell him, but I'd rather spend the evening with you than with him."

She laughed and scooted even closer. They rode the rest of the way in silence, lost in their own thoughts.

Clyde heard the wagon coming up the lane. He looked up and saw that it was James.

"Hey Clyde," James yelled from the wagon. "I've come for the shoes you made for me, before we head out to the farms." Clyde carefully laid the tools he was working on to the side of the fire and stood. Marge jumped down from the wagon, curious to see what Clyde was doing. The smell of the heated metal and wood fire filled her senses. The wood pavilion where Clyde worked was hanging full of his creative ironworks which thoroughly intrigued her.

"Well, well, Marge, you clean up pretty nicely." Then turning to James, he said, "Are you really going to ride out of town with her? How do you think that is going to sit with your farmers? You know, she actually looks like a girl now that she's cleaned up a bit and won't be mistaken for a fellow. I don't know, James, I think you are making a big mistake. Besides, in what way do you think she's going to be able to help you?"

Marge whirled around and got in Clyde's face. "Listen, Clyde, you don't know anything about me, and I'll have you know that I'm capable of learning a trade and tougher than any other girl you've ever met. So get off my case, will ya!"

She stomped back to the wagon and waited for James. Clyde, taking a step backwards, let it go and went to get the horseshoes he had made for James.

As James was paying for the shoes, Clyde said, "I just don't understand, James, what this is all about."

"You don't have to understand, Clyde, and honestly, I'm not sure I understand all that's happening either. But let's not allow this to get in the way of our friendship. In fact, why don't you come over Monday night and let's get back to some semblance of what we had before Lily passed."

Slapping James on the back, Clyde said, "Okay, sounds good. See you then."

As they rode through town, heads turned as they noticed that James had someone sitting on the seat next to him. They stretched their necks to see if they recognized who it might be. People were asking one another who they thought the girl was sitting alongside James. But no one seemed to have seen her before.

Immediately the gossip wheel started turning. "Lily hasn't been gone a week, and he's already got him a girl," they murmured amongst themselves.

Ignoring their stares, James told Marge that she was going to have to act like she knew what she was doing while working with him to make a good impression on the farmers.

"They have put a lot of confidence in my work, and I want to continue to earn their confidence and respect," he told her.

"Well, I don't know what you want me to do. I've never done anything like this before."

"Stay close to me, and at least act like you know what you're doing. And don't strike up any conversations with them." James had some legitimate concerns about how this was going to work.

As they approached the first farm on his route, he pulled the wagon alongside the barn, and both jumped down. "Get my toolbox, while I talk with Ernie to see what he needs done today."

"Good afternoon, James, I'm so glad to see you today, and so sorry to hear about your wife," Ernie said, while shaking his hand.

"Thanks, Ernie, but life goes on, and that's why I'm here today, to get on with my business." Marge came around the corner with his toolbox and set it down beside him. Gesturing between Marge and Ernie, he said, "I want to introduce you to a helper I've taken on. Ernie, this is Marge. Marge, Ernie." Ernie extended his hand to her, and she awkwardly extended her hand. She wasn't the hand-shaking type of person. "She's going to help me get caught up with the work that I've neglected to take care of since I was off for a week." Ernie eyed Marge up and down but came back to reality when James asked, "So, is it the workhorses that need to be checked this time?"

"Yes, and I bought a couple of sheep at the auction last week that need their hooves trimmed. I have them penned up over there under the oak tree." He pointed to the tree and began walking away. "Well, I'll let you get to work. I've got to get back to fixing the fence I was working on, so just holler at me when you are finished, and I'll settle up with you."

James was relieved that he wasn't going to hang around to chat while he did his work, as he needed to show Marge the ropes a little to get her feeling comfortable around the animals. He was interested in showing her the ways that she could be a help to him.

Ernie didn't go back to mending his fence, but rather went straight to the house where his wife, Bess, was washing clothes.

"You're not going to believe this, Bess," Ernie began, "James came today with a helper."

"Well, what's wrong with that?"

"Bess, it's not just any old helper, it's a young girl."

Bess stopped what she was doing and barked, "Why in the world would a young girl want to do the filthy job of cleaning hoofs and shoeing horses in stinky old barns?" She went to the window and peered out but was very disappointed when she couldn't see anything. "Ernie, didn't his wife just pass away recently?"

"Yes, that's why he didn't come by earlier this week. This just doesn't seem quite right. But I've got to get back to working on the fence."

By the time Bess went out to hang up her clothes, James and Marge had moved from the barn to the sheep that Ernie had penned up under the oak tree. Bess could hear them before she saw them, laughing and sounding like they were having a good time. As she peered out around the sheet she had just hung on the line, she finally spotted them and proceeded to take her time hanging up the remainder of the clothes so she could watch them. Finally, Bess went back to the house, and thought to herself, *When I finish with my wash, I need to go down the road and tell Clara about this.* Shaking her head, she whispered, "She's not going to believe this."

Clara was just as surprised and interested in the news as Bess was. "You know Bess," Clara said, "I always pitied Lily. Whenever we had functions at church or picnics in the park, she always would come alone with her girls. She never said anything, but you could tell she wished she had a companion with her, like the rest of us. She ended up hanging out with the single ladies. She and James just didn't seem to have many things in common."

"That's such a shame, and now here he is with a young girl laughing and throwing around flirtatious words. Right in my backyard! I tell you, it's just not right."

It didn't take long for the word to spread from farm to farm that James had a young girl working with him. He was able to take care of several more farms on his route before he needed to head home, and by the time he got to the last one, there was a coolness that he felt with the farmers that he hadn't sensed before. He brushed it off as being later in the day than he usually worked, and the farmers being busy taking care of their evening chores. Heading back to town, James remembered he needed to stop by the market to get some items so that Emily could make lunches for school and food for her to fix supper with during the week. *Next time*, he thought, *she can come to the market with her own grocery list.*

When they made it into town, just as they did when they rode out of town in the morning, heads turned, and whispers were heard. James told Marge to stay in the wagon. He did not want to subject her to possible ridicule from those who were quick to speak their minds. As he entered the market, the people who would usually strike up a conversation with him met him instead with disgust. He went about gathering the different items he needed and was quick to pay and leave. He definitely felt the tension, and wondered how he was going to put a stop to the weirdness. He handed the groceries to Marge, hopped up into the seat beside her, took the reins, and headed home. He decided to stop and talk to Clyde before going home to see if he had heard any gossip from anyone during the day. James hated the silent treatment he was getting from everyone. This was so unusual for him. He was usually the one who knew what was going on all over town and the one that everyone would get their news from. Clyde invited them to stay and eat with him. Reluctantly, James consented, only because he really needed to get some advice from him.

"How was your first day back on your route?" Clyde asked.

"It wasn't bad. Still have some catching up to do. What's really bothering me though is how I'm being treated by the townspeople. All the weird stares and silent treatment. I guess they have a problem with me having a young helper sitting beside me so soon after Lily passed."

"Well, what do you expect?" Clyde asked.

"Have you heard anything today, Clyde?"

"I did have to make a run into town to make a delivery, and I was asked if I knew who you had with you today."

"And what did you tell them?"

"I told them that as far as I knew, you hired a helper. That is all there is to it, right, James?"

"Uh, oh, uh, yes of course, Clyde. What would make you think anything different?"

Marge piped up and said, "Well now, James, we could really make them talk if you wanna. I mean, I think that would be kinda fun, don't ya think? If they're gonna talk, might as well give them somethin' to talk about. What do ya say there, Jamie Boy?"

"Stop that kind of talk Marge," James chastised her, and quickly changed the subject. Turning to Clyde, he said, "Amanda is bringing Emily back home Sunday and I have to figure things out. What do you think I should do? Do you think I should tell the girls on Sunday about Marge staying in the barn?"

"That's a decision you're going to have to make, as far as when to tell them, but you know you will eventually have to tell them."

"Yeah, you're right. It's giving me a headache. Come on Marge, we need to get home. Thanks, Clyde for sharing your supper with us."

On their way home, James told Marge, "I don't think I'm going to say anything to the girls about you unless it gets brought up. But if it does, and it probably will, given everyone's reactions in town, I'll just admit to having a helper but not that you are staying in the barn."

That really didn't sit well with Marge. "When are ya gonna stop being embarrassed 'bout having me around? After all, your wife is gone, and you are free to do whatever ya want or feel like doin'."

"Yeah, I know, but you don't understand. I have to keep some sense of peace in the family. It's been hard on them having just lost their mama. They have always been very protective of her and now to her memory."

## Chapter 12

Sunday morning found Amanda up at the crack of dawn, fixing everyone breakfast and preparing Sunday dinner, just like her mama used to do. But today she was preparing a picnic-type dinner because she was taking it to Papa's after church. They were taking Emily home today and planned to all eat together. Amanda was still apprehensive about leaving Emily there, and Sarah didn't make it any easier on her because of her distrust in Papa. However, they all agreed to give it a try.

It wasn't long until she heard the pitter-patter of little feet on the floor above her and then clumping noises coming down the stairs. Charlie and Willy came into the kitchen with their hair askew, yawning, and wiping their sleepy eyes. They were up earlier than usual this morning, but Amanda was ready for them and ushered them up to the table. Just as she was placing their bowls of oatmeal in front of them, Emily came into the kitchen.

"Good morning, Emily, would you like a bowl of oatmeal too?"

"Sure, that sounds good."

Amanda continued, "How are you feeling this morning? Are you ready to go home to your own room and go to school in the morning?"

"Yes, I've already packed up my things, and I'm so excited to see my friends tomorrow."

Jake came in from milking and was surprised to find everyone already up and sitting around the table. Amanda got up to get his coffee and fix him a breakfast plate. She reminded him of the plans for taking Emily home after church and eating dinner together with Papa.

"I'll need to stay for a while after dinner so I can get Emily settled and make sure everything is ready for her to go to school."

Jake told her that he would have to come straight home after they ate to take care of things around the farm, but that he didn't mind coming back to get her and the boys later in the evening. She was fine with that arrangement and asked him to help get the boys ready for church.

She looked at Emily and said, "Go ahead and get dressed and bring your things downstairs."

Jake told her to put her things by the door and he would take care of getting them in the buggy. "Gonna really miss you, Emily," he told her. "You are such a joy to be around, and the boys are especially going to miss you."

"Yeah, Jake, I know, and I'm going to miss all of you too."

"You know Emily, you can come here anytime you want."

"I know, and I'm sure I'll take advantage of that from time to time."

"Okay," Amanda said, "I'll clean up the kitchen and get the dinner packed up so we can get to church before the service is over."

Laughing, Jake said to the boys, "I'll race you up the stairs," and they jumped down from the table and started running.

They arrived at church just as the service was starting, so they quietly went inside and sat down. Everything seemed normal until it was time for everyone to shake hands and greet one another. Amanda suddenly realized that she was being ignored by some of the people around her.

Her best friend, Anna, came to her, gave her a hug, and said, "Don't worry, Amanda. I'm sure there is an explanation. We'll talk after church."

"What in the world are you talking about?" she asked as Anna slipped away. Amanda didn't hear anything the preacher said because her mind was going crazy trying to figure out what Anna meant by 'an explanation'. *For what?* She wondered.

After the service ended, she told Jake to look after the boys because she needed to find Anna and talk to her about something. She found Anna talking with some other ladies, and as Amanda approached, the ladies moved on, leaving Anna standing alone.

"Anna," Amanda started, "what in the world were you trying to tell me during the greeting time? What needs an explanation?"

About that time, Emily came running to Amanda with tears streaming down her face saying, "Let's go Amanda! We need to go home and see what Papa has done!"

Putting her arm around Emily and pulling her in close, she said, "No, now just wait a minute. Anna, you need to explain to me what is going on, and right now."

"Well, I guess you really don't know."

"Know what?" Amanda demanded.

"Your Papa was seen leaving town yesterday with a young girl sitting awfully close beside him, just like she belonged there, and then came back into town in the evening with her still sitting by his side. It seems a little inappropriate don't you think, Amanda, given that your mother just passed last week." Amanda was infuriated and, taking Emily by the hand, she went to find Sarah.

"Sarah, did anyone say anything to you about Papa?" Amanda asked.

"No, but I've been busy putting up tables for the ladies' auxiliary meeting in the morning. Why?"

"Well, Anna told me some disturbing news about Papa," and she proceeded to tell Sarah everything she had heard.

Then, turning her attention to Emily, who still had tears streaming down her cheeks, she asked, "What did you hear, sweetie, that has you so upset?"

Trying her best to hold back her tears, she said, "I heard some ladies talking about Papa having a girlfriend."

Sarah was so angry that Amanda had to calm her down. Then they went out to the buggies, where they met up with the men. Jake and Harry, seeing the girls so upset, questioned them about what was going on. After telling them what she had heard, Amanda went to Sarah, who was still fuming.

"Listen, we don't know the whole story until we talk to Papa. Maybe there is a reasonable explanation. Let's all go see Papa and get to the bottom of this. I have plenty of food for all of us, so please, Sarah, come eat with us so we can get this resolved."

"No, absolutely not! Papa is the last person I want to see right now. I've told you before how I feel about Papa taking advantage of Mama, and how he never really cared for her. All Papa thinks about is himself and this is just another example of that behavior. You all go on, and I'll come see you in the morning after I finish my chores. You can tell me all about what Papa has done this time. It will confirm what I've been trying to tell you all along, you'll see."

Amanda and Jake, along with Emily and the boys, crawled into the buggy and headed to see Papa, and Harry and Sarah headed to their home. On the way, Amanda consoled Emily by telling her that she felt confident that Papa had a reasonable explanation and all would be okay.

"Do you remember how Mama taught us the importance of not doing anything that appeared wrong or inappropriate?"

"Yes."

"Well, this is a good example of that, Emily. Papa may not have done anything wrong but seeing him with a girl or lady sitting by his side so soon after Mama passed could give people a reason to think poorly of Papa. Do you see where people may get the wrong impression and could be wondering if he had this *girlfriend* on the side while still with Mama?"

Emily was silent for a few seconds taking in what Amanda was saying and then said, "Yeah, I guess you're right. But do you think he did have a girlfriend, Amanda?"

"No, I don't think that he did, and we need to give Papa the benefit of the doubt until we hear the whole story."

As they pulled up, Amanda noticed Papa coming from the barn with a frying pan in his hand. She thought it strange, especially when she saw him quickly set the pan down behind a pile of logs lying near the path before he walked over to the buggy.

"Hey, can I help carry anything into the house? Hope you brought some good food. I'm starving."

The boys jumped down from the buggy and ran toward the house. Jake started unloading the wagon, and as he set Emily's bags down at James' feet, he said, "Here, you can help Emily into the house with her things."

Papa picked up her bag and walked toward Emily, who was expecting a hug, but instead, he just said, "It's about time you're back home. I sure can use your help around here."

Emily and Amanda's eyes met. Amanda shrugged her shoulders and motioned for Emily to go on into the house. Amanda thought that Papa could have at least given Emily a hug and made her feel welcome, but he was more interested in feeding his starving belly and thinking about all the work that Emily could do for him. *Could there be some validity to how Sarah feels about him?* Amanda wondered.

"Papa," Amanda asked, "what were you doing with that frying pan you were bringing in from the barn?"

"Oh that? You know, Clyde and I spend time together out there, and we cook up some things now and then on the old pot belly." He then hurried on toward the house.

The house felt cold, but it was more than just the temperature. "Why don't you have a fire started in the wood stove?" Amanda asked. "Did you spend the night in the barn?"

"Yeah, it was really late when Clyde left, and I just didn't feel like coming back to an empty house."

Jake offered to get a fire started while Amanda and Emily started getting the dinner on the table. Papa seemed a little nervous as he flitted around the kitchen.

"Hey, boys," Papa said, roughing up their hair, "let's go find the toy box and see what we can find. How does that sound?" They trotted off to the toy box that was in the sitting room. Amanda, Emily, and Jake all looked at each other.

"That's not like Papa at all," Amanda said. "I think he wanted to get away quickly to keep from having a conversation with us."

"He is acting a little guilty, I think," Jake replied.

"Let's just enjoy our lunch before we ask any questions," Amanda said, and Jake agreed.

"Dinner is ready," Amanda announced. It didn't take her calling everyone to dinner the second time. The chairs scraped across the floor as everyone found a place to sit at the table. Jake asked the blessing for the food and started passing the chicken.

"Oh, fried chicken," Papa said. "I haven't had this for a long time. You even made macaroni and cheese. Wow, Amanda, you can bring dinner every Sunday."

"Well, thanks, Papa, but we won't be eating here every Sunday. You are welcome to come to our place for Sunday Dinners."

"Nah, there is too much that needs done around here for me to waste an afternoon out and about."

"It wouldn't be a waste of time, Papa," Emily piped up. "You would be spending time with family, and that's important."

"Well, Emily, you'll be here, and you are family. We can spend time together."

"I'm not going to be here every weekend, Papa, because I will want to spend some weekends with Amanda and Sarah and some with my friends."

"Humph, well, we'll see about that," Papa grumbled.

Amanda quickly said, "Eat up, everyone, and enjoy." *Yes*, Amanda thought, *enjoy the food because what's coming, I'm afraid, won't be so enjoyable.*

Willy and Charlie finished their dinner and were excused to go play. Amanda knew this was the time to have the dreaded conversation. She began by saying, "So Papa, who did you have in the wagon with you when you went to work the other day?"

Dropping his fork onto his plate, making a loud clank, he said, "What, what do you mean? What are you talking about? Oh, yeah, I almost forgot. I got me someone to help with my backlog of jobs since I've missed a week of work."

"How did that work out for you?" Jake asked.

"Oh, it was a great help to me."

"Are you going to keep *him* on with you?"

"Yeah, I probably will."

"What's *his* name?" Jake kept inquiring.

"Oh, what's that got to do with anything? Anyway, I've got to get up from here and get some chores done. Thanks, Amanda, for such a good dinner, and Emily, you can help her clean things up around here. I'll be back in before you go to bed, and we can talk about what to expect next week," and out the door he went.

*That's enough for now*, Amanda thought, *but Papa, we're not done yet. You have a lot of explaining to do.*

Jake excused himself to head home to do his chores. "When do you want me to come back for you and the boys?"

"Give me a couple of hours."

"Okay," Jake said, kissing her on the cheek before heading out the door.

"Now, little Miss Emily, let's get these leftovers put away and then go up to your room and check things out," Amanda suggested.

"I've already taken my things up and everything looks the same as I left it."

"As it should," Amanda said.

"Amanda, what do you think about Papa going along with Jake assuming his helper was a man?"

"He just wasn't being truthful, Emily. And did you notice how quick he was to leave when Jake asked what his helper's name was?"

"You know Amanda, if Papa plans on keeping his helper, we are bound to find out it's a girl and soon. I am going to make sure of that."

"I'm glad you will be here, Emily. You can keep your eyes and ears open and report to us what's going on, but please be careful."

"Oh, I will Amanda, don't you worry."

———••••••———

The next morning, Emily woke up early, excited to get back to school and see her friends. She was a little apprehensive about what the talk might be among them because of what she experienced at church on Sunday. Nonetheless, she was excited to get some sense of normalcy back in her life.

She came down the stairs with a little bounce in her step, and as she entered the kitchen, she noticed her papa coming in the back door. "Wow, Papa, it's early and you are already up and dressed. Where have you been?"

"It doesn't matter where I've been, just put on some coffee."

Emily thought it strange that he was up and dressed, yet seemed to have just woken up, but then again, she thought he must have just had a bad night. He went into his bedroom, and when he came back out, she noticed he had changed his clothes. When he sat down at the table, Emily said, "Papa, you didn't come in last night before I went to bed. You said that you would come in and we would talk about our week."

"Well, I'm here now, so talk."

"What is going on Papa? Where were you last night? You just now came home, didn't you?"

"Oh, all right," he grumbled, "I fell asleep in the barn last night, if you must know. Clyde came over, and we got to playing cards until late, and when he left, I just laid down and fell asleep."

*Yeah*, Emily thought, *that's not a likely story. He probably passed out from too much to drink.* "Well, I'm going to fix my lunch and head out for school. It's a beautiful morning so I'll be walking. What are you going to be doing today, Papa?"

"Humph, same ole same ole. I'll be working the farms in the next county, which will take me a while, so I won't be home until late. When you get home from school, you can fix supper and just leave some on the stove for me, and I'll get it when I come home. You make sure to fix a good amount now. I'm sure I'll be plenty hungry when I get home." Thinking all along that he needed to have enough food to share with Marge.

# Chapter

# 13

When Emily got to school, Beth and Ruthie Ann ran up to greet her and gave her a big hug. Nearly everyone expressed how glad they were to see her and told her how sorry they were about her mother. She did notice a few being standoffish but decided not to let them ruin her day and took her seat. The teacher, Ms. Minard, welcomed the class, and especially Emily since she had been absent for a while, and expressed her condolences. Emily sat up straighter, nodded, and thanked her. At lunch, she asked about the new building being built beside their one-room schoolhouse.

"What is that building?" she asked Ruthie Ann.

"Oh, you haven't heard? They are making a new school building, separating the younger children from the older ones."

"That will be really nice," Emily said. "Especially since our one room is getting overcrowded."

Emily was curious about the building and asked if anyone had gone over to see it. Not waiting for anyone to answer, she started over to take a closer look. There was a crew working hard. She noticed one man in particular. He looked her way, waved, came down off his ladder, and went over to her.

"What are you doing here, young lady," he asked. "We don't want anyone getting hurt."

"Oh," Emily sheepishly said, "I'm not going to bother you. I just wanted to see what it looked like inside. I understand it will be a school room for the older children which I'll be part of when it's finished."

The bell rang signifying the lunch break was over and Emily turned to go.

"See you around," the man said and turned back to continue working. As he headed up the ladder, he thought to himself, *She's a pretty little thing.*

After school and before going home, Emily drifted back over to the new building hoping to maybe see that nice man that talked with her at lunch. "I don't even know his name," she said to herself.

---

As Emily's first day back at school proved to be a little different, James' morning was out of the ordinary as well. Especially when Marge suggested, as they were heading through town, that they stop and get some lunch to take with them. She thought it would be fun to have a picnic somewhere along the way.

James looked at her and said, "What do you have up your sleeve?"

"Oh, you will see, just get some things to make sandwiches and something to drink."

James stopped and obliged her. As they made their way out of town, he explained to her that they were going to go into the next county. Even though it was a little farther out than he normally would go, he wanted to see if he could drum up some new business.

"There are some big farms out that way. It's a far piece but a nice peaceful country road takes us there," he explained to Marge.

When they started down the beautiful tree-lined road, Marge scooted closer to James and said, "It was really nice cuddling up close to you last night. I ain't never slept close to no man before."

"Well now," James said, "that's just between you and me."

"I know for now, but when can it be a for real thing?"

James responded with an emphatic, "Never!"

"Oh, come on now Jamie," Marge whispered in his ear.

"Now stop that kind of stuff, Marge," he said. But at the same time, enjoyed her little games of flirtation.

They rode on in silence until they got to the first farm. James pulled into the lane, jumped down and told Marge to hang tight. He went to see if he could find someone to talk to about how he could benefit them with his services.

Finding an old man in the barn, he called out to him, "Hello there, sorry to bother you, but are you the owner of this fine farm?" he asked.

The old man looked up a bit startled and said, "No, I used to be, but now it belongs to my son."

"Well, I'm James Miller, the local farrier from Stone County. I am spreading out this way and trying to let the farmers know what services I can provide them. Is your son where I can talk with him?"

"No, he's plowing the upper nine acres today getting ready to plant corn. I will certainly tell him about you stopping by. We used to have a man who came by on a regular basis, but he hasn't been here for six months or better. I know my son will be glad to know there is someone else we can use."

"That sounds good. Tell him that I also have connections with the vet in Stone County and can help in areas involving care for the animals as well. I'll be back out this way next week and will stop by. If he wants to set up some work to be done, we can talk then. How does that sound?"

"That will be great. I'll be sure to let him know. James, you said, right?"

"Yes, and your name is?"

"I'm John Turner and my son's name is George. I'm so glad you stopped by. I'll be sure and tell him you'll be back next week."

"Thanks, Mr. Turner."

James returned to the wagon where Marge sat waiting. He hopped up onto the seat and said, "Margie, baby, I think we may have us a new customer. Take this notebook and write down this address and to revisit Mr. George Turner next—"

"Wait," Marge said, holding up her hand, "I don't know how to do any of that stuff. I don't know how to write all of that."

"Oh, for goodness' sake, Marge, give me the book, I'll do it myself."

"I may not be able to write, but there are a lot of other things I can do," she said flirtatiously. Looking at her, he softened.

As he continued meeting the different farmers along the way, James' excitement grew. They all were saying the same thing that Mr. Turner told him, and most of them were interested in his services. He had several who set up appointments with him, and one even had him do some work for them on the spot.

Marge was getting hungry for lunch and was thinking about the picnic that she had in mind. "Are you ready for some lunch, Jamie?" she asked.

"Guess I am. Just been so excited about my new contacts that I've not even stopped to think about lunch. I'll see if there isn't a nice place to pull over in the shade and we'll eat."

Unbeknownst to James, Marge had put the quilt that he had given her from the house, in the back of the wagon. When they stopped, she pulled it out along with the bag of groceries. She spread the quilt out on the ground away from the road in a nice secluded little spot.

"Oh, and what do we have here?" James said, joining her after tethering the horse.

"Come sit down," she said patting the quilt beside her, "and I'll make you a sandwich."

They sat in silence eating their lunch. James broke it by saying, "You know the man at the last place we stopped asked me if you were my wife," and laughed so hard he nearly choked on his sandwich.

Annoyed by his laughter, Marge said, "I don't see what's so funny about that. You know, it could become a real thing."

James stifled his laugh and said, "Oh you think so, do you?"

"Yes, I do. I really like being with you and you seem to enjoy having me around. Doesn't that count for something?"

"Yeah, I guess you're right. But what would people say? Anyway, we've only just met. Don't get ahead of yourself. My girls don't even know about you."

"We really need to talk about that, Jamie. I can't stay in the loft of the barn forever, you know." Silence once again enveloped the moment as they finished their lunch. Marge slid closer to James, put her head on his shoulder and whispered in his ear. James looked down at her, their eyes meeting each other.

"Kiss me, James."

Something stirred within James, and he couldn't resist the temptation. He kissed first her forehead, then her nose, and finally found her lips as they embraced and fell back on the blanket. Both were lost in the moment.

"I've never felt this way before," Marge told James. "I want to be with you forever."

"But you're a child, you can't be much older than Emily."

"So what, does that really make any difference?"

"I guess it wouldn't, if you were in love."

"Well, do you love me, James?"

Just then, the old mare whinnied and stomped her foot on the ground. James shot straight up and, coming to his senses, said, "We gotta go, Marge. Gather up things and take them to the wagon. We've still got to visit a few more farms before we head home."

# Chapter 14

Emily, promising Amanda to keep an eye on things, did just that, and some time later at a Sunday dinner, she filled her in. She told her about seeing Papa on numerous mornings coming in from the barn wearing the same clothes he had on the day before. It was so strange.

"Did you ask him about it?" Amanda asked.

"Yes, and when I did, he gave me some story about Clyde coming over and falling asleep in the barn. Now, Amanda, I haven't seen Clyde's horse around there for quite some time."

"That is strange, Emily, because Clyde always tethered his horse right in front of the barn, in plain sight."

"Another thing, Amanda, when I fix dinner, he wants me to always make extra because he says he gets really hungry after working all day. I know he can't be eating all that I fix by himself. If it *is* for his helper or for Clyde, why doesn't he just say so?"

"Have you seen anything of his helper around the barn?"

"No, but she's still around because a couple of the girls at school talk amongst themselves, but loud enough for me to hear, making snide remarks about seeing Papa and his *girlfriend* in town. I just try to ignore them, but honestly, it hurts me."

"I'm so sorry that you have to put up with the guff from Papa's actions. On a sweeter note, let's call for the boys and enjoy some apple pie together."

"That sounds wonderful."

As Emily and the boys were finishing their pie, Amanda said, "Before Jake takes you home, I'm going to get some leftovers ready for you and Papa to eat later."

Emily said, "Don't forget to make extra for Papa and his *big appetite*," and they both laughed.

Emily got into the buggy with Jake and started on her way home. As much as Emily would have liked to stay longer at Amanda's, she was anxious for Monday and another day at school when she could see the nice carpenter man she had become friends with. All she thought about was how he made her feel. The fact that he was older than she was didn't make a difference to her. Just the thought of his handsome suntanned face and blue eyes, which seemed to glisten when he smiled at her, made coming home and putting up with Papa bearable.

The steady rhythm of the buggy wheels on the road was comforting. She relaxed and became lost in her thoughts.

*I know Ruthie Ann thinks I shouldn't be hanging around the construction site so much after school. She keeps telling me that spending so much time with my friend is going to cause people to talk, especially since he's so much older than me. She says she doesn't understand why I would want to be doing that instead of spending time with her and Beth. Secretly, I just think she's jealous because she asks me so many questions about him.*

Her thoughts were interrupted when Jake said, "We're here." Putting his hand on her shoulder, he added emphatically, "You *do* understand that you are welcome at our home anytime. I know things are somewhat rough for you right now."

"Thanks, I appreciate that, and I know."

She jumped out of the buggy, and Jake handed her the bundle of leftovers. Waving goodbye, she went into the house and straight to the kitchen to put them away. As usual, Papa was nowhere to be seen. She stoked the fire to heat up the cold house, then went upstairs to her bedroom.

She finished her homework, prepared her things for school the next day, and got ready for bed. Not feeling hungry for the leftovers that Amanda had given them, she lay down on her bed and let her thoughts drift to her carpenter man. *I don't know how or when I'm going to tell my sisters about him*, she thought to herself, and drifted off to sleep.

## Chapter

# 15

Emily had been visiting her carpenter friend for a while now. They had exchanged first names some time ago, and she knew him to be Lester, and that he was from New York. School was about to be out for the summer, and she was going to miss watching Lester work and spending time with him. She had begun to feel comfortable talking with him and felt like he was a real friend. Papa got home much later than school let out, affording her time to hang around after school until Lester had finished working for the day.

Today was no different. She ventured over to the nearly finished school building where the men were working. Lester spotted her and waved. She walked over and hoisted herself up onto the porch where she sat, dangling her legs over the edge. She opened her lunchbox and finished the sandwich she hadn't eaten at lunchtime. Anxiously, she sat swinging her legs back and forth as she waited for him to finish his work. She didn't know why he would want to waste his time on a kid like her, but she was glad that he did.

A short while later, however, it felt like an eternity to Emily, he sauntered toward her with his lunchbox under his arm and his hat in his hand. He looked tired and older today than she remembered him. He came over to the porch and leaned against it facing her.

"How was your day, little missy?" he said, greeting her with a smile.

"It was great. I enjoy school and I am not looking forward to being out for the summer. It's what keeps me busy and my mind off things at home."

"What's going on at home?"

"My mama passed away a while back and Papa doesn't come home much. He stays out in the barn with his friend and sometimes just sleeps there. Your friendship means a lot to me. I go home to an empty house every day since Mama passed. So, spending a little time chatting with you gives me something to look forward to. But now that school is almost out for the summer, I will really miss these times."

"Well, little missy, I really look forward to visiting with you each afternoon as well. Just because school is out doesn't mean we can't still get together sometimes."

"But you are about finished with the new school building, which is really nice, by the way, and then what? If you go back to New York, I'll never see you again."

He reached over and put his hand on hers and said, "Whoa, slow down now. Don't get ahead of yourself. Who said I was going back to New York when we finish this building?"

Blushing from the touch of his rough hand on hers, she asked, "You're not?"

"No, I have a contract with the county. After we finish the school, we will be working on the courthouse. They want some renovations done. That means I'll be staying around for a little while."

Emily sighed, and a sense of relief swept over her. "Oh, that's really great. Where are you and your workers staying while you are here?"

I'm at the Country Inn, and the other fellows all live close by. I won several general contracting bids that the county had listed. One of the things that helped me win them was that I would use local construction workers, which would provide jobs for the locals, and instead of just overseeing the job, I would work right along with the men."

"Very interesting, what's the name of your company?"

"It's my firm, and it's called Granger's Construction Firm."

"I take it your last name is Granger?"

"Good guess! I am Lester Granger. By the way, what is your last name, Emily?"

"It's Miller. My Papa is a farrier and assists the local vet from time to time. I used to ride with him occasionally to watch him work. We have ridden by the Country Inn many times, but I've never been inside. How is it?"

"The Inn is a fine place. They give me free breakfast each morning and pack a free lunch for me. Then, for a price, of course, they have a good evening menu to choose from."

"Speaking of evening meals, I need to get home and fix supper for my papa and me. He comes home starving, and if I don't have something fixed, he gets plenty upset. Besides, I'm sure you have plenty of other things you need to be doing other than sitting here talking with me."

"No, that's not true, but I understand you need to get home. Would you let me give you a ride in my truck?"

"You would do that? I've never ridden in a truck before. So yes, Lester, that would be great."

They gathered up their lunchboxes and walked to the truck. Lester stepped ahead and opened the door for her. *He makes me feel so special and doesn't treat me like a child,* she thought. As she was getting into it, she looked around, hoping that no one saw her. The last thing she wanted was for this to get back to Papa. Lester started the truck and swung in beside her. She felt so proud to be riding in a truck, let alone sitting beside Lester. The ride home was short but thrilling.

"You can just let me out at the lane to my house, and I'll walk the rest of the way. Thank you so much for the ride."

"You are very welcome. Anytime I can be of service, let me know. You know where to find me. I'm either working on the school building or at the Inn."

She gathered her things, opened the door, and climbed down.

"Thanks again," she said and closed the door.

She stood looking down the road as he drove off. She couldn't believe that she had just ridden in a truck. Very few people in town had an automobile, mostly businessmen, and it was very rare to see a truck. She started down the lane toward her house, excited to tell someone about her experience. But it soon dawned on her that she couldn't tell anyone. She certainly couldn't tell Papa because she didn't want him to find out about Lester, and she couldn't tell Amanda or Sarah because they definitely wouldn't approve. She couldn't even tell Beth or Ruthie Ann, at least not yet. *I guess it's just my little secret,* she thought and skipped the rest of the way home.

## Chapter 16

The days flew by. James spent more and more time with Marge. They went out every day to the farms and worked alongside each other and grew closer and closer. Deep down, he knew the feelings that he had for Marge were wrong, but he couldn't help himself. He was so lonely, and she was such good company in the evenings. They would sit in the barn together, drinking from his stash, joking, and laughing, something he'd never done with a woman before. He loved the way her body felt pressed against his when they would fall asleep in the barn together. He couldn't help how he felt when he kissed her lips, even though he knew he shouldn't be doing it. It got harder and harder to keep the secret from Emily and the other girls.

Clyde was upset because he wasn't being invited over for drinks anymore and would complain about it. James would tell him that he had gotten a lot of new farms to take care of and he was simply coming home so tired all he wanted to do was go to bed and sleep. Clyde wasn't buying that story and knew the real reason was Marge. It really put a wedge in his and James' relationship. This left James having no one to talk to about everything. He was confused and just wasn't sure what he should do. The time wasn't right to tell the girls yet, but he knew that Emily had some suspicions. He tried to play dumb and avoid her, but school would be out for summer soon, and she would be home all day roaming around. He knew that he needed to make sure that she didn't stumble onto Marge in the barn or find her things in the loft. He decided to put a latch on the barn door, too high for Emily to reach, knowing that Marge could climb in and out through the window like she did before, if she needed to.

Emily had to be creative in coming up with ways to spend time with Lester without anyone finding out now that school was out for the summer. She knew that until the school building was done, she could still go there and watch him work while Papa was gone. But it became more of a challenge when it was finished, and Lester was working on other jobs in the county. Beth and Ruthie Ann knew Emily's secret and provided a good excuse for her to walk into town most days. She would see them occasionally but mainly met up with Lester. As time went by, she wanted more than that. She began leaving the house at night after Papa went into the barn with his supper because she knew he wouldn't be back in the house until late into the night, if at all. She and Lester decided that she would walk to the edge of town in the evenings. He would meet her there, then they would go somewhere together. Most of the time, he would buy her dinner, and they would go to a park or the lake. She loved just being with him, it didn't matter what they were doing or where they went. She discovered that they were both gravitating toward each other, more and more. They would hold hands, or she would sometimes lay her head on his shoulder, which made her feel like that was where she belonged. It felt so comforting to be near him. She found that she could tell him anything, and they would talk for hours. She didn't know how long she could keep it a secret.

## Chapter

# 17

It was a hot Saturday afternoon. Summer was in full swing, and the sun was beating down on what was once Mama's luscious garden. Papa had gone into town to visit Clyde and check on some horseshoes that he was making for him. So, with Papa not around barking orders, Emily would have the afternoon to do whatever she wanted to do. The longer she looked at the garden area overrun with weeds, the more she thought of Mama and the wonderful memories she had of working in the garden with her. She thought Mama would be pleased if she kept up with the gardening, so she decided to try her hand at weeding the garden and maybe plant something for the fun of it. Mama had a special place in the barn where she always hung her gardening tools, so she headed to the barn to get them. She pushed on the large sliding barn door but realized Papa had put a latch on the door that was above her reach. She wondered why he had put a new latch on it and especially so high. She checked the back door and found the same thing, except that latch was even higher. So she went back to the front door where fortunately, there wasn't a lock on it. She jumped up thinking she could reach the latch enough to swing it open, but after several attempts she realized it was no use.

Marge, who was inside cleaning James' tools to get them ready for the week ahead, heard the noise. Realizing someone was coming, she quickly gathered anything that belonged to her that would give away her presence and headed for the stairs to the loft. Upon reaching the bottom of the stairs, she hesitated. The noise had stopped. *Have they given up and gone away?* But then she heard the banging again and continued hurrying up the ladder.

Emily walked around the barn looking for something that would help her reach the latch. Under one of the trees, she found an old bucket that when turned upside down, would give her the height she needed to unlatch the barn door. She carried it to the door and carefully stood on it, hoping it wasn't too rusty to hold her. She stretched as tall as she could and after several tries, she got the latch to release. None too soon, because just then the bucket kicked out from under her, and she ended up sprawled on the ground. Not hurt, she got up quickly, brushed herself off, gave the bucket a good kick, and proceeded to open the barn door. She slid the wooden door open, walked in slowly, and stopped for a moment to wait for her eyes to adjust to the dimness in the barn. As she waited, she thought she heard a rustling noise above but dismissed it as some birds that she had disturbed. She walked over to the area where the garden tools were hanging. Just as she started to remove the rake from its hook, she heard another noise coming from above. She stopped and wondered if she should go up in the loft and see for herself what was making the noise. She removed the rake and walked slowly, tiptoeing quietly toward the back of the barn. She peered into the old hay room where the ladder was that led to the loft. She was half afraid of what she might find but wanted to know what the noise was that she was hearing. She put her foot on the first rung of the ladder, rake in hand. With her free hand, she grabbed onto the ladder and pulled herself up. She stopped when she heard a soft bump. Scared, Emily jumped down and took off running toward the open door and ran all the way to the house, leaving the barn door open. Out of breath, she sat down and thought how silly she was. She decided it was just a cat or some kind of animal and nothing to get herself so riled up about. She would just tell Papa when she saw him, and he could check it out.

Emily went about weeding the garden platz, reminiscing about the many good times she and Mama had working in the garden together. "I miss you, Mama, so much," she said to herself. Just then, the sounds of Papa's wagon creaking up the lane brought her thoughts back to the noises she heard in the barn, reminding her that she needed to tell him about it. He pulled the wagon around to the back of the barn. Seeing Emily in the garden, he gave her a wave and jumped down. He unharnessed his old faithful mare, led her into her stall, gave her a bucket of cool water, and threw in a pitchfork of fresh hay. Instead of him heading into the house as Emily expected him to, he walked around to the front of the barn and went in through the open barn door.

*Oh, my goodness, I left the barn door open when I came running out. Papa is probably going to be upset with me for leaving it open*, she thought. She dropped her rake and started running to the barn so that she could explain to Papa what she heard and why she left the door open.

To James' surprise, Marge came running to him and threw her arms around him at the same time as Emily came bursting through the open barn door. Emily came to a jolting halt and stood dumbfounded. Marge quickly dropped her hands from around James' neck and took a few steps back. James stood, running his fingers through his hair, looking at the very awkward scene before him.

Before he could say anything, Emily screamed in disgust, "Oh, I hate you! I hate you!" and ran out the door, never stopping until she got to her bedroom, where she slammed the door and barricaded herself in by sliding her bureau in front of it.

"Marge, what have you done? Why did you leave the barn door open?"

Grabbing onto his arm, she said, "But I didn't, Jamie, I promise."

Yanking his arm out of her grasp, he growled, "Get your hands off me! I don't have time for this. I've got to go straighten things out with Emily," and started for the door.

"Well, ya better straighten things out with more than Emily, I'm telling you, Mr. James Miller, or I'm out of here, ya hear?" she yelled after him.

James had only one thing on his mind. He had to get to Emily and try to make some sense of all of this to her. He ran into the house calling for her. She remained silent, locked in her room. James went up the stairs, walked over to her closed door, and knocked ever so lightly.

"Emily, my sweet baby girl, open the door. We need to talk. I can explain everything. Please, let's talk." Emily lay across her bed, sobbing into her pillow. James heard her sobs and said, "Please, sweetie, don't cry."

Emily lifted her tear-drenched face out of her pillow and screamed, "Don't 'sweet baby' me! I'm not your *sweetie*. You don't care anything about me. You only think about yourself!" She pushed her face back into her pillow and continued to sob.

"Okay, okay, Emily, I get why you feel that way, and you are right to feel that way. It wasn't until after Mama was gone that I realized how little time I spent with her. I regret the times I spent in the barn with my drinking buddy Clyde, but hear me out, okay? Please open the door." He waited, with no response. "I'm not going anywhere, Emily, until you open the door and talk with me."

About fifteen minutes had passed when he reminded her, "I'm still here Emily."

Leaning against the wall, he slid himself down just outside her door. He sat, his elbows resting on his knees with his head in his hands, waiting for some kind of response. *What in the world have I done?* he thought to himself.

Emily knew she couldn't stay in her room forever, and she didn't want Papa to be sitting outside her door all night. She didn't know why, but she wanted to talk with Lester. *I need to see him*, she thought. *I know he would know what I should do.* She also thought about how she was going to tell her sisters about what she saw. She knew for sure that Sarah would want to strangle him because she already had him pegged as an egotistical, manipulative man who used and abused Mama. Emily was curious, though, about who it was that had her arms around Papa's neck. Pondering that for a brief moment, she sat straight up in bed and said to herself, "Oh, now I get it, she must have been the cause for the noise I heard in the loft today." And with that, she decided to let Papa talk and see what excuses he was going to give her. She got up from her bed, pushed the bureau back and opened the door. Her legs weakened from the raging emotions she was experiencing, she dropped to the floor.

Papa turned to face her, "Oh Emily, I don't know where to start."

"Well, I'll tell you where you can start, Papa. Start by telling me who was hanging on your neck when I entered the barn."

"Okay I will. Her name is Marge, and she is my helper. You know the one that the whole town has been talking about."

"Yes, the whole town, Papa, but you haven't even had the decency to tell your family that your helper was a girl. Why, Papa, did you let us hear it from outsiders and deal with the snickers and shunning that we heard and felt? Why Papa? Did you feel guilty? Is there a reason for you to feel guilty? From what I saw, she looks like way more than just a helper. Why was she in our barn? She was in there all day while you were gone, wasn't she?"

Looking down at the floor, he said, "Uh no, she just walked up right before you came in."

"Oh Papa, Papa, just stop!" Leaning over and pounding the floor, she continued, "You're lying to me, and you know it. Don't make it any worse than it is. I went in there earlier today to get the rake to weed the garden platz and I heard noises coming from the loft. I thought it was birds or a rat or something. I started up the ladder to the loft with the rake to see what it was when I heard a thump that scared me so bad that I ran out of there as fast as I could. I was planning on telling you about it when you got home. But now I know she was the '*rat*' in the loft. So, don't lie to me anymore."

"You're right, Emily. She's been staying in the loft for a while because she doesn't have any place of her own."

Emily's mind quickly went back to that early morning when she was in the kitchen fixing breakfast, and Papa came in the back door, sheepishly, and went to his room. *So that's where Papa had been*, she thought. *He spent the night with her.*

She became so angry, she screamed, "Get out of here, you disgust me! Go, I don't want to talk to you, and I don't want to see you!" and slammed the door in his face.

Reluctantly, he picked himself up off the floor and slowly descended the stairs. He knew Marge was waiting for him to return. He had some decisions to make. He could send Marge packing and make things right with Emily or tell the girls about Marge and be willing to suffer the consequences. The thought of sending Marge packing tore at his heart. *How can I do that*, he thought. A lonely sadness overwhelmed him. And at that moment he realized he had real feelings for Marge, more than he ever dared to admit to himself. *If the girls can have their happiness and go on with their lives without Mama, why can't I?* he thought.

When he entered the barn, Marge was sitting with her arms crossed and looking like she was mad at the world. "Well, so what happened?" she asked. "Am I out of here?"

"No, but we need to talk."

"You're right about that, mister," she spouted. "If I'm gonna stay here, we're gonna get truthful with each other. How do you see me, James? Am I just a helper and someone to keep you company, or do you have feelings for me? If you do, then you better man up and not be so afraid to tell your family about me. I'm getting tired of trying to stay hid and really tired of sleeping in the loft," she ranted on and on. "So, what's it gonna be, James?"

"Marge, you know you are more than just a helper to me, but there are so many obstacles in letting you become more than that. I have three daughters who have recently lost their mother."

"Not that recent, James," Marge interjected.

"I know, but it's still fresh to them."

"There will always be somethin', James. They just gotta get over it."

"Also, Marge, you know that you're only a year or two older than Emily. How's that gonna sit with them, or the towns-people, for that matter?"

"James, if we both love each other, then who cares?"

"Well, do you love me, Marge? Or am I just someone who's taken you in, and given you a job, and food to eat?"

"I love you, Jamie, haven't I shown you that?"

"Yes, Marge, I guess you have."

"Then the question is, do you love me, James?"

"You might say I have tendencies in that direction. You are growing on me, you know."

"Well then, you've got to tell your daughters, or I'm just gonna move into the house and let them find out on their own."

"No, you can't do that, Marge! I just don't know how to handle all of this, but I do know I want to be with you. I've got to figure out how to come out with everything. But I promise you, I will. It's been a long day and I have a lot to think about. I'm gonna go fix us something to eat and I'll be back."

"I'm going with you."

"No, you can't! Emily is at the house, and she's already so angry with me she told me she didn't even want to see me."

"Well, she already knows about me, so it won't hurt nothin'. I'm coming to the house with you."

Emily sat in her room, thoughts running through her mind. She wanted to get out of the house but where would she go? *I could go live with Amanda but then I would be too far away from Lester, and I couldn't bear the thought of not seeing him on a regular basis.* Her thoughts kept going to Lester, and she longed to talk with him. She looked out of her bedroom window. *It's still light out. I think I could make it to the Country Inn before dark. It's only about a 30-minute walk.*

She changed into a peach-colored summer dress. It was one that Mama had made for her. "Oh Mama, I so wish you were still here with us," she cried. "Everything has become a mess." She washed her face and combed her hair before going downstairs. As she started down the stairs, she heard Papa coming in the kitchen door.

"So, what do you have for us to eat Jamie?"

Emily stopped in her tracks. *Jamie? No one calls Papa Jamie. Is that the girl who was in the barn?* She peered around the stairs toward the kitchen. *What is she doing in our house?* She was even more determined to dart to the door and run to Lester. As she did, she heard her papa yell.

"Where are you going, Emily?" But it was too late for an answer. She was already out the door slamming it behind her.

Papa started after her, but Marge caught his arm. "Let her go. She'll be okay. Besides Jamie, we now have the house to ourselves."

Papa couldn't help but feel somewhat guilty but also a sense of relief. "It is nice to finally get you into the house, Margie. I could get used to this."

Emily ran most of the way, but when she got close to the Inn she suddenly thought, *what if he's not here? What if he doesn't want to see me? What am I going to do then?* But she was willing to take those chances. She stopped running and before entering the Inn, she wiped her face, patted down her hair, smoothed her dress, and stood as tall and mature as she could. Hands shaking, she pushed the door open, walked up to the desk, and asked to see Lester Granger.

"And who should I tell him is calling," the clerk asked.

"Emily."

"Emily who?" he inquired.

"Just tell him Emily, he'll know."

She wasn't prepared for all of that, and she was feeling embarrassed. She looked around the big dining area and actually spotted him sitting at a table all by himself. He looked up and their eyes met. He immediately got up and walked toward her.

"Oh, Mr. Granger, this girl here is asking for you."

"Thanks, I got her," he said to the clerk.

"Emily, what in the world are you doing here? How did you get here?"

"Oh, Lester, I mean Mr. Granger," looking at the clerk. Quietly, so no one would hear, she said, "There's big trouble with Papa and things at home."

"Come over to the table with me. Are you hungry? Can I get you something to eat?"

"No thanks, but I could use a drink of water."

Lester motioned for the waitress. "Could you bring the lady a glass of water please?"

"Lady, you called me lady."

"Yes, I did because that's what you are to me. Now what is bothering you? Does your Papa know you are here?"

"No, and he must never know." She looked around the room nervously, to see if there was anyone she knew.

Lester asked, "Do you want to go somewhere else?" just as the waitress brought the water. He thanked her and told her to put his dinner on his tab.

"Drink your water, and we'll go for a ride. Then you can tell me all about what's going on."

Lester suggested that they go to the little ice cream shop at the other end of town where they could spend time talking while enjoying ice cream.

Emily felt safe when she was with Lester. She trusted him to keep whatever she told him confidential and didn't hesitate to share all that was on her mind. She told him all about what happened earlier and how she felt like running away.

"I am so angry with Papa right now. I don't even want to see him, let alone talk to him. He has lied to us, hidden things from us, disgraced the family, and has shown no respect for our mama." Lester remained quiet and just let her talk. "Papa is all about himself and has always been that way." She got quiet and a tear spilled out of her eye and tumbled down her cheek.

Lester handed her a napkin and in a soft voice said, "Emily, you have had a rough day today. A lot has hit you all at once, which has been very unfortunate. I understand why you feel angry at your papa right now, but I think you need to try to let it rest until tomorrow and sleep on it. Tomorrow is Sunday, doesn't your sister pick you up for church?"

"Yes, Amanda comes by every Sunday and then we meet Sarah and Harry at church. I can hardly wait until I see them to tell them what has happened."

"Okay then, I think you will feel better after you confide in them. I'm sure they will know how to handle things and will help you get to the bottom of it all. Together, as a family, you can work through this. What do you think?"

"Yeah, I guess you're right. Thanks for talking with me Lester. I just didn't know what to do."

"Well, I'm glad you came to me. I feel privileged that you felt comfortable enough to talk with me about things that are bothering you. I know you don't have any answers yet, but do you feel like you have calmed down enough that you can go back home, go to your room, and get some sleep?"

Reaching over, he put his hand under her chin, pulled her face to his, and said, "Our problems are always handled best after a good night's sleep. Trust me, okay?"

Emily melted at his touch and said, "Okay."

"It's getting dark, and we have to get you home before your papa comes looking for you."

Emily was jolted back to reality. "Oh my, I was so caught up in our conversation I hadn't noticed."

She really didn't want to exchange the comfort she was feeling with Lester for the hostility at home, but knew that she had to get back there and hopefully without Papa noticing.

# Chapter 18

"Come on, Jamie. I'm hungry. What do ya got to eat?"

James slid a chair out from under the table and slumped into it. His body expressed his frustration as he held his head and ran his fingers through his hair.

"I don't know what there is to eat. Besides, I'm not even hungry."

"Well, I am, and I need to find somethin'. You're making too much of all this. She'll come home. When she does, you need to be the man, stand up to her, and tell her how it's going to be, whether she likes it or not. Emily is just a kid—"

"Wait just a minute, what do you mean 'just a kid,'" James interrupted up, the hair at the nape of his neck raising a bit. "She's nearly your age. Do you think of yourself as 'just a kid'?"

"Well, no, but I've been around a lot more than she has. She's been protected by her sisters and her mama. I've had to fend for myself. None of them have seen the world like me." She floated around the room waving her arms and continued, "It's time you let Emily and the girls see that there is a life outside of this." She went over to James, put her arm around him, and tried to nuzzle his neck.

"Get off of me," he said and pushed her away. "I need something to drink."

He stood up abruptly and headed out the door to retrieve a bottle from his stash in the barn, leaving Marge staring after him, frustrated.

She took the opportunity to explore the house and quickly ascended the stairs. As she gazed into each of the rooms, she felt as though Lily was watching. The quilts, pillows, and even the curtains were all reminders of her. Marge went back downstairs and into James' bedroom.

She saw all of Lily's things in the room as if she were still there. She took a few of Lily's clothes, put them up to herself, and danced around the room. "I could get used to wearing these," she said to herself and threw them on the bed. She noticed Lily's brooches lying on the bureau next to her picture. "This is just too much. He needs to clear Lily from this room. She's gone, and all this stuff of hers must go too." She heard James coming back from the barn, so she quickly grabbed the clothes she had thrown on the bed and threw them behind the door.

"Well James, you decided to come back, have you?"

He sat his bottle of whiskey on the table and plopped in his chair. "Yes, I did." Looking around the room, he asked, "Did Emily come home yet?"

"No, and quit worrying about her. It's you and me now, and that's the way it should be." She went to the ice box and pulled out some meat. Then proceeded to make them both a sandwich with the fresh bread on the counter before she sat down next to him. "Did Emily make this bread?" she asked.

"Yes, she's a good little baker. She learned well from her mama. She really misses her," James answered, taking a few drinks from his whiskey bottle.

Marge, so tired of hearing about Mama, pushed the sandwich under James' nose and said, "Here, eat your sandwich with *Mama's* bread."

Agitated with her, James snapped, "I told you I'm not hungry. I just want things to be alright with Emily." He tipped the bottle and took a few more gulps. Then, turning his head and looking into Marge's eyes, he said, "If Lily were only here, she would know what to do."

That was all Marge could handle. She stood up, placed her hands on her hips, and angrily said, "I've heard enough about Lily, James. She ain't here, so figure things out yourself. Let Lily go, will ya?"

James jumped up and knocked his chair onto the floor. Clearly, having had too much to drink, he staggered over to where Marge was standing, and yelled in her face, "Don't you come in here telling me what to do! Do you understand? Or you can go back to where you came from."

That is the last thing Marge wanted. She composed herself, picked up his chair, and said, "Now, now Jamie, you don't mean that. Come on now, sit back down here."

Nearly falling into the chair, he said, "I've got to go find Emily. She's my baby girl. I can't let anything happen to her." Trying to stand, he told Marge, "I'm going to go get the wagon hitched up and go try to find her."

"James, you can't do that. It's getting dark, and it looks like it could rain any minute."

"That's all the more reason I need to find her and bring her home."

Once again, Marge tried to convince him not to go. "You are too drunk to be out on the road in your wagon."

He slung his arm at her, pushed her out of the way, and said, "There you go again, telling me what to do," and stumbled out the door swinging his whiskey bottle in the air.

Realizing she couldn't stop him, Marge let him go. She sat there looking at her half-eaten sandwich. *What have I gotten myself into?*

In a drunken stupor, James hooked the old mare to the wagon, crawled into it, and said, "Come on, old girl, we got to go find Emily." He turned the horse in the direction of their lane and headed out.

## Chapter

# 19

As Lester and Emily were leaving town and heading onto the country road, it started to rain. Lester drove slower due to the twists and turns in the road and diminishing visibility. They hadn't gone too far when the lights from Lester's truck shone briefly on a horse and wagon coming in their direction. Emily, wondering if that could possibly be her papa, leaned her head close to the window to see if she could make out who it was. Sure enough, she recognized Papa's mare and saw Papa holding the reins.

"That's Papa!" she exclaimed to Lester. "He shouldn't be out in this weather. He's probably out looking for me, or maybe he's going to see Clyde. Regardless, he won't be home to lecture me on why I shouldn't have run off like I did."

By the time they reached Emily's house, the rain was letting up. Lester, knowing that James wasn't home, drove down the lane to the house instead of letting her out where he usually did. He stayed watching her until he knew she was safely in the house, then turned the truck around and headed back into town.

He rode toward town, thinking about Emily and how much he cared for her. He knew she was a lot younger than he was, but when they were together, that didn't seem to matter. He was lost in his thoughts when he noticed a horse running loose alongside the road. He slowed to keep from hitting it. As he did, he noticed a wagon that had tumbled into the ditch and was lying on its side with its wheels still spinning. His mind flashed back. He remembered Emily saying that the horse-drawn wagon they had seen on the road earlier was her papa. Fearing it could possibly be him, he pulled off the road, leaving his truck lights on to shine on the wagon. He jumped out and ran toward the wagon. He realized that the horse he saw running along the road was the horse that had broken free from it. Going closer, he heard someone groaning.

"I hear you. I'm coming, hang in there!"

James didn't know how long he had been in the ditch, but when he heard someone calling to him, he rallied and yelled, "Help me my legs are trapped under my wagon!"

Lester slid down into the ditch and discovered the man's legs were, in fact, pinned under the wagon. He tried to lift the wagon off the man's legs, but it was too heavy. The strong smell of liquor wafted to Lester's nostrils. The bottle of whiskey that James had taken with him lay broken beside him. Lester once again tried lifting the wagon but to no avail. Lester knew he needed to go for help. Since there was little to no traffic on this country road, he knew he couldn't wait for someone to pass by who would be able to give him a hand. He thought of the men who worked for him and knew that any one of them would help, but he knew John's place was the closest, so that's where he needed to go.

Feeling sure this was Emily's papa, but having never met him, he asked, "What's your name, Sir."

"James, James Miller," he replied weakly.

Lester knew he needed to get help, and quickly. "I'm going for help. Do everything you can to stay awake. I'll be right back." Lester, seeing that the man had fallen asleep, slapped him on the cheek and again said "Wake up, stay awake, I'm going for help. I'll be back."

Lester scrambled up the side of the ditch, grabbing handfuls of grass as he went. When he got back up to the road, he looked around for the horse, but by now it was nowhere in sight. He got into his truck and headed into town to John's house, which was just inside the town limits.

When he reached John's house, he jumped out of his truck and ran to the door. He pounded on it frantically until John opened it.

"Sorry to bother you man, but I need your help. There's been an accident. A horse-drawn wagon went off the road into a ditch a little way out of town, and a man is trapped under it. I tried, but I couldn't lift it off of him. Do you have a pole that would be strong enough to pry the wagon up enough to drag the man out?"

"Yes, I think I do. Give me just a minute to get my boots on, and I'll fetch it from the barn and be right with you."

"Thanks, John, but hurry. I think the man was losing consciousness when I left him."

As Lester waited, he thought of Emily and how he was going to have to tell her about her papa. Just then, John threw a pole, along with a rope and his tool bag, into the back of Lester's truck.

"Grabbed a few other things I thought we may need."

"Good idea. Let's go."

When they returned to the accident, both men jumped out of the truck. Lester headed toward James, while John gathered the tools.

"James, are you still with us?" Lester called out, but there was no response. Sliding down the ditch, he called out again and he heard a faint groan. "James, hang in there. I've brought help, and we will get you out of this mess."

Both men went to work. Lester grabbed the pole and said, "I'll lift up on the wagon, John, and you try to drag him free."

John nodded, "I'm ready when you are."

Lester placed the pole under the side of the wagon close to where James lay. He put his shoulder under it and started lifting with all his strength. He had only lifted the wagon a few inches when they heard a loud cracking sound. The wagon came back down on James, and he screamed in pain.

"So sorry man," Lester said, "but the pole broke."

"Now what?" John asked."

"Do you think that the both of us could lift the wagon enough for him to slide out on his own?"

"Maybe, it's worth a shot."

Lester turned to James and said, "James, do you think you can shimmy yourself out from under the wagon if John and I lift it up?"

"I don't know, but I can try."

"Okay then James, we're going to give it all we got, and you give it all you got, and let's get you out of here."

The two men were able to lift the wagon. Grunting, Lester told James to drag himself out.

"I'm trying but I can't," James replied.

"I can't hold this much longer," John told Lester.

"I know, neither can I." To James, Lester urged, "Give it one more try."

"I'm trying, but I think my arm is broken and I can't use it to pull myself out."

"Okay then, we will have to let the wagon back down and think of another solution," Lester said to John.

"I agree," John said. "So, listen James, the wagon is coming back down. We are going to let it down as easy as we can. Hang in there, okay?"

I'm trying," James moaned.

Lester and John let the wagon down as easily as they could but, even so, it went down on James a little harder than they had planned, and James yelled in pain. The two men put their heads together and decided to use the rope that John had the forethought to bring.

"If we tie one end of the rope to the wagon and the other to your truck, maybe you can pull the wagon up enough for me to pull him out. What do you think?" John asked.

"Good idea! Let's give it a try. You tie up the wagon, and I'll handle the truck."

Lester maneuvered the truck into a position that would pull the wagon straight up. He was concerned that the truck was blocking the road, but since he hadn't seen anyone come by the whole time he was tending to James, he decided that it would be okay if they hurried.

"Are you ready John?"

"Yes, we're ready down here."

"Okay, here we go."

Lester slowly moved the truck forward. First, the rope jerked a little until it finally straightened and became taut. He moved the truck forward until he heard John call out to him.

"Whoa, that's good."

John put his arms under James' arms and slid him out from under the wagon. Lester held the truck steady until he heard John yell again, "He's out."

Lester carefully let the rope go slack, and the wagon bumped down on the ground.

"Is everyone okay?" Lester yelled to John.

"Yes, we're good down here."

"Then untie the rope from the wagon so I can move the truck off the road."

Lester was anxious to get the truck off the road because, even though there hadn't been any traffic, he didn't want someone to come along and run into him, causing even more injury. Once he got the truck moved, he slid down into the ditch to assess the situation with James.

After John pulled him from the wagon, James slumped lifeless partly from relief that he was out, but more from his head injury.

"I think he needs medical attention," John said. "Where all do you hurt, James?" But James didn't respond.

Lester slapped his cheek and said his name loudly. "James, we're not losing you now. Stay with us."

James rallied a bit and in a dazed voice said, "My head, oh my head."

Lester agreed with John that he needed to get to a doctor quickly. "James, we are going to take you to the hospital to have you checked out. You may have some broken bones."

"Lester, how are we going to get him up out of the ditch when we have a hard time getting out ourselves?"

"We figured out how to get him out from under the wagon, I'm sure we can figure something out."

They stopped for a moment and looked around as if they would magically find something that would do the trick. That's when Lester spotted the broken pole.

"That's it," he said.

"What's it?" John asked.

"That pole. It's broken in half. We can use the rope to make a makeshift stretcher."

They went to work laying the two pieces of pole parallel with each other and stretched the rope from one pole to the other creating a cradle. They tied a rope handle on one end of the homemade stretcher, turning it into a sled of sorts.

"Boy John, I am so glad you thought to bring rope. Once we get him on this stretcher, we're going to have to pull him at an angle up the side of the ditch, so it won't be so steep that he slides off."

*Shattered*

They laid the stretcher next to James and carefully lifted him onto it. James groaned in pain, but they kept moving forward with their plan.

"John, I'll pull the stretcher, and you stay at the side of it to keep James from tumbling off and push as much as you can."

They started up the ditch. It was a slow process but eventually, they got him up and over to the truck.

"John, let's keep him on the stretcher because we can't put him into the truck without causing him more pain and possibly more injuries. So, let's just lift the stretcher up and slide him into the back of the truck. You ride with him, and I'll drive very slowly to the hospital."

"I think that's a good idea," John said.

They lifted James into the truck, got him settled, and headed to the hospital.

Once they got there, while James was being assessed, Lester struggled with how and when to tell Emily about her papa's accident. He decided to see what the doctors had to say about James' injuries before he left to tell her. *Possibly, they'll release him*, he thought, *and I'll be here to take him home.* But that was not the case. The doctor came out and told them that James' legs were just badly bruised and had some bad abrasions but not broken. His Arm was. They would set the break and cast it, but they were mostly concerned about his head injuries and were going to keep him overnight for observation.

Knowing they were keeping him overnight and James wouldn't need a ride home, Lester decided to go and inform Emily of the accident.

Lester told John, "I know where James lives, and after I take you home, I'll go there and let his family know about what happened."

John wondered how Lester knew James but didn't inquire.

Letting John off at his house, Lester said, "Thanks, man, for your help tonight. I couldn't have done it without you."

"No problem, was glad I could help." As he was closing the door, he said, "See you Monday."

## Chapter

# 20

When Emily walked into the house after Lester brought her home, she was appalled to see Marge in the kitchen. Marge came running toward her with her hands in fists down by her side, yelling, "Where have you been? Your Papa has gone looking for you and he was in no shape to be out on the roads. If anything happens to him, it will be all your fault!"

Emily shot back at Marge, "First of all, get out of my face, and secondly get out of my house! What gives you the right to be in my house telling me what to do or not do? You need to get out right now!"

"I'm not gonna go nowhere," Marge barked, "James brought me here, and I'm staying until he gets home. At least I care about him, even if you don't."

"How dare you say that? You know nothing about me, our family, or how we feel about Papa. You are not welcome here!"

"Well, little smarty pants, you're gonna have to get used to me being here 'cause I ain't going nowhere."

Emily stomped past Marge and went to the kitchen. She fixed a glass of milk, got a few crackers from the pantry, and went to her room to get away from her. She was so angry but knew she couldn't do anything until Papa got home. She sat on her bed and thought about her visit with Lester. He gave her a sense of calmness and helped her work through things that were troubling her. She drank her milk and ate her crackers, then got ready for bed. She was tired from her hike into town. The altercation with Marge didn't help matters. Although she was worried about Papa, she was more angry at him than worried. She didn't want to see him or talk with him when he got home. To help ease her worry, she said to herself, "I know Papa is okay because I just saw him on the road. Eventually, when he doesn't find me, he'll come home."

To be sure she wouldn't be disturbed, she once again slid her bureau in front of her bedroom door. Feeling somewhat safe and secure, she lay down and soon fell asleep.

The next thing she knew, she was suddenly awakened by a truck pulling up the lane to the house. She sat up, rubbed the sleep from her eyes, and wondered what was going on. She didn't know how long she had been asleep, but it was still dark outside. She got up, put her ear to the door, and listened to hear what she could. She heard someone knocking on the door and waited to see if Papa was home and would answer it.

She heard Marge yell, "Coming," and heard her open the door.

A man's voice said, "Good evening, may I please speak to Emily?"

Emily heard the voice and knew immediately that it was Lester. As she grabbed her robe and pushed the bureau away from her door, she heard Marge loudly demanding answers from him.

"What is this about? Does this have something to do with James? Tell me, talk to me."

Lester recognized the girl who was demanding answers from him as the girl that Emily was so disturbed by and very calmly said, "I need to speak with Emily, please."

Emily was already coming out of her room when Marge yelled, "Emily, get down here, there's a man that wants to talk to ya."

Moving down the stairs, Emily very anxiously asked Lester, "What's wrong, what's happened?"

Quietly, directing his attention to Emily, he said, "Emily, it's your Papa. He's okay, but he had an accident. Shortly after we saw him, his horse and wagon went off the road and into a ditch."

"Oh no," Emily exclaimed, "where is he now?"

Marge went into a frenzy, "What do you mean 'when you saw him'?" Turning to Emily, she shouted, "Why didn't you tell me you saw him? You knew I was worried about him! I told you if anything happened to him it would be your fault!"

"Wait just a minute," Lester said, "you need to calm down. We are not blaming anyone for what happened tonight. It was an accident."

Turning to Emily, he continued, "Emily, let's step outside and I'll tell you what happened."

Emily was so glad that Lester stood up for her. She quickly started out the door, happy to be getting away from Marge.

This infuriated Marge even more because she wanted to know all the details. She put her foot in the door to keep it from closing and yelled, "I have a right to know what happened since I'm the only one who really cares about James around here."

"Marge," Emily shot back, "you are nothing to this family and have no right to know anything."

Turning to Lester, Emily asked, "Would you take me to my sister's house please? We need to let them know about what has happened, and they will know how to deal with this."

"Of course, but do you want to grab some clothes first?"

"No, I have clothes at Amanda's. I don't want to go back inside the house with that tramp in there. I just want to get away from here."

While they were walking to the truck, Marge continued ranting and demanding to know where James was.

Ignoring her, Lester opened the truck door and said, "Just get in the truck, Emily, and I'll tell you what happened on the way."

## Chapter

# 21

Lester told Emily all about the accident and how he and John had rescued Papa as they made their way to Amanda's house. It was after midnight by the time they arrived, and the house was dark. Amanda and the family had long been asleep. Lester allowed the truck lights to shine on the porch as he walked with Emily to the door.

She tried it, but it was locked, so she pounded on it calling out, "Amanda, open the door, it's Emily."

Jake awoke first, startled, he sat up and listened for what had woken him. He heard the pounding on the door and the faint voice calling for Amanda. He softly touched Amanda, waking her gently so as not to startle her, and said, "Someone is at the door. I'm going to see about it."

Amanda, waking up and hearing Jake, sat up, grabbed her robe, and followed right behind him. When she heard what she knew to be Emily's voice calling her, she stumbled and nearly fell down the last few steps in her hurry to reach the door. Jake unlocked it, and upon opening it, they both saw Emily standing there in her night clothes with a man standing beside her.

Scared nearly to death, Amanda grabbed Emily's arm, pulled her away from the man, and brought her inside.

"Emily, for goodness' sake, what is going on? Are you alright? What's happened?" The questions tumbled out of her mouth all at once.

"It's Papa," Emily said, falling into Amanda's arms.

"What sweetie, what happened to Papa?"

"He's had an accident and he's at the hospital," she explained.

At that point, Jake turned to Lester and said, "And may I ask who you are, and what you are doing here with Emily?"

"Oh, this is a friend of mine," Emily quickly interjected.

Lester extended his hand to Jake and introduced himself. "I'm Lester Granger, sorry to meet you this way." Shaking Lester's hand Jake introduced himself as well. "I'm Jake, come on in."

"Let me turn off my truck lights," Lester said, "and I'll be right in."

Emily went on to explain, "He's the one who found Papa and took him to the hospital. Then he came to the house to tell me."

"Tell you what exactly?" Amanda asked, as she ushered her to a chair at the table.

"My friend Lester was driving, headed into town when he spotted a horse running along the side of the road. Then he spotted a wagon turned over in the ditch, and he stopped to help. It was Papa. He got him out from under the wagon and took him to the hospital."

About that time, Lester came in and told them in more detail about taking James to the hospital.

"I stayed at the hospital with James to see if he needed a ride home," he said. "But they told me that James' left arm was broken and needed to be set. There were only lacerations on his legs. However, they wanted to keep him overnight because of his head injury. I knew he had quite a bump on his head because while my friend and I were trying to get the wagon off him he was going in and out of consciousness. They think he'll be fine but wanted to keep him for observation."

"Wait, wait, wait," Amanda said, rubbing her temples. "I'm totally confused. How did you know it was Emily's papa and how did you know where she lived? I don't understand."

"Oh, Amanda, I'll tell you all about it, but first, I need to tell you what's going on at home. Papa's so-called *helper*, the one who people have been seeing him all over town with, is at the house and she is just making herself at home. Earlier today, I saw them in the barn together, and she had her arms draped around Papa's neck. I couldn't run to my room fast enough. Papa came upstairs and tried to talk to me about what I saw and explain things away, but I knew he was lying. Oh, Amanda, it was so awful. I got so angry that I told him I didn't want to talk to him or see him. And now if something happens to him, I'll never forgive myself for being so hateful toward him."

"Hush that kind of talk now and tell me what happened next."

"He left and went back out to the barn, I guess to his little *girlfriend*. I felt terrible and needed to talk to someone. I thought about Lester, who has been a good friend and a good listener. He is the contractor in charge of building the new school building and doing the renovations at the courthouse. I knew he was staying at the Country Inn, so I decided to walk there and see if I could find him. As I was coming down the stairs to leave, Papa and that girl he calls Marge were coming in the back door, so I made a beeline for the front door, but not before Papa saw me. He started yelling at me, asking where I was going. I didn't stop to answer. I went out the door and ran most of the way into town.

"I found Lester, and he was so kind to listen to me and calm me down. We talked for quite a while, and then he offered to drive me home since it looked like it was about to rain, and it was getting dark. On our way home, we passed Papa going into town. I knew he was probably out looking for me or going to see Clyde. I was just glad he wasn't going to be home when I got there because I didn't want to get into things with him again. When I got home, Marge was in the house, and she screamed at me, 'Where have you been? Why did you stay gone so long? Your papa is out looking for you and if anything happens to him, it's gonna be all your fault.' I'm so sorry, Amanda." And with that, Emily broke down and cried.

"Now, now," Amanda told Emily, "none of this is your fault, so you get that out of your head right now."

"That's what I told her," Lester said. "It was only an accident." He continued with his story, "I was leaving Emily's house, going back into town, when I saw the wagon in the ditch and knew it was the one Emily had said was her papa's. James was pinned under the wagon, and I had to go for help to be able to raise the wagon off him enough to pull him out. But the good news is that he's safe now and will be alright. The wagon is still in the ditch, and I'm not sure where his horse went."

"Hopefully she went back to the barn," Jake said. "I'll take care of finding the horse and getting the wagon out of the ditch. Thank you for taking care of James, getting word to Emily, and bringing her to us."

"Yes," Amanda agreed, "but I still don't know how you two became friends. I'm sure Emily will explain that later."

"Well, now that I know Emily is in good hands, I'll go. But if there is anything I can do to help with getting the wagon out of the ditch, let me know. It's not going to be an easy task because the embankment is very steep."

"Okay, thanks so much, but we'll take it from here," Jake assured him.

Giving a tender glance in Emily's direction, Lester said, "You take care now."

Jake showed Lester to the door and thanked him again for everything. Amanda recognized the glance and kind words that Lester gave Emily to be somewhat affectionate and was disturbed by it, but didn't say anything.

After Lester had left, Amanda and Jake just looked at each other as if to say, "What just happened?"

Emily just sat slumped in her chair, feeling the heaviness of all that had taken place over the last twenty-four hours. She had pulled her feet up and sat there hugging her knees, staring at the placemat in front of her. Amanda put on a pot of water and dropped a cheesecloth bag of loose tea into it to make some hot tea.

Breaking the silence, Amanda said, "Jake, we have to let Sarah and Harry know what's happened, but I don't know if we should tell them tonight or wait until morning."

"Well, I'm going to need Harry's help early in the morning to get the wagon out of the ditch and find Papa's horse. If we don't tell them until morning, we'll waste valuable time."

Amanda agreed and added, "While you and Harry are checking on the wagon, the rest of us need to go to Papa's house and check on things. We need to see what that Marge girl is up to and then go to the hospital and check on Papa. Hopefully, we can bring him home."

As Amanda was waiting for the pot of tea to boil, she remembered that it was Sunday. Thinking of all the things that needed to be done, she knew there was no way they would be able to make it to church.

Mama's words drifted into her mind. *Sunday is the day of rest, the day we go to church and worship God.* Then she would add, *that's what the good book tells us to do.*

"Well, Mama, today we have an emergency we have to take care of, and I know God will understand," she whispered to herself.

"Did you say something, Amanda?" Jake asked.

"No, I'm just talking to Mama. I miss her so much." The water was hot, and she poured three cups of tea and carried them to the table. She set a cup of tea in front of Emily and encouraged her to drink it.

"It will make you feel better," she said. "Everything will look different in the morning. We're a family and we take care of each other. We'll go see Papa in the morning, and when you see that he's okay, you'll feel better."

Emily stirred from her stupor, dropped her feet to the floor, and sat up. She thanked Amanda for the tea, and then said, "Oh Amanda, what are we going to do to get that tramp out of our house? When I told her to leave, she looked at me with mean eyes and said, 'Well little smarty pants, you're going to have to get used to me being here because I ain't going nowhere.'"

"We'll see about that, Emily, now drink your tea."

Jake got up and, looking at the clock, said, "Well, since this is going to be a sleepless night for me, I'm going to go to Sarah and Harry's place now and break the news to them."

"Okay, tell them to come on over in the morning and I will fix us all breakfast before we get on with everything."

Jake left, leaving Amanda and Emily alone.

"Emily, are you ready to talk to me about Lester and tell me how you know him?"

Taking a sip of her tea, Emily said, "Yeah, I guess so. I met him at school. He and his men were building the new school building. During lunch and before going home from school, I would go over to see the progress that was being made. You know, Amanda, I will be assigned to that new building this fall when school starts."

"Yes, I know, Emily, you are growing up too fast."

Emily continued, "Lester would always recognize me and come talk with me. He was always so kind and never put me down or acted like I was just a kid. By the time school was out for the summer, I felt extremely comfortable talking with him, and I shared some of what was going on with Mama passing and Papa being so demanding."

"He does seem like a very nice man, but Emily, you know nothing about him, and to confide in him so easily could be dangerous."

"But Amanda, I do know something about him. He's from New York and has his own company called Granger's Construction Firm. I know he has been nothing but kind to me. He's doing the work not only on the school building but also doing all the renovations to the courthouse. He has hired local workers to help with the projects, which he explained to me helped him win the bids."

Amanda thought to herself, *Child, what do you know about winning bids?*

"He is staying at the Country Inn in town, and that is where I found him and talked with him about Marge and Papa. That's when everything started happening, that has brought us here, tonight."

"I'm so glad he was such a help with everything, and I'm reminded of Mama telling us that the good book says, *Everything works together for good to those who love God*. And it seems like that definitely happened in this case because things could have gone in a much different direction. I hate to think what would have happened to Papa if Lester hadn't seen his wagon and stopped to help. But Emily, please don't get too friendly with him. After all, he will be finishing his projects one day and going back to New York. What will you do then?"

They both sat quietly drinking their tea. When they had finished, Amanda told Emily, "It's going on three o'clock, how about going up and getting into bed to get a little sleep? I may lie down for a little while myself. I'll call you and the boys down for breakfast around six."

"Okay, Amanda, I'll try, but I don't feel like sleeping."

She made her way up the stairs to the room that she called her home away from home and climbed into bed. She closed her eyes, but all she could see was Marge screaming at her and blaming her for Papa's accident. So much had transpired in such a short time, and it all kept swimming around in her head. She at least rested a bit even though sleep evaded her.

It wasn't long until Jake came back from seeing Sarah and Harry. He went upstairs and found Amanda in their room trying to get a little rest.

"Oh good, you're back, how did it go when you broke the news?" Amanda asked him.

"They were shocked, of course, and Sarah had to know all the details. I told them we all would have to work together to get everything done. Harry said he would gather up a few things that may help us with getting the wagon out of the ditch, and Sarah said she would help you with whatever needed to be done."

"Good, what time did you tell them to come for breakfast?"

"I just told them early, and Sarah said when I was leaving, she would see us around five."

"Oh dear, that's good, but five will be here before you know it. This night has been a wash."

# Chapter 22

At the house, Marge was like a cat on a hot tin roof. She paced the floor, frustrated that she didn't know what was happening to James.

"I don't even know where he is or how badly he's hurt," she fumed. She walked all around the house, looking in all the rooms. When she came to Emily's room, she stopped and yelled, "It's your fault, you little brat. You just wait until the next time I see you, you'll wish you had never walked out that door!"

All of a sudden, she heard a commotion outside. She ran downstairs, went to the kitchen window, and looked out, but it was pitch black. The cloudy, rainy sky concealed the moon, and she couldn't see a thing. She listened and heard the noise again. Grabbing a lantern, she said to herself, "Nothing scares this old girl," and went out the back door to find out what the commotion was. She stood on the stoop holding the lantern high, so its beam shone in front of her. She listened to see where the noise was coming from. It sounded like it was in the stable, out back of the barn. She stood still, thinking. *Could it be Jamie?* She heard Lester say that he had had an accident, but she didn't know what kind of accident or how bad it was. *Maybe he's found his way home.* She picked up a shovel that was leaning against the house, just in case it wasn't him. Slowly, and quietly, she started walking to the stable area. Suddenly, she heard a horse snort and kick the water bucket. It made her jump, but then she thought for sure it was James putting up his old mare.

"James," she called out, but no answer.

Just then a horse came flying out of the stable, started going in circles, and kicking up its heels.

*Shattered*

"James," she called again, but still no answer. It was then that she realized the old mare had broken free from the wagon and had found her way back home. She put down the shovel and set the lantern on a fence post. Then, she slowly started toward the mare, trying to take hold of the reigns that were dragging on the ground.

"Come on, girl," she coaxed over and over in a gentle voice until she finally got close enough to grab her reigns. "There now, come on, and let me get you some fresh water."

Marge led her into the stable, closed the stall door, got a bucket of water, and set it down for her to drink. She was so thirsty she drank nearly all of it. "My goodness, you were really thirsty."

She took an old towel that James kept for wiping her down when they came back from their rounds each day, from a hook, and began wiping her neck and back, talking to her all the time. "There now, doesn't that feel better? Oh, how I wish you could talk. You could tell me what happened to James." She continued wiping until the mare calmed down, and Marge felt comfortable leaving her. *Well, there is absolutely nothing I can do tonight*, she thought, picking up the lantern. She walked into the barn and headed to her loft bedroom. With the excitement over, she began to realize how tired she really was. *I might as well try and get some sleep until tomorrow when hopefully someone will come and let me know what happened.* She started to climb the ladder to the loft when she stopped. "Why am I going to the loft when there is a perfectly good bed in the house that no one will be sleeping in tonight?" she said to herself.

She came down the ladder, went back inside the house, and into James' bedroom. She had been in there before looking around and remembered seeing his wife's clothes in the bureau drawers. She started looking through them until she found a pretty, soft flannel nightgown. She pulled it out and laid it on the bed while she undressed. As she pulled it over her head, she thought, *Now I know how a lady must feel.* She rubbed her hands down over the gown, smoothing it over her body, turned down the covers, and crawled into bed. The mattress was so soft, nothing like her pile of hay that she had been sleeping on. Her body melted into the softness of the mattress, and it wasn't long before she was sound asleep.

## Chapter 23

Sarah and Harry arrived at Amanda and Jake's house around five in the morning. Amanda was just dragging herself out of bed. Jake was up and out doing his morning chores, and Harry found him in the barn.

"Hey Jake, how are you this morning?"

"I'm fine, Harry, but what a night. I'm glad you brought your wagon. We can throw everything we think we might need in it."

They discussed how they should go about getting James' wagon out of the ditch. Each had ideas, as they both had been thinking about it during their sleepless night. Harry suggested using Jake's set of working mules to upright the wagon.

Jake agreed, "My mules are pretty good workers, so I think they will do us just fine. We can tie them to your wagon, Harry, and bring them along behind."

"Sounds like a plan, Jake, and since we don't know what condition the wagon is in, we'll need to take tools to repair it if need be. I brought some heavy-duty rope and a pry bar but figured you would have the rest of the tools that we might need."

"Yeah, I've already gathered up some. They're lying there in the corner. You can go ahead and throw everything in the wagon."

Harry gathered the tools, and said, "Hopefully, the wheels didn't come off, because then we will have another problem."

Jake agreed. "Yeah, you're right about that. However, I do have an extra wheel behind the barn. If you go grab it and throw it in the wagon, I'll go ahead and hitch up the buggy for the girls so it will be ready for them when they are ready to go check on the house and James."

*Shattered*

After loading the wagon with the extra wheel and tools that Jake had set aside, Harry looked at Jake and said, "Okay, finish up what you're doing there, and I'll meet you in the house. I just realized how hungry I am."

Sarah, seeing that Amanda hadn't been downstairs yet, put on a pot of coffee and started the bacon. She was just starting to scramble a bowl of eggs when Amanda came downstairs and entered the kitchen.

"Oh Sarah, good morning, I see you've started breakfast. That's so kind of you. I'm still reeling from the nightmare of last night. I really wish it had been a dream."

"I know," Sarah said. "You've got to tell me all the details. Jake told us some when he came over, but you know men, they don't tell you everything."

While Amanda stirred up the pancakes, she told Sarah what she knew about the girl that Papa had brought to the house.

"You mean the girl who is supposed to be his helper?"

"Yes, but according to Emily, she's more than just a helper. She spotted Papa and her in the barn together, and she had her arms around Papa's neck."

Sarah went into a rage, "Are you serious? He never stops hurting our family! I just can't understand him. So, what are we going to do Amanda?"

"Well, we will go to the house and make sure she is gone, and then go and check on Papa. Hopefully, he's well enough that we can bring him home. Depending on how he is, maybe we can get some answers from him."

"Oh yes," Sarah agreed, "we need answers, that's for sure."

"I'm also concerned about Emily and this man who brought her here last night."

"What do you mean Amanda? Who is he?"

"Emily claims he's a good friend of hers. He seemed like a very nice man, but he's nearly as old as Papa. Well, not really, but he's way too old for her."

"I see. Where did she meet him?"

Just then, Harry came into the house, with Jake shortly behind.

"Yum, something smells mighty good in here and I'm starved," Harry declared, rubbing his belly.

"Good, we have plenty of food. Sarah, will you take care of things here while I go upstairs and wake Emily and the boys?"

When Amanda went upstairs, she was surprised to see that Emily was already up and dressed.

"Good morning, my sweet girl. Did you get any sleep at all?"

"Maybe a little, but I'm just anxious to see how Papa is and take care of things at the house."

"Sarah and Harry are downstairs, and breakfast is almost ready. As soon as we finish breakfast, we'll be heading that way. Come with me to wake the boys. They will be so excited to see you."

They both walked to the boy's bedroom. Amanda shook each of them. "Wake up boys, breakfast is ready." It took the boys a few seconds to wake up. They wiped the sleepy sand from their eyes with the back of their fists and stretched before opening their eyes to the morning light. Emily went over to their bed, and as soon as they saw her, they jumped up and bounced up and down on their bed. "Emily!" they both squealed at the same time, surprised to see her. They gave her hugs so tight, it nearly took her breath away.

"Oh my goodness," she said. "I'm glad to see you too, but I'm hungry. How about you? Go get washed for breakfast."

Emily told Amanda that she would bring the boys down when they were done.

"Okay, but hurry now, we've got a lot of things to do today."

The plans for the day were solidified over breakfast. Jake and Harry would take care of getting the wagon out of the ditch and finding Papa's horse, while the girls would take care of things at Papa's house and go check on him at the hospital.

Harry and Jake left right after they finished their breakfast.

"Be careful boys," Sarah told them. "We don't need any more excitement around here."

Amanda explained to Charlie and Willy that their grandpa had had an accident with his wagon last night and assured them that he was okay but was in the hospital. "We're going to go see Grandpa and hopefully bring him home to his house today, while your papa and

Uncle Harry get Grandpa's wagon out of the ditch. Because we have this emergency that needs to be taken care of, we won't be going to church today. So, when you finish your breakfast, run on upstairs and put on your everyday clothes as quickly as you can so we can get going. Come down as soon as you're ready."

Emily offered to go up with them and help move them along.

"Thanks, Emily, that would be a great help. And Sarah, if you don't mind finishing cleaning up the kitchen, I'll go get the horse and buggy and bring it around front."

# Chapter

# 24

It was a little after seven when they pulled up to Papa's house, and everything was quiet. The girls wondered what they would find when they went inside.

Jumping down from the buggy, Emily said, "She better not still be in there, that's all I have to say."

Amanda and Sarah were thinking the same thing but didn't say it out loud. They helped the boys down from the buggy and all headed for the house. Emily opened the door slowly, looking around as she did, and stepped inside.

"Well, it appears she's gone for now at least, which is a relief."

The door opening and Emily's voice, woke Marge. She had all intentions of being out of there before anyone came back, but she realized she had overslept. *What am I going to do now*, she thought to herself. On the far side of the bed there was just enough room to walk between the bed and the wall, so all she knew to do at this point was to quietly roll off the bed into that space. Hopefully, no one would see her. She had just lowered herself to the floor when she remembered her boots and clothes lying on the floor on the other side of the bed. So, she squeezed herself under the bed far enough to reach them and pull them under. While doing so, one of her boots hit the foot of the bed. By this time, the girls had made their way to the kitchen and heard the noise.

"What was that noise?" Sarah said with a start.

"I don't know," Amanda said. "It sounds like it came from Papa's room." Entering, she saw the bed in disarray. "It looks like someone slept in here last night, the bed is a mess."

"Oh, never mind that, Papa never makes his bed," Emily said.

Amanda looked around, saw nothing out of place, and went back to the kitchen. "I don't know what that noise was, but everything seems to be okay."

Marge was as quiet and still as a mouse and was glad when she heard Amanda say everything was normal.

"Where do you suppose Marge is?" Sarah asked.

"Oh, she's probably in the barn waiting for Papa to come home," Emily surmised. "But I'm not going out to find her."

"At some point," Amanda said, "we need to meet her and find out what Papa's intentions are with her and what to expect. But for now, we've got to go see about him, and hopefully bring him home."

"I'll stay here with the boys while you and Emily go," Sarah offered. "I hope Papa is okay and all of that, but I'm not anxious to see him."

"Okay, maybe you can find something to make lunch with so everyone can eat when we get back."

"Sure, I'll find something."

## Chapter

# 25

On their way into town, Emily and Amanda saw Harry and Jake still trying to get the wagon up onto the road. They stopped to check on them.

"So, how's it going?" Amanda called down to them.

"We're getting there, but one of the wagon wheels was broken so we had to replace it," Jake yelled up from the ditch. "I'm so glad we thought to bring an extra wheel along. Now we are going to see what those two work mules can do for us."

"Have you seen Papa's horse?" Amanda inquired.

"No, haven't seen her, but haven't looked for her yet."

"Well, be safe, and good luck getting that wagon up this steep embankment. Emily and I are heading in to check on Papa. Sarah is staying with the boys and fixing some lunch, so I'll see you fellows at the house later."

Amanda clicked her tongue at the horse, and they rode on into town.

Emily said, "Wow, no wonder Papa got hurt, that is a steep ditch."

"Yes, it is, but we'll soon see how he is."

Amanda led her horse-drawn buggy to the hospital, tied the horse to the hitching post, and asked Emily, "Are you ready for this? You do know that he will have a cast on his arm, and he may not be able to walk well since his legs were badly hurt."

"Yes, I know, I just don't want him to be mad at me and yell at me. I'm glad you are with me."

As they opened the door to the hospital, the smell of alcohol and disinfectant filled their nostrils. The open room was filled with people coughing and babies crying, all waiting their turn to be seen by a nurse or doctor. Amanda and Emily went straight to the nurse's station.

"Excuse me, we're here to check on James Miller who was brought in last night and kept for observation. Could you please tell us if he is able to go home, or can we at least see him?" After the nurse checked his file, she told them they could see him and explained how to get to the room. "The nurse that has been taking care of him will meet you there and will go over everything with you."

"Thank you," Amanda said, and started down the hall to find Papa.

"I don't like this place, Amanda," Emily said. "It's so cold, and everyone is moving around so quiet like, and it smells funny. It's just spooky to me. I sure hope Papa is alright and can get out of here today."

"Yes, and I do too."

When they got to Papa's bed, he was sitting up eating.

"Well, there's my girls. Did you come to take me home?"

"Yes, if they are ready to discharge you. How are you feeling?"

"I feel sore all over. My arm is broken as you can tell, and my legs are pretty bruised and scraped, but I'll be fine in a few days. I'm ready to go home."

The nurse saw them and came to talk with them. "Is this your father?" the nurse asked.

"Yes, and we've come to take him home if he's able."

"Yes, we mainly kept him to watch for any side effects from his head injury. He had quite a bump, but everything seems to be okay. After signing these papers, you can take him home."

"That's great, and thank you."

Amanda signed the papers, and the girls carefully walked Papa to the buggy.

Looking at Emily, Papa said, "I see you made it home, young lady."

"Yes, Papa, and you didn't need to come looking for me. I'm not a child anymore. I can take care of myself."

"Let's not get into this now," Amanda said. "Just be thankful that everyone is okay."

"Yes, I suppose you're right," Papa said.

Emily breathed a sigh of relief when she heard Papa agree with Amanda. But Papa had a lot of questions about how he got to the hospital, and what happened to his wagon and old mare. Amanda decided that if he couldn't remember how he got there, that he either had a really bad head injury or was really drunk.

"There's time for all those questions to be answered, let's just get you home," Amanda said.

It was a little hard for Papa to crawl up into the buggy, but with the girls' help, he got in and settled. On the way home, Amanda pointed out where he had gone into the ditch. She was glad to see the wagon was gone.

"Harry and Jake came early this morning and got your wagon pulled out. I'm sure they're probably at the house with it now. Sarah stayed at the house to make everyone lunch."

"Good," Emily said. "I'm starved."

"Not me, little girlie. I just had something to eat before I left the hospital."

As they were nearing the house, James started remembering that Marge was at the house when he left to go find Emily. "Is everything at the house, okay?" he asked.

"Everything seemed fine," Amanda said. Nothing more was said the rest of the way home.

# Chapter

# 26

Marge's body was aching from lying on the hard floor without moving for so long. She wondered if she should try to sneak out of the house while Sarah was in the other room playing with the boys, or if she should just show herself and get it over with. She knew that she had to face the girls at some point and one at a time might be better than facing everyone at the same time. She heard Sarah announce to the boys that she needed to go to the kitchen and see what she could scrounge up for lunch. With that, Marge knew that sneaking out of the house was out of the picture. She tried shifting from one side to the other and in doing so banged the wall with her elbow. Once again, Sarah heard the noise coming from Papa's bedroom. She stopped what she was doing and entered the room.

"Who's in here?" she asked.

In a split second, Marge decided now was the time to show her face. Marge raised herself up from the small space between the bed and the wall.

Sarah jumped back with fright and yelled, "Who are you, and what are you doing in Papa's bedroom?"

"Who are *you* and what are *you* doing here?" Marge replied.

"I'm Sarah and this is my family's house. You had better explain yourself right now."

"Well, I'm Marge, James' friend. He invited me here."

"How dare you sleep in my Mama's bed! Get up from there and get out of here! No, wait! Do you have my mama's nightgown on?"

Sarah recognized the gown and became so angry that she grabbed her by the arm, causing Marge to stumble as she pushed her out of the bedroom and then shoved her into a kitchen chair. Before Marge could react, Sarah grabbed her by the shoulders.

"You're not going anywhere you, you vagrant trespasser," she stammered, searching for the right words, "until Papa comes home, and I get an explanation."

The boys, frightened by all the commotion, ran to the kitchen to see what was happening. "What's going on?" they asked Sarah.

"Everything is alright, boys," she tried to reassure them.

"Who is that lady?" Charlie asked.

"Well, for starters, she's no lady. I'm not sure who she is. She tells me she's a friend of your grandpa's. I'm taking care of things, don't worry. Just go, stay in the other room, and play with your toys."

Reluctantly, they trotted off.

Marge wiggled in her chair and tried to stand. Sarah just kept pushing her back into the chair. She remembered seeing a jump rope hanging in Emily's room and she called to Charlie, "Come here a minute please. I need you to do something for me."

Both boys, eagerly, came into the kitchen to see what she wanted.

"Charlie, I need you to go upstairs to Emily's room and find the jump rope that's hanging on a hook and bring it to me, please."

"What do you need a jump rope for?" he asked.

"Never you mind, just run and get it for me."

Before she knew it, both boys were headed up the stairs, Willie right on Charlie's heels. They found it and proudly presented it to her.

"Thank you, boys. Now go back to the toy room and stay until your momma comes back. She'll be here soon." *I sure hope so anyway.*

She tied Marge to the chair with the rope. Marge continued to kick, trying to stand, so Sarah took tea towels and tied her legs to the chair as well. If Sarah hadn't been so angry, she would have had to laugh at the sight of her.

"You untie me right now, or I'll—"

Sarah interrupted, "What, what will you do to me? Nothing, that's what you are going to do. You are going to sit right there until Harry, Jake, Amanda, Emily, and Papa get home. That's right, all of us, and we're going to get to the bottom of you being a so-called '*friend*'. It appears to me you are more than just a friend. The thought of you sleeping in my mama's bed repulses me. And who do you think you are wearing my mama's clothes?"

Even Marge began to see herself as a ridiculous sight and felt embarrassed. "Please, let me explain. Untie me and let me get into my own clothes. I promise I'll stay right here. When James comes home, he'll explain everything."

"Do you think I would untie you just on your word? How do I know you are telling the truth? I don't even know you. Oh no, girlie, you're staying right there. How old are you anyway?"

"I won't tell you my age or anything else until you untie me," Marge said defiantly.

"Well, I'm not going to untie you, so you can just sit there and keep your mouth shut."

Sarah got busy fixing lunch, trying to ignore Marge. She put on some coffee and made sandwiches. As she did, she slammed things around on the counter harder than necessary, emphasizing to Marge how angry she was.

It wasn't long before Sarah heard Harry and Jake's wagon coming up the lane, and she saw them head to the barn. They wanted to see if perhaps James' horse made it back to its stall and were pleased to see the old mare content and munching on hay. As they came out of the barn, Amanda's buggy pulled up.

Sarah was relieved to see Papa in Amanda's buggy. *Boy, he has a lot of explaining to do when he comes through that door,* she thought to herself.

Papa opened the door and the boys ran to give him a hug, only to be pushed aside when he saw Marge tied to the kitchen chair.

"What in tarnation is going on here?" James exclaimed.

Emily, coming in behind Papa, gasped at the sight. She knew that was Marge, and she recognized her mama's nightgown.

"That's for you to tell us, Papa," Sarah said, standing with her hands on her hips. "What *is* going on here?"

Amanda, along with Harry and Jake, walked in the door just as Papa stumbled to the table and yelled for Sarah to untie Marge immediately.

"What is this all about Sarah?" Amanda asked, rushing toward the boys to protect them. "What have you done?"

"The only thing I've done is find this" —she pointed at Marge— "this girl on the floor in Papa's bedroom hiding under the bed."

All eyes went to Papa. Marge spoke up and said, "Alright, alright, I'm James' friend. When Emily left and I was alone here, I thought it would be okay if I slept in a soft bed instead of the hard barn floor while I waited for James to come home. I didn't mean no harm." She looked at James for some support.

"Untie her right now," James demanded, "and I'll explain everything."

Sarah reluctantly untied her. James ordered Marge to go to the bedroom and put on her own clothes.

Marge pushed the chair over, stomped to the bedroom, and pulled the door closed, leaving it cracked enough so she could hear what James was going to say to the girls.

He started by saying, "Now, girls, this isn't what it appears."

Sarah, bending over the table and getting into his face, yelled, "How dare you say this isn't what it appears? We aren't dumb, Papa. It's exactly how it appears. Don't lie to us anymore. Your secret is out, and you better tell us the truth."

"Well, I guess you're right, I owe you the truth," he said sheepishly. "It's a long story."

Amanda jumped in, "We just want to know what your intentions are with this girl. You have been lying to us and hiding things from us for a long time now. We deserve to know what exactly is going on."

James was silent, and Marge standing next to the door, strained to hear what he was going to say.

"We're waiting, Papa," Sarah said.

"Well, it's like this. Back when I was in the barn making Lily's box, I heard noises coming from the loft. When I went up the ladder to see what it was, I found her hiding in the hay. She told me that she was part of the gypsy clan that the police ran out of town a while back and she had decided she wasn't going with them, so she hid in the woods. When it got cold, she found our barn and crawled in the loft to get warm. What was I going to do? I couldn't turn her out in the cold with no place to go and with no mother or father. I knew it wouldn't look right for me to have a female hanging around especially just after Lily had passed, so I kept her hid as long as I could. Finally, I had her go with me to my jobs as my helper. That's when things started getting out of hand. Everyone started gossiping and telling stories."

"Well, what did you expect, Papa?" Amanda chastised. "By keeping it a secret, you caused our whole family grief and embarrassment. And now, after what Emily saw in the barn, and with Sarah finding her in your bedroom with Mama's clothes on, it seems to me that the gossip wasn't too far-fetched. What are you thinking?"

Sarah spat, "He is only thinking about himself. Just like he always has and continues to do. I'm tired of it. He doesn't care about us, he only cares about himself."

"So, what are you going to do, Papa?" Amanda asked him.

He sat there for a moment shaking his head. Then finally, he slapped the table with his good hand, and said, "Well, she's not going anywhere."

When Marge heard James say that, she opened the bedroom door and skipped into the room smiling. She put her arms around James' neck and gave him a kiss on the cheek. Looking up at the girls, she said, "I win, you lose."

Fire shot from Sarah's eyes as she stood at the counter where she was fixing lunch. She spun around, still holding the knife she was using to slice the loaf of bread, and looked at the two of them. She shook the knife at Papa and screamed, "You traitor, I hate you!" She dropped the knife on the floor and ran to Harry. "Take me home, I never want to come here again."

Amanda tried to stop her but knew she meant what she said. She felt the same way, but controlled herself, for Emily's sake. Emily had run to her room and slammed the door, as she had done so often lately, and once again, shoved her bureau in front of it.

Jake grabbed a few sandwiches that Sarah had made and took them and the boys outside, leaving Amanda alone with Marge and Papa. Amanda sat down at the table across from Papa. They sat in silence for what seemed like an eternity to James because he knew Amanda was hurt and was going to ask questions.

"Papa," she finally said, "What did you mean when you said she isn't going anywhere?"

"Just what I said, Amanda. I'm not sending her away."

"So, does that mean she's going to continue staying in the barn and remain your helper?"

At that, Marge piped up, "What, and let that comfy bed in there go to waste?"

"I wasn't talking to you, Marge. Sit down and be quiet. Papa, I asked you a question. What exactly did you mean by that?"

"Well Amanda, I'm lonely and I need her. And like she said, I mean, there's no use for her sleepin' on the hard floor in the barn when there is a comfy bed in here."

Silence enveloped the room once again. "So," Amanda said calmly, "What I'm hearing is that you are going to bring Marge into the house to live and sleep with you in your bed. Is that right?"

"Yes, that's what I'm going to do."

Turning to Marge, Amanda asked, "How old are you?"

Sitting up straighter in her chair to appear taller, she said, "bout seventeen I reckon."

"About seventeen," Amanda repeated looking at Papa. "Papa, you have a daughter upstairs who will be sixteen soon. Do you realize that? How do you think this will make her feel? Where do you see her in this new life you are making for yourself?"

James, looking at Amanda with surprise, said, "Well, why would this make anything different? I would think that Marge and Emily could become friends, and Marge would be company for Emily."

Amanda pounded the table with her fist, scooted her chair out, stood up, and said, "I thought you had more sense than this, Papa. I've gone to bat for you with Sarah many times, but this is just too much. I can't believe that you would ever think that Marge could become friends with any of us. Do you really expect Emily to be okay with this arrangement? Do you realize you are choosing this girl, this *Marge*, over your very own daughters? What is wrong with you, Papa?"

Marge said, "He's in love, that's what's wrong with him."

"Oh, please," Amanda said in disgust, "you are too young to know what love is and Papa, well, you are just disgusting."

With that, Amanda grabbed some sandwiches and milk for Emily and stomped upstairs to talk with her.

Emily, alone in her room, had a little time to herself to think. She knew that she needed to talk with Lester. He would be able to calm her anger. He had done it before, and she knew he would tell her what to do. She wondered how she was going to get to him without anyone knowing. She didn't want Amanda to know that she felt the desire to be with Lester. Amanda had already told her what she thought of her being friends with a man so much older than she was.

She had agreed that he was a genuinely nice man to have pulled Papa out of the ditch but emphasized how dangerous it was to hang around a man you know nothing about. *Well, I know more about him than you think I do,* Emily thought to herself.

Amanda jolted her out of her thoughts by knocking on the door, telling her to open it.

"I brought some sandwiches that Sarah made for us and some milk."

Emily knew that Amanda was going to try to persuade her to go home with her. As much as she wanted out of that house, she knew she had to stay there if she wanted any chance of seeing Lester. Sliding the bureau away from the door, she opened it and told Amanda to come in. Amanda set the sandwiches and milk on the bureau. Emily threw her arms around Amanda and held on, rocking back and forth with her before she pulled away and said, "Amanda, what a mess Papa has made."

"I know, sweetie, as much as I've tried, I can't get him to see that the choices he's made have pushed his family away from him, or maybe he knows and just doesn't care. He is determined to move her into the house, and nothing is going to change his mind. I know Sarah will never darken this doorstep again, especially if Marge is here and part of Papa's life. As for me, well, I am done with Papa as well. He has chosen her over us, so as far as I am concerned, let her deal with him and take care of him. Now, how about you? You can pack up all your things and move in with Jake and me. The boys will be thrilled."

Pretending to be thinking about her decision, she took her time and then said, "No Amanda, I'm going to stay right here, for now anyway. I want to keep an eye on things and see if he really is going to do what he says. I will stay out of their way but keep my eyes and ears open."

"I'm shocked, Emily, that you want to be anywhere near the two of them."

Emily felt like her heart was beating out of her chest in fear that Amanda would put two and two together and conclude that she wanted to stay there so she could see Lester. However, that was the farthest thing from Amanda's thoughts. She had no idea that Emily was so emotionally connected to Lester. Emily tried to be nonchalant about her decision and added, "Besides, I can keep you posted on what is happening here."

"If you're sure Emily, but we'll stop for you every Sunday, and if you change your mind, you can let me know. Besides, you know you have a birthday coming up that's just around the corner, and I want you to be with us to celebrate your 'sweet sixteen'."

Amanda left the house without another word to Marge or Papa. Jake was patiently waiting for her, but the boys, not so much. They were bored and anxious to go home, but not as anxious as Amanda was. It had been such an exhausting day for everyone, and she felt a strong desire to be in her own home where she could feel some sense of normalcy while she processed the events of the day.

---

After dinner, Jake realized how exhausted Amanda seemed, and told her that he would take care of the boys for the rest of the night so she could have an evening to herself.

"Oh Jake, that would mean so much to me. I just need to collect my thoughts about everything that has transpired today."

"I know, Amanda, I'm taken aback by all of this myself. You just go and take care of yourself, and I'll take care of the kitchen and the boys."

Amanda went over and gave him a kiss. "Thank you, honey, you don't know how much that means to me."

He held her in his arms. "You know I'm always here for you and with God's help, we'll get through this."

Amanda, so grateful for an understanding husband, went to her room and got ready for bed. She felt a strong desire to settle down in her comfy rocking chair, the chair where she kept the quilt her mama had made for her, and where she often went to meditate. It meant even more to her now that Mama was gone. Before going to her chair, she

*Shattered*

picked up Mama's Bible that she kept on the stand close to her bed. She stood there for a moment holding it close to her chest as though embracing Mama. She nestled into her chair with the quilt draped over her shoulders, feeling Mama's arms around her. She put her head back and closed her eyes.

Letting out a huge sigh, she prayed, "Please Lord, give me wisdom to know how to fix this mess that Papa has put us in. I feel such a heaviness upon my shoulders to make things right, but I can't. There's not only my husband and little ones to take care of, but now, Papa and his shenanigans are tearing our family apart. And then there is Emily. I feel responsible for her now that Mama is gone. She needs guidance and a sense of security. It just seems like more than I can handle." She sat in silence for some time.

Finally, her eyes fell on her Mama's Bible lying on her lap. She flipped through the pages. Not knowing where to look for words of wisdom, she noticed scriptures that Mama had underlined. She started reading them. *Oh, Mama, what precious treasures are here for us to find,* she thought and continued reading.

On and on she went flipping through the pages and finding more and more treasures. She felt the tension she was feeling when she sat down slowly melt away. "Oh Mama," she said, "now I know how you made it all those years putting up with all the things that Papa put you through. No wonder this book was so precious to you." She bowed her head as the tears streamed down her face. "Thank you, Lord. Thank you for Mama who loved your word and passed on to us the verses that got her through her difficult times. They've touched my heart and have given me the peace that I needed tonight. I know that you will be with me in the days ahead and with your help I will get through this."

She hesitated, not wanting to leave her chair because she felt such peace. She slowly got up, moved to her bed, and was sound asleep when Jake came to check on her.

# Chapter

# 27

Emily, in her room, pondered how she could get to Lester without Papa knowing she was gone. She couldn't wait until tomorrow. She needed to see him today. She knew about what time he ate his dinner at the Inn and decided that would be a good opportunity for her to find him there - like she had before. She thought about how he made her feel like a lady and how he had a way of comforting her.

It seemed like forever to Emily until it was finally time to try and catch Lester at dinner. "I've got to get out of here," she said to herself. She decided to carefully, and as quietly as she could, slide the bureau away from her door and crack it open enough to listen to what Papa and Marge were talking about. What she heard nearly made her sick - the way Marge was calling her papa *Jamie* and *sweetie pie*. She waited in silence for what seemed like an eternity, hoping that they would move into the bedroom, or better yet, go out to the barn. Finally, she heard Papa say that he needed to lie down for a little while because his arm was hurting.

"You know, Marge," Papa said, as he pushed his chair away from the table, "this has been an incredibly stressful day."

"I know Jamie, but look what we accomplished. The girls now know about me and how we feel about each other, and we are here together. I don't have to worry about hiding anymore. Here, let me help you to the bed and get you settled."

Emily knew that if she was going to go find Lester today, this was her chance to leave the house unnoticed. She waited until they were lost in conversation, then slipped down the stairs and out the door. Feeling a sense of relief, she hurried into town to find Lester. She found him in the dining room of the hotel just as she suspected. He was kicked back, engrossed in his newspaper, and drinking a cup of coffee before dinner. She nodded to the hotel clerk, pointed to the table where Lester sat, and continued to his table. Lester did not see her approaching and was surprised when she snapped the paper with her fingers.

"Emily," he said, startled. "What a pleasant surprise. What brings you here?"

"Well," she said as she pulled out a chair across the table from him and sat down. "A lot has happened at home since I saw you last."

"Oh, and what might that be?"

"This morning, while Jake and Harry were taking care of getting Papa's wagon out of the ditch, Amanda, Sarah, and I went to the house to check up on things. Everything seemed fine. There was no sign of that crazy girl, so Sarah stayed at the house with the boys while Amanda and I went to the hospital to bring Papa home. When we got home with Papa, Sarah was in a rage. While she was working in the kitchen fixing everyone's lunch, she heard noises coming from Papa's bedroom and went to investigate. Much to her chagrin, she found Papa's mystery girl hiding on the floor between the bed and the wall."

Lester stifled a laugh and said, "Oh my, that must have been a sight."

"And to make things worse, she was in Mama's nightgown. It made Sarah so angry that she took her and tied her up in a chair in the kitchen until we all got home. Of course, when we walked in, there she was as big as day. Papa was so surprised he didn't know what to think or say. But their secret was out, and they had no choice but to admit what was going on between them. They both made it very clear that, regardless of how we feel or what we say, their intentions are to stay together and that includes her moving into the house with him. I am so disgusted and don't know what to do. I can't do this Lester," she said as tears welled up in her eyes. "I just can't watch that evil girl living in our house, sleeping in Mama and Papa's bed. It makes me sick to my stomach."

Reaching out and taking her hand in his, he asked if she would feel better if she left the house and went to live with Amanda.

Emily grew silent and stared into space.

"What is it, Emily? What are you thinking? Talk to me. You know you can tell me anything."

After what seemed like an eternity, she turned and looked Lester in the face and said "I can't do that because it would be taking me away from you. By staying home, I know that I can come into town and see you when I need to talk. I couldn't do that if I lived so far out of town with Amanda. I don't know what I would do if I couldn't see you."

"Emily, listen. My job here will be finishing up before long, and I'll be going back to New York. What will you do then?"

Silence once again enveloped the conversation. Emily sat with her hands in her lap and her head down, trying to fight back the tears that were already rolling down her cheeks.

Lester took a sip of his now cold coffee and, handing her a napkin, he very quietly asked, "Would you want to go to New York with me?"

Emily raised her head and looked directly into his eyes. She whispered, "Do you really mean that Lester?"

"Well, you've just told me how much you want to be with me, and you know I love being with you too, so that sounds like a reasonable solution. What do you think?"

"Oh, Lester, that would be wonderful. I just couldn't imagine not having you in my life."

"But Emily, there is just one problem that I see, and that is getting your Papa to agree to it. You know you are only fifteen."

"Almost sixteen," she interjected.

"Ok, but still a minor, and we must have your father's approval."

"Why do we have to ask him? He doesn't care anything about me. All he cares about is being with Marge."

"Well, maybe it won't be a problem with him, but we still have to ask."

"But I don't understand why."

"Because it's the law, Emily. I can't take a minor out of the state without the parent's approval."

Emily sat quietly, fiddling with the napkin she used to wipe her tears. She wondered what her papa might say when they told him of their plans. *He might say good riddance, but what if he gets angry and refuses to give his permission? I could just run away, and he would never know where*

*I was. But then, what would Amanda and Sarah think of me doing that, and where would I go?* She couldn't imagine being away from Lester. Nothing else mattered to her. She was so desperate to be with him that she was willing to do anything, right or wrong, to make that happen.

"Lester, what if he won't give his permission? What will you do?" she finally asked him.

"I don't know Emily. I really don't know. How sure are you that you want to go with me?"

"Oh Lester, I've never been more sure of anything in my life, but how sure are you that you want me to go with you?"

"I love you my little lady, and you coming with me would make me the happiest man around. But you know there is a big age difference between us, and I'm not sure what your sisters will think about this, even if your papa did give permission. I don't want to come between you and your sisters."

"Let me worry about them, it's Papa who we need to get past first."

"Well then, why don't we go to the house and talk with your papa? We won't know unless we ask, will we?"

"I don't know," Emily said, "it's getting late and it has been a crazy long day. I'm not sure this would be the best time to ask him."

"Emily, I'm not sure there would ever be a 'best time' to ask him. Maybe catching him in the vulnerable state of mind that he's in tonight will be the best we could ever expect to get. What do you say, Emily? Or are you having second thoughts?"

"No, there are no second thoughts. I guess you're right."

# Chapter

# 28

They rode in silence back to the house, but Emily scooted closer to Lester feeling a sense of belonging. As they drove up the lane to the house Emily looked up at Lester and with tears in her eyes said, "I'm scared."

He took her hands in his and again asked her if she was sure this was what she wanted. Assured she was certain, he said, "Let's go in now and see what he has to say. What we do then will depend on how he reacts."

James heard the truck pull up. "Who could that be coming around here now?"

Marge got out of bed, went to the front window, and looked out.

"Oh, it's that man that Emily hangs around."

"What do you mean by 'that man that Emily hangs around'?"

"You know, the one who rescued you and took you to the hospital. She said he's a friend of hers."

"I'm going to need to have a talk with that girl. And he can just go back to wherever he came from, 'cause he's not seeing Emily tonight. Besides, she's probably sound asleep." Coming out of the bedroom James said, "I've not heard anything out of her, have you, Marge?"

Just then, Emily came through the door with Lester right behind.

"Emily," Papa said in shock, "what were you doing out of the house? You were supposed to be in your room. You didn't ask if you could go out."

"No, Papa, I didn't! I left while you were so engrossed with your new little girl here. I want you to know that I will not stay in this house as long as she is here. I went to talk things over with Lester, as I have done many times in the past, which you've known nothing about. You know why? Because you don't pay any attention to me or care about anything around here except for your little Marge."

"Now you just wait a minute, girlie," James started.

"No, Papa, '*you just wait a minute*' because we need to tell you our plans."

"Plans? What are you talking about?"

Lester knew it was time for him to take over the conversation at this point.

Clearing his throat Lester began, "James, how have you been feeling since your accident? You know you are an incredibly lucky man to have not gotten hurt worse than you did. There was a huge rock lying only a few feet from where you landed. If you had hit your head on that rock, you would have been a goner.

"Oh, you poor baby," Marge said, rubbing her hand over James' back. "That would have been terrible. What would I ever do without you?"

Distracted somewhat from the conversation at hand, he said, "Now, now, Marge, I'm okay, and nothing happened to me that a few weeks won't fix."

Emily felt nauseous and nearly gagged. She knew for sure that she could not stay in this house any longer than she had to. She glanced at Lester as if to say, "Get on with it."

Lester got the hint and continued the conversation gently, leading into the question he needed to ask. "Your daughter" —nodding toward Emily— "is a very fine young lady."

"Yeah well, I don't know about the lady part, but she is a good daughter." He then added, "Most of the time."

"She is a lady in my eyes, James, and I think very highly of her."

James started squirming in his chair. "You do, do ya?"

"Yes, I do, and the reason I'm here is to talk to you about marrying her."

Emily's eyes got as big as saucers, and she nearly choked. She didn't know that was part of the plan, but it sure sounded good to her.

"Marrying her?" he screamed. "What are you talking about man? She's just a child."

"In case you haven't noticed, she is much more than a child, James. We have both grown to enjoy each other's company and have expressed our feelings for each other."

She stepped closer to Lester, he grabbed her hand giving it a squeeze, which gave Emily the confidence she needed to continue the conversation.

"Papa, I'm not a child. I have a birthday coming up."

"Yeah, I know, and you're going to be what, fourteen, fifteen?"

"No, Papa, sixteen."

"Oh my," he said settling back down in his chair and running his fingers through his hair.

Marge recognized that as a sign of him needing some comfort. She went over to him and put her arm around his shoulder. Bending down, she whispered in his ear, "You know, Jamie, that would get her out of our hair, and we wouldn't have to worry about her or any of your girls anymore. We could live our lives in peace."

"Oh, I don't know," he continued. "Look at you, Lester, you are a grown man, probably twice her age, and she is just a child. No, I can't let that happen."

"Now, now," Marge said, patting him on the back.

"No, no, no I can't allow her to go off with a man that much older than her. How would that look, tell me?"

That opened the door to a great argument for Lester to pursue. "How do you think it looks for you, a man of your age living with a girl of Emily's age?"

"Well, that's different."

"And how so, James?"

Emily was standing taller and feeling proud of Lester for sticking up for her like he was doing. She felt the urge to lash out at Papa but allowed Lester to fight this battle for her.

Lester asked again. "How so, James?"

Papa remained still, but under his breath, he whispered to himself, "No, no, no," over and over.

Lester finally broke the silence, "I don't think the authorities would look too fondly on you harboring a young gypsy girl and taking advantage of her, now would they, James."

The hair stood up on the back of James' neck at the thought.

*Shattered*

Marge knew that wouldn't be good. She let out a whimper and moved even closer to James. He knew Lester was right. *What am I to do?* He thought to himself.

"I'll bring the marriage consent papers to you in the morning, and when they are signed, we will be on our way. You and Marge can continue as you are."

"Oh, Jamie," Marge begged, "please sign the papers, please. I can't leave you. I need you. Let Emily go. She's only trouble."

Slamming his fist on the table and turning his head sideways, he glared up at the two standing hand in hand, and said, "Okay, you fools, bring the papers but no more talk of the authorities, is that clear?"

Emily was filled with mixed emotions. She was happy that he had said yes, but angry that he had called them fools, especially considering what he himself was doing. She leaned forward, looked Papa in the eyes, and hissed, "We are not fools, and if you think that *we* are, then what does that make you?"

Quickly pulling Emily back, Lester said, "Yes, sir, and we both thank you very much. I will be here in the morning with the papers."

Turning to Emily, and leading her towards the door, he said, "Let's go get you some dinner and talk, shall we?"

Lester and Emily went out to the truck where they could talk in private. As soon as the truck door shut, Emily blurted out nervously "Lester, you never said anything to me about marrying you."

"Well, how else did you think I would be able to take you with me to New York? You do still want to go with me, don't you?"

"Oh yes, you know I do, Lester, but marriage?"

"Well, I guess I should have asked you first, but I just assumed that you knew that's what I meant when I asked you to go to New York with me." Taking her hand and pulling her close, Lester said, "So, Emily, I'm asking you now, will you marry me?"

"Oh yes, of course, Lester. If you're sure this is what you want."

He leaned toward her, looking into her beautiful green eyes, and said, "I've never been more sure of anything in my life."—he gave her an assuring kiss— "Now let's go get some dinner."

Emily felt like she was floating on a cloud, and nothing could wipe the smile from her face.

At dinner, Lester explained that he would go to the courthouse and get the papers for her papa to sign as soon as he got the crew up and running with the day's work.

"Oh Lester, I sure hope that Papa doesn't change his mind. What would we do then?"

"Let's not get ahead of things, Emily, but if he does, we'll cross that bridge when and if it comes."

"I've got to tell Amanda and Sarah about all of this. I'm not sure how they are going to feel about it."

"Don't worry about that now. After we have the signed papers in hand, we will go and tell them together."

"I've got to tell Ruthie Ann too. She would never forgive me if I didn't." Sighing, she added, "I'm *so* not looking forward to going back into that house tonight."

"I know, Emily, but you must. Just ignore anything you see or hear and go straight to your room. Get your things ready for me to put in the truck when I get there in the morning. Perhaps that will be the last time you have to step foot back into that house. Speaking of that, I need to get you back there so you can get packed up and get some sleep."

"No sleep for me tonight, I'm sure, Lester. I'm too nervous and excited to sleep."

*Chapter*

# 29

Marge danced around the kitchen table. She was happy to be rid of the little twit who kept stirring things up between them. James, however, was in an entirely different mood. He was angry that Lester had him over a barrel when it came to going to the police. He was upset at Marge for getting him into this mess and felt defeated from losing the battle to keep Emily at home.

"Go get me my liquor bottle," he ordered Marge. "In fact, now that everyone is gone you can bring in the whole stash."

Marge danced her way out the door to get his liquor, repeating in a sing-song fashion, "Everyone is gone, everyone is gone."

When Marge came back with his liquor bottles, she found James lying across the table moaning. He was in pain. Pain from the happenings of the day and pain from his broken arm that was swelling beneath his cast.

"Give me something, Marge, quick. Marge was more than happy to oblige, since she already had a nip herself.

---

By the time Emily got home, Marge and James were so absorbed in each other and their liquor that they didn't even notice her entering the house, thankfully. She hurried up the stairs and ran to her room. Inside, she quickly closed the door and, as usual lately, slid her bureau in front of it. She could still hear the loud talking and laughter coming from downstairs, which made her very irritated. In the privacy of her room, she sank down into her bed. Her head spun with all that had just happened. She knew she needed to gather the rest of her belongings, at least what she wanted to take with her anyway. A lot of her things were already at Amanda's house, so she didn't have too much to worry about. With a sigh, she took the quilt from her bed, made a nap sack out of it, and began loading it with her clothes and personal things. After she was satisfied that she had everything gathered, she laid down on her bed exhausted and drifted off to sleep.

The sun coming through her window woke her. She jumped out of bed, afraid she had overslept and possibly missed Lester. She listened at the door and, not hearing a sound, she removed the bureau, and quietly went downstairs. All was silent. She tiptoed to Papa's room and peered in, where she found Marge and Papa both lying across the bed with their arms and legs entangled. "Disgusting. A disgrace is what it is," she said softly to herself, so she didn't wake them.

Looking at the old pendulum clock hanging on the wall, she saw that it was nearly eight o'clock. She wondered if Lester was really going to be able to get the papers that he talked about the night before. What if thoughts swirled in her head. *What if he couldn't get the papers? What if Papa changes his mind and refuses to sign them? What if...* She went to the ice box, got out the milk, poured a glass, and took it back to her room to wait for Lester. The minutes clicked by so slowly she couldn't stand it. It was now nine o'clock and she just knew Lester would be there any minute. Nervous, she decided to take her quilt nap sack downstairs because, regardless, she was not staying in this house one more night. She hauled it out into the hallway, lifted it up over the railing, and let it drop with a thud to the floor below.

The noise roused James, and he yelled, "Who's out there?" Not hearing anything, he woke Marge and untangled himself from her. "What was that noise, Marge?"

Irritated that she had been disturbed, she just turned over and ignored him. Moaning and grunting, he slowly unfolded himself and crawled out of bed. Emily was just entering the kitchen when she saw a nasty, disheveled-looking creature emerging from the bedroom. If she didn't know it was Papa, she would have screamed and run out of the house. But instead, she waited to see what he was going to do.

"Coffee! I need coffee NOW," he bellowed.

"It looks like you need a whole lot more than coffee, but as for the coffee, you will have to get it yourself or have your beloved, lazy Marge fix it for you. I'm leaving, don't you remember? For good this time."

"Yeah, yeah, I hear you." "He stumbled to the table and fell into a chair. "MARGE!" he yelled. "Get out here and get the coffee going, NOW!"

Slinking out the door, she hoarsely said, "Coffee? I don't know how to make coffee. You always brought it to me," and turned around and went back to bed.

Emily, while amused at this little scene, was also slightly worried about what was going to happen next. She was saved from having to find out by the rumbling of Lester's truck coming up the lane. She ran out to meet him and briefly told him of what was happening inside.

"If he needs coffee, Emily, then we have to get him some or he'll never sign these papers," Lester said, waving them in his hand. "Let's do whatever it takes so we can get out of here."

Upon seeing them enter the house, James yelled, "What are you doing here Lester?"

Emily and Lester looked at each other and knew they had their work cut out for them.

"I'm here with the papers that you agreed to sign last night."

"Papers? What papers?"

Emily's heart sank. She was afraid this wasn't going to go well.

"The papers that allow me to take care of your precious daughter, Emily."

Emily quickly said, "Papa, do you want me to make some coffee for you?"

*Way to go Emily, Lester* thought.

"Oh, coffee. Ah, yes, coffee. I need coffee. Please, Emily, please do."

Emily had to get a hot fire going to fix the coffee, so it took a while. In the meantime, Lester tried talking calmly with James about things that would take his mind off his hangover and his need for coffee. He thought he was doing a pretty good job of it when finally, the coffee was ready, and Emily set a hot cup of it in front of Papa.

Taking a big whiff, he told Emily, "Get a cup for my buddy here."

Emily raised her brow and looked at Lester, biting her lip to keep from laughing. "Your buddy, huh? Sure, coming right up."

Lester let James take a few swigs of coffee and sober up some and then he produced the papers for James to sign. "Well, 'buddy', here's where we need to sign these papers. You sign there, and I'll sign here, and we'll be good."

James took the papers and started reading. He was silent for a long time and asked for another cup of coffee. Emily was getting nervous. Everything had been going so well, but now she didn't know what to expect. Finally, he said, "So if I sign these papers, you won't go to the authorities about Marge, right?"

"That's right James. And you sure don't want me to do that, do you?"

"No, so give me the damn pen."

Emily held her breath while Lester handed him the pen. After he signed, she exhaled a big breath and dropped into the chair beside Lester. "Thank you, Papa."

"Yeah, well, be gone with you," he pushed papers toward Lester, and yelled, "MARGE!"

James refused to shake Lester's extended hand, but it didn't bother Lester. He just wanted to get out of there before he changed his mind. "Let's get your things, Emily, and get out of here."

## Chapter 30

It was mid-morning, and Amanda was busy with her Monday morning chores. The dirty clothes she had sorted lay in piles on the back porch waiting to be washed. The laundry tub filled with water was heating over the fire out back, and the boys were playing in the yard with the dog when she heard Lester's truck coming down the lane. *What in the world is he doing here?* she wondered. Then she saw the passenger door open and Emily running toward the house.

"Emily, what is going on? Are you alright?"

"Oh," grabbing Amanda's hands, "Amanda, I'm more than alright. I'm just so happy. Papa signed papers for me and Lester to get married. We're getting married, and I'm moving to New York!"

Looking at Lester for some kind of explanation, Amanda said, "Wait, wait just a minute. What are you telling me? What is going on here? You two are getting married?"

"Yes, that's right. James just signed the papers this morning and Emily wanted to come straight here to let you know and explain everything."

Stepping aside and motioning them into the house she said, "Well, get in here and start explaining because you've got a lot of that to do." She poured each of them a cup of tea and sat down with them at the table to hear what they had to say.

Amanda was shocked upon hearing all that had transpired since the last time she had seen Emily. To Amanda, this marriage sounded like an out for Emily, a quick fix, so to speak, but she was not convinced it was a valid solution. She had so many questions. She struggled to wrap her head around everything and with the idea of Emily, so young, leaving home and going so far away with a much older man.

After the shock had subsided a bit, Amanda said, "Emily, you know that just because these papers have been signed doesn't mean you have to get married."

"Oh, but I want to," she gushed.

Amanda continued, "Let's take some time to talk this over with the rest of the family and look at all the options we now have since Papa has released you from his care. We all need time to process this."

Lester spoke up and said, "I totally understand Amanda and I need to get back to work anyway, but I want you to know that I definitely love this little lady and promise you she would be well taken care of." Looking at Emily he continued, "How about I give you a couple of days with your family and I'll come back Wednesday evening. We can talk about everything then."

Amanda agreed that was a good idea and said, "Why don't you plan on coming for dinner? That would be a good time for all of us to discuss this."

"Sounds like a plan." Giving Emily a hug, he said, "Don't worry, everything will be ok, you'll see."

After Lester left, Amanda said, "Come here, little sister, and give me a hug. We've got a lot to talk about. But for now, help me finish up this laundry."

Emily, flitting around with excitement, helped Amanda finish the laundry, and said, "I'm just so excited. I can't wait to tell Ruthie Ann and Beth. I know they will be surprised."

"Whoa! Slow down, little sister. Don't get ahead of yourself."

---

When the laundry was finished and the morning chores done, they sat down to talk. Emily went on and on about how Lester made her feel and was always there for her. She barely stopped to take a breath. She told Amanda about all the time they spent together while Papa was busy with Marge. When Emily was finally done talking, Amanda suggested

*Shattered*

they go over and see what Sarah had to say about it all. So, Amanda, Emily, and the boys got into the buggy and headed over to see Sarah.

Over Sarah's freshly made bread pudding, they filled her in on what had transpired over the last few days. Sarah took the news better than either Emily or Amanda dreamed she would.

"All I can say is that Papa has really messed up good this time. When you said that she doesn't even know how to make coffee, it almost made me laugh. You know what, they deserve each other. As far as you marrying Lester goes, I was only a year older than you when I married Harry, and we are still happily married to this day. If you really love him like you say you do, and if he feels the same way about you, then I don't see any reason for you not to get married if that's what you both want. I'm so glad you are out of Papa's clutches. My only concern is that you will be so far away. You must promise to stay in touch."

"Oh, I most definitely will. I'll miss you all as well. Then I have your blessing, Sarah?"

"You certainly do. You don't have to worry about me standing in your way. But of course, you will have to win over big sister here," she said, gesturing to Amanda.

"I'll be talking to Jake this evening," Amanda said. "I'm not totally against it, but there are a lot of things that will need to be worked out. Lester is coming to dinner Wednesday night, and I would like to have you and Harry join us so we can all talk things over with him. Would that be alright with you?"

"That sounds good. You can count on us."

Before leaving, Emily went over and gave Sarah a big hug. "Thank you, Sarah, for understanding."

On their ride home, Emily asked Amanda if she would take her into town to see Ruthie Ann. She was anxious to tell her the news and to see her reaction.

"I can't do it today because we need to get home and prepare for our evening meal. However, I do need to go into town tomorrow to run some errands and pick up groceries. You can come with me, and while I'm doing that, you can visit with her."

"That will be great," she said. "I can't wait to tell her. She is going to be so surprised."

When they arrived home, Emily helped Amanda in the kitchen all the while talking nonstop about Lester, the wedding, and New York.

"I know you are excited, Emily, about this possible new adventure, but don't forget we need to talk things over with Jake this evening and get his opinion. So, I think you should slow your thinking down a bit. He may think differently about Lester, or perhaps he may think this isn't the right time for you to be going off with him. We only want what's best for you, that's all."

Reluctantly, feeling a little deflated, she said, "I know Amanda."

At dinner, Emily sat nervously waiting for Amanda to drop the news on Jake, when Jake said, "Emily, how are you? I didn't expect to see you here this evening. Is everything all right?"

Emily looked at Amanda and smiled. "I'll let Amanda tell you why I'm here."

"Well, I had a surprising visit this morning from Lester and Emily who shared some interesting news. Papa signed papers for them to be married."

"What? Wait! He wouldn't do that in a million years."

"Well, he did, and Lester and I couldn't be happier," Emily told Jake, excitedly.

"I just don't understand how this happened. I want to talk with Lester about this. I want to see if he's as excited about this as you appear to be."

"I've invited him to dinner Wednesday night along with Sarah and Harry so we all can talk about this and get everyone's opinion," Amanda told him.

"Well, that's a good idea, Amanda, and in the meantime you and I will talk about this," Jake said, shaking his head.

It seemed to take forever for Wednesday dinner to arrive. She missed Lester so much and found herself wanting to be with him more and more. She tried keeping herself busy by helping Amanda around the house and playing with the boys. Her visit with Ruthie Ann had been a positive one. Emily was glad that she understood the situation she was in and supported her decision.

Setting the table for the Wednesday night dinner, Emily asked Amanda, "So, are you on board with things any more since talking with Sarah and Jake?"

"I'm getting there, but I have some major questions for Lester. He's not going to take you away from us without me knowing exactly where you will be and how I can get in touch with you. I also need to know his true feelings for you."

## Chapter

# 31

Dinner went well. Everyone talked about everything except what they were actually there for. Finally, Sarah blurted out, "So, Lester, you want to marry our little sister and take her away from us?"

There was silence. Then Lester said, "Well, Sarah, when you put it that way, it sounds like I'm a mean person. However" —looking at Emily and taking her hand— "It is true that both Emily and I would greatly appreciate the family's blessings on our marriage."

"Well, you certainly have mine and Harry's blessings. Anything to get Emily out of the clutches of Papa. I want to see him flounder in the mess that he created."

Jake interjected, "Sarah, this is not about vengeance against your papa. We all know that he has made poor choices and they have been hurtful to our whole family, but I know you remember your mama saying, *Vengeance is mine, says the Lord.* Your papa will have his day, but it's not ours to get even. The issue at hand is what is best for Emily."

"Oh, I know Jake, but I'm just so angry at him."

Amanda wanted to get the conversation back to what was important, so she asked, "Lester, what are your true feelings about Emily?"

"Hopefully you've seen that I care immensely for Emily's well-being, but it goes deeper than that. I truly love her and want to be a place for her to feel safe and secure."

"Well, Lester, there is no question that Emily has fallen for you in a great way too. Another question I have is, where in New York do you live?"

"I have a little two-bedroom bungalow that's just waiting for a lady's touch in Clinton, New York. I feel sure Emily will love it there. All of you would be more than welcome to visit any time. I would like to assure you, Sarah, that I'm not taking her '*away from you*.'"

"Well, that's good, I didn't mean it like it sounded. So, Emily, you've been quiet, are you ready to make this move?"

"Yes, Sarah, I am."

"Well then—" Sarah started.

"Wait just a minute, I want to hear from Lester how he got Papa to agree to sign the papers," Jake interrupted.

"That's a good question, Jake," Lester said. "I had him over a barrel. I reminded him that he was harboring a young gypsy girl nearly Emily's age and asked him what he thought the police would do if they found out about it. Marge went to crying and begged him to sign the papers. After promising him that if he signed the papers, I wouldn't say a word to the police, he begrudgingly took the pen and signed."

"That's a good one, Lester. I'll give you that," Jake said, and they all agreed. "I do admire your proven integrity in the business world and the human kindness that you have demonstrated to our family. Do you promise to live up to those traits going forward with Emily?"

"Yes, sir, I promise."

"Then, Sarah," Jake said, "Continue on."

Laughing, Sara continued, "With Jake's approval, let's take a vote. Is everyone in agreement for them to be married?"

They all nodded in agreement and said yes.

Emily said, "Finally," and laid her head on Lester's shoulder. Looking up at him, she said, "I love you."

"I love you too Emily."

Amanda pushed away from the table, "Well, with that settled, Sarah, come help me serve dessert."

The comfort of the warm peach cobbler set the mood for solidifying the exciting plans moving forward.

Amanda addressed Emily and Lester, "What are your thoughts about when this wonderful event will take place?"

"Well, Emily and I haven't had time to discuss dates, but I do know that my job here will be finishing in two weeks, and I'll need to return home then." Looking at Emily, he continued, "So if you want to go with me, the wedding needs to be rather soon."

"The sooner the better works for me." Emily said excitedly, and then added, "Amanda, you and Sarah will have to help me with the plans." The girls both agreed and said they would love to.

Two weeks didn't give them very much time to do all the things they wanted to do, but they would put their heads together and make it happen.

"First things first," Amanda said. "We have a sweet sixteen birthday to plan."

Sarah spoke up, "Oh, I have an idea. How about combining the Birthday Party and the Wedding Party into just one great big celebration? What do you think about that Emily?"

"That sounds wonderful to me."

Amanda also agreed, "Okay, let's set a date."

They decided a week from Friday would give them time for all the planning and preparations and then a few days together after the wedding to say their goodbyes. Emily was ecstatic and Lester was just as thrilled.

That Sunday, unbeknownst to Emily, Amanda talked with both the mothers of Beth and Ruthie Ann. She made plans for Gladys, Ruthie Ann's mother, to bring the girls out to her house on Tuesday, for the day, to help Emily with her wedding plans. When Emily found out, she was thrilled. The girls spent a lot of time laughing and had a great day sharing their ideas for the wedding. They decided how she should wear her hair and suggested she wear a circle of flowers on her head. Emily was so grateful for their help, but she was even more grateful to have a fun day with her friends before she had to leave them.

Each evening after work, Lester came to visit Emily and the family. They kept him abreast of all the plans.

"Your part," Emily informed him, "is to make all the necessary arrangements for us to be married at the courthouse on Friday morning so we can have our big celebration in the afternoon and evening."

"I think I can handle that, my little wife-to-be," he said with a big grin on his face.

*Chapter*

# 32

Emily woke early. She jumped out of bed, and with a big yawn, arched her back and stretched her arms in the air. "This is my wedding day," she said happily. She went to the window and looked up at the cloudless sky, "What a perfect day this is going to be."

It was a beautiful summer morning. The sun was shining, and the birds were singing as Emily and her sisters walked into the courthouse to meet Lester. Emily was wearing a pink sleeveless summer dress that made her look and feel like a lady. Her hair was pulled back with a ring of wildflowers adorning the top of her head. She carried a beautiful bouquet of pink roses and white daisies that Sarah had arranged for her.

Lester greeted the ladies and then turned to Emily, "Good morning my love. You look beautiful."

Emily, blushing, said, "Good morning. You look mighty handsome yourself."

Lester turned to the man standing next to him, "Allow me to introduce you ladies to my good friend, John Peters. He's the fellow that helped get James out of the ditch and to the hospital."

"Oh, so glad to meet you. Thank you so much for your kindness," Amanda said, extending her hand. Emily and Sarah greeted him as well, agreeing with Amanda.

"You are so welcome. I'm glad I could help. But now it's my pleasure to stand with Lester on this joyous occasion."

"Everything is all set," Lester announced. "They will call our names when they're ready for us.

It wasn't long until they heard, "Lester Granger and Emily Miller, please make your way to room 219."

Lester took Emily's hand and whispered, "It's time, my lovely bride. Are you sure this is what you really want?"

"Yes, Lester, more than anything," she said, as she put her arm in his.

"Well then, let's get on with it," he said.

Amanda and Sarah both had tears in their eyes when they heard the judge say, "I pronounce you husband and wife. You may now kiss your bride." They couldn't believe their baby sister was married.

Sarah was the first to congratulate them and gave Emily a hug. "Mama would be so proud of you, Emily. It feels like she's here."

Papers were signed and filed with the court. Then they left the courthouse with smiles on their faces.

Walking down the steps, Lester said, "My beautiful bride and I are going to have a bite to eat in town. We'll meet you at the house later if that's okay with you, Amanda."

"That will be perfect. It will give us time to prepare for the party. The few guests we have invited will be arriving around four, and John, you are certainly welcome as well."

"Thank you, ma'am, I appreciate that. I wouldn't miss it for anything. Lester can tell me how to get there."

Amanda, reaching down to hug Emily, said, "Sounds good, then we'll see you around four. I'm picking up Ruthie Ann and Beth. They wanted to help with the decorations."

# Chapter 33

As a surprise for Emily, Lester had the restaurant at the inn where he was staying prepare an elegant table for two with linens and china. In the center was a vase of red roses and a place card that read *Reserved for Mr. and Mrs. Lester Granger.*

Emily gasped when she saw the arrangement and just stood there with her hand over her mouth. Finally, after taking it all in, she said, "Oh Lester, you are the sweetest. I can't believe you thought to do all of this."

He pulled out a chair for her and slid into the one across from her just as the waiter came to their table. Handing them both a menu, he said, "Congratulations, Mr. and Mrs. Granger, on your wedding day." Emily was beaming from ear to ear with joy.

While they were waiting for their food, Lester pulled out a tiny box from his jacket pocket and placed it in front of her. "This is for you, my love."

"Lester, what have you done now?"

"Just open it and you'll see."

She very carefully opened the box and to her amazement, she found the most beautiful ring she had ever seen. It was an exquisite purple amethyst ring. She gasped and said, "Oh Lester, It's beautiful."

"Well, I hope it fits you. Here, let me put it on your finger."

"Oh, it's perfect. Thank you, Lester, I'll never take it off."

"You are now officially mine, my sweet Emily."

She could hardly wait to show the ring to Sarah and Amanda and tell them all about what Lester had arranged for them at the restaurant.

They ate their food slowly, gazing into each other's eyes. When they finished their meal, they headed out to Lester's truck.

As they were leaving the hotel, out of the corner of her eye, Emily noticed a horse and wagon that looked like Papa's. She took a second look, and sure enough, it was Papa with Marge sitting right beside him. They were pulled up beside Lester's truck.

"Oh Lester, this can't be happening. I can't deal with him today of all days."

"Now, don't you worry, Emily. I'll take care of him. You wait right here."

Lester walked over to the wagon and asked James what he was doing there.

"I knew that was your truck and I wanted to talk with you about Emily," James answered.

His breath reeked of liquor, and Lester knew he would have to tread lightly with him so as not to make a scene.

James began saying over and over, "I need my Emily to come home. I need her."

"Emily will not be going home with you. We are married now, and it is my responsibility to take care of her and protect her, not yours."

"Married you say? Well, we'll see about that."

"There's nothing for you to see about, James. That's the way it is. You have no business here. So, you just be on your way now."

"I will not!" James said emphatically.

"James," Lester said sternly, "I suggest you leave right now, or I will walk across the street to the courthouse and report you for harboring your little gypsy-friend here, and they will throw you in jail. Is that what you want?"

Stammering, James said "Jail? Did you say jail?"

"Yes, that's right. If you don't want that to happen, you better go home NOW! Do you understand?"

Marge became very nervous and said, "Jamie baby, we need to go on home now. Here, let me take the reins and you just sit back and relax."

As Marge pulled the wagon back onto the street to head home, Lester saw James shake his fist at him and heard him say, "You'll pay for this."

Lester went back to where Emily was waiting and found tears running down her cheeks.

"This was supposed to be a *perfect* day, but Papa has ruined everything. He will never change."

"Now, now, Emily, he's gone, and he hasn't ruined anything. Forget this even happened. We are happily married, have had a wonderful afternoon, and now we're off to celebrate our wedding - and your sweet sixteenth birthday. We can't forget that."

"You're right, Lester. I refuse to let Papa spoil our wonderful day. Let's get out of here."

## Chapter

# 34

Amanda, Sarah, and the girls outdid themselves with the decorations. The house was decorated with white paper bells and crepe paper ribbons that hung everywhere from the ceiling. The boys were proud of their contribution of the paper chains that draped from the mantel. There was a sign that read, *Happy Sweet Sixteenth Birthday* and another one that read, *Congratulations to the Newlyweds*. The table was covered with a pink linen tablecloth, and centered in the middle was a beautiful three-layer cake decorated with white frosting and pink roses. There was an array of finger foods and casserole dishes that filled the rest of the table.

Besides the family, there were numerous friends from church, a few close friends from Emily's school, and of course Ruthie Ann and Beth. She was pleasantly surprised to see all of them.

"The house looks great, Amanda. You and Sarah have made this such a special time for Lester and me."

"We helped," the boys chimed in.

Emily, giving the boys a hug, said, "I can see that. You boys are so sweet. Thank you so much."

Noticing the ring, Amanda grabbed Emily's hand and asked, "What's that on your finger?"

"Oh, isn't it beautiful, Amanda? Lester surprised me with it and a scrumptious dinner at the hotel. I'll have to tell you and Sarah all about it." Looking around, Emily said, "I can't thank you enough for everything."

The party was in full swing. Some people with their plates full were standing around the table as if to guard the food. Some were enjoying each other's company, talking and laughing. And some were dancing and singing to the music of the fiddlers that Sarah had arranged for entertainment. Everyone was having a grand time. So much so that Emily forgot about the run-in with Papa, but not Lester.

At an inconspicuous time, Lester pulled Harry and Jake aside to tell them about the encounter he had with James and Marge before leaving town. "I just wanted you to know so you can keep an eye out for him. Just not sure what he might do. Of course, he was drunk and may not even remember it by morning. But if he causes problems, all you need to do is threaten to turn him in to the authorities for harboring his little gypsy-friend. That shuts him down every time."

"We're so sorry you had to deal with him on your wedding day," Jake said, "but glad you told us. We will definitely keep an eye out for him and use your advice if we need to."

Amanda had the boys ring bells to announce the cutting of the cake. "Everyone, gather around for cake! Emily, you and Lester cut the cake and give each other the first bite, then Sarah and I will serve it."

"Oh, this will be fun," Lester said mischievously.

"You better be nice," Emily replied playfully.

When the party was winding down, Lester told Emily, "I have reserved a special room at the hotel for us tonight. When you're ready, we'll excuse ourselves and go."

Emily looked at him with wide eyes and, in a bit of a panic, said, "Oh" —pausing to take a deep breath— "Um, that sounds great." Looking around anxiously for her sisters, she added, "Excuse me for a minute, I need to find Amanda and Sarah."

She hadn't even thought about the living arrangements. When she found the girls, she told them what Lester had said about getting ready to leave and the hotel.

"I didn't think about this part, Amanda. I'm scared."

"We prepared a little suitcase of clothes for you to take. Let's go upstairs to get it and we can talk," Amanda answered.

Upstairs, Emily peppered them with questions and listened intently to the answers. By the time she was done, she was feeling more comfortable.

"Thank you both for all you've done for me."

As she came down the stairs with her suitcase, her head was spinning. She couldn't believe this was really happening. "This was the best day of my life," she said to herself. She paused at the bottom of the stairs and bowed her head. *Thank you, Lord, for this day that means so much to me. If you can, would you please give a message to my mama? Tell her I miss her and so wish she could have been with me to celebrate today, and let her know how much I love her.* She then composed herself and with suitcase in hand, she enthusiastically went to find Lester and announce they were leaving.

Arm in arm with Emily, Lester said, "I'd like to say thank you to all of you for making Emily's and my wedding day so special. However, we are heading out, but please continue what you are doing and enjoy."

Emily said, "I also want to say, I can't thank you all enough for coming today to celebrate with Lester and me. Thank you all for your support, your love, and for making this day so special."

They all raised their glasses to them and yelled their congratulations. Emily threw a kiss to everyone as they headed out the door amidst the guests clapping and cheering.

*Chapter*

# 35

Amanda and Sarah were pleasantly surprised to see Emily and Lester walk into church that Sunday. Amanda motioned to them and slid the boys closer together, making room for them to sit. Emily gave her sisters both a hug and then settled down into her seat beside Lester as the congregation began singing the first congregational hymn. Emily sensed the stares of some but ignored them as she sat even taller and scooted a little closer to Lester.

After church just as Emily assumed, Amanda invited them to eat Sunday dinner with the family. "I was hoping we could come for dinner," Emily said.

"Well of course, you know you and Lester are always welcome."

At dinner, Lester reminded everyone that he and Emily would be leaving on Wednesday for New York.

"Oh my, so soon?" Amanda asked. "Emily, please give us your last couple of days here to wrap up loose ends and say our proper goodbyes. Why don't you stay here with us until Lester is ready to go?"

Emily looked at Lester and asked, "What do you think about that?"

"If that's what you want to do, that will be fine with me because I'll be busy gathering my tools and packing up the truck plus dealing with final inspectors most of the time anyway."

"Well then, it's settled. You'll have to put up with me another couple of days."

Laughing, Amanda said, "There won't be any putting up with you, Emily. It will be Sarah's and my pleasure. To start with, I think we girls should visit Mama's gravesite before you go."

"Oh, I would love that! Yes, please. Let's do that."

The next afternoon, Sarah came to Amanda's house so they could all go to the grave together, while Jake watched the boys.

"Before we go," Amanda exclaimed, "I want to grab Mama's Bible and take it with us. There are some special verses I want to share with you that I discovered Mama had underlined."

As they were heading to the horse and wagon, Emily picked a bundle of daisies and roses from Amanda's flower bed to put on Mama's grave. On their way, they started reminiscing about the good times they remembered with Mama.

"She was a very special lady to have put up with Papa all those years, and I, for one, would have never done it," Sarah said.

They tied the horse to a big oak tree that shaded Mama's grave, spread out a quilt and sat down. A kind of hush came over them, and they sat for a moment in their own thoughts. Emily broke the silence with, "Oh we love you Mama, and miss you. A lot has happened that I wish you could have been here to share with me, but had you been here things would be different. It would break your heart if you knew what Papa has done."

"That's for sure," Sarah agreed.

Amanda opened Mama's Bible and began reading some of the verses that were underlined.

"Wow!" Emily said with tears streaming down her face. "That was just as if Mama were here with us. Her memory will live on forever."

It was a fast and furious three days trying to capture every moment with Emily. A lot of laughter and chit-chat filled the house. Their most memorable time together, though, was when they visited Mama's grave.

Wednesday morning came all too soon, and it was time for Emily to leave. Lester's truck was loaded with his tools and scaffolding, with barely any room for Emily's things. By pushing and shoving things around, they made everything fit. Sarah and Harry, Amanda and Jake, and the boys were all gathered in the front yard to give hugs and kisses as they said their goodbyes to Emily and Lester.

Just before they pulled away, Amanda yelled, "Wait! I almost forgot something." She ran into the house and came out with Mama's Bible.

She handed it to Emily and said, "I want you to have this. Take part of Mama with you and never forget her teachings from this book."

"Oh, Amanda, are you sure you want me to have this?"

"Yes, keep it close and remember to read it."

"Oh, I will. Thank you so much, Amanda."

## Chapter 36

The long and tiring ride to New York gave Emily and Lester time to talk about things that, up until now, they hadn't even had time to think about. Emily's future was a big mystery to her. She had many questions for Lester about what it was like where he was taking her, what the town was like, what kind of a house he had, whether there were neighbors, and what they were like. She was bombarding him with questions, but all were important to her. She was excited about her new adventure but at the same time a little fearful of the unknown. Lester assured her that she would fit in just fine, and not to worry about anything. As they neared their destination, Emily sat up straighter and put her nose closer to her side window. The street was lined with trees that shaded a row of houses that basically looked alike except for their different colors. She also took note of the number of vehicles that lined the street or sat in driveways.

"My oh my, Lester," she said. "I've never seen so many cars and trucks in my life."

"Yeah, well, remember, Emily, this is New York. You'll see a lot of things here that you didn't see in your little secluded town. We're not far now." He began pointing out different places. "There's Websters, which is our main shopping store. You can buy everything there, from groceries to home goods, furniture, and tools. Across the street is the community church that may interest you, where you will be able to make friends. Down that side street is Dublin's Garden and Feed, a garden shop where you can buy seeds or seedlings if you want to plant a garden. I have a nice yard out back that has plenty of room for one."

"Oh, that sounds really nice. I will definitely be interested in that."

They drove just a few more blocks and he pulled into the driveway of a small bungalow. It looked just like all the other houses she saw coming into town, except this one was painted a light green with white shutters and a dark green door. Its roof looked like all the other houses as well, tin with notable rust spots. It had a nice porch across the front of the house. She noticed a cluster of empty clay pots piled in the corner next to an old wicker chair that a calico cat jumped out of when they drove up.

"So, this is home, Emily, what do you think?"

"Well, it's tiny, but it looks inviting."

They walked to the front door. Unlocking it, he said, "Wait right there, my beautiful bride." He threw the keys into the house and went to Emily, swooped her up, gave her a kiss, said, "Welcome home my love," and carried her across the threshold.

As he was putting her down, she looked up at him and said, "Thank you, Lester, for marrying me and bringing me here with you."

Looking around, she found the inside small and rather manly. There was a small kitchen, living room, and two bedrooms. It had only the basics, a table with two chairs, an old upholstered chair with an old ottoman, a bed with a saggy mattress, and material nailed to the window frames covering the windows. The floors were of old, worn, and cracked linoleum. Her heart sank for a minute, but she knew that with a few touches of her own, she could make it a comfy and homey space.

Lester went over to his comfy chair and turned on the floor lamp.

"Oh, Lester, we have electricity?"

"Yes, my love, and plumbing" —He walked to the kitchen sink and turned on the faucet— "No more fetching water or going to the outhouse my dear."

Come here, let me show you." He took her into the bathroom and said, "Push that lever." When she did, she jumped back as the water came rushing into the toilet.

"Wow, this is great!"

"Wait, there's more." He led her out to the back porch. Throwing his hand out, he said, "Ta-Da, and here my sweet lady, we have an *electric* washing machine."

"Oh, this is so great. I can't wait to write Amanda and tell her about all this."

It wasn't long before the neighbors came over to introduce themselves. They came bearing a tray of oatmeal raisin cookies, Lester's favorite. Lester introduced Emily as his new wife to Gloria and Esther. They both looked surprised, their eyebrows raised a tad.

Emily saw the look on their faces. *They're thinking I'm too young to be a wife.* She quickly held out her hand and, in her most mature voice said, "I'm so glad to meet you ladies, and thank you so much for the cookies. They look and smell so delicious. We'll have to get together sometime and get better acquainted."

When they first arrived at their home, Lester told Emily, "I want you to know that you can go to Websters and buy whatever you need to run the house and whatever you want to make 'this house' a home. I have a running tab there and you can just have them add it to my tab."

She took him up on that and didn't waste any time. She washed the windows, put up proper curtains, scrubbed the floors, and purchased a braided rug for under the table along with matching rugs to place over the most worn spots in the linoleum. Lester helped her pick out a rocking chair, a side table where she kept her mama's Bible, and a lamp. The bedroom got a sprucing up too. She bought a new mattress and dressed the bed with new sheets and a new bedspread. As a finishing touch, she folded the quilt that her mama had made for her and placed it at the bottom of the bed.

Emily wasn't used to having close neighbors, but it wasn't long until they became her very good friends. Having them to talk to and do things with helped with her homesickness for Amanda and Sarah.

Gloria and Esther helped her make plans for a vegetable garden, and discussed canning the produce, as it became available.

Things were going smoothly for several months, and Emily was happy until one morning at breakfast when Lester said unexpectedly, "I'm glad you have made friends with the neighbor ladies, sweetie, because I have won the bid on a job in North Carolina that will take me away for about four months."

"Four months?" she shrieked. "What are you talking about? What am I going to do here by myself all that time? You never talked with me about this."

"Emily, I don't feel like I need to ask for your permission to bid on or accept a job. You knew that I worked away from home, or I would have never met you. Remember?"

"Well, I just didn't think about that. But now that you are married, can't you find jobs that will at least let you come home on the weekends?"

"Emily, I'm not going to argue about this with you. I will go wherever the jobs take me. You will need to get comfortable around here, meet people, and get involved in activities, because this is the way it's going to be."

Emily left the breakfast table, went to the bedroom, and cried. This was their first real argument, and she was not happy. *Oh, if I could only talk with Amanda.* Emily stayed in the bedroom until Lester left for work. She did not even want to see him right then.

When Lester came home from work, he went over to give her a kiss, but she shoved him away.

"Really, Emily. You're still miffed at me?" There was just silence. "Aren't you going to talk to me tonight?" he asked.

"I have nothing to say."

With firmness in his voice, he said, "You're pouting like a child, Emily. Did I make a mistake marrying someone so much younger than myself?"

At that, Emily swung around from the stove where she was fixing his dinner, put her hand on her hip, and just glared at him for what seemed like forever to Lester. Finally, she said, "Well maybe you did." She tore off her apron, left the dinner on the stove, and stomped out the front door.

It wasn't long before she calmed down and admitted to herself that she was acting childish. She knew she had to go back and face him. She opened the front door and found him sitting alone at the table eating dinner as if nothing had ever happened.

"Well, I see you got your dinner," she said.

"Yes, and it's very good. Why don't you fix a plate and come eat with me?"

It was an awkward moment for her, but she went to the stove, dished up her dinner, and sat down across from him. "I want you to know Lester," she began, in her most grown-up voice, "you angered me when just out of the blue, you told me you were going to be going away for an extended time without discussing it with me first. I will admit that I was acting childish, but you hurt me when you accused me of pouting like a child. I think I have proven to you over and over and in numerous ways that I am not a child, and I didn't appreciate that at all."

"You're right, Emily, and I apologize for not discussing the job thing with you. It's just that I've never had to take others into consideration when taking a job out of town before. I'll do so in the future. And as far as me calling you a child, that was uncalled for, and I'm sorry. Will you forgive me?"

"Yes, of course, but we both need to communicate better."

"I agree. Now come give me a kiss."

## Chapter 37

Lester had been gone for a month when Emily noticed she wasn't feeling well. She was sick to her stomach and had no energy. Gloria and Esther came to check on her, brought her homemade chicken noodle soup and home remedies, but nothing seemed to help.

After about a week, Esther asked Emily, "Do you think you're pregnant?"

"Pregnant!" she gasped. "Oh no, oh my goodness, do you think I am?" That was the farthest thing from her mind. "I am late, now that I think about it."

"I wouldn't be surprised," Esther said. "We will have to keep an eye on you and see. In the meantime, try eating some crackers and broth for your upset stomach, and just rest."

After a few months, she went to see Dr. Spriggs.

"Looks like you'll be having a Spring baby," he told her. "I suspect sometime in April, but you being so young, it may come early."

She was excited and couldn't wait until Lester got home so she could tell him the news. She wrote a letter to Amanda and sent it the next day. Oh, how she wished she could talk to Amanda.

Time seemed to pass so slowly until Lester finally finished his job and came home. She had been planning on how she was going to tell him and was so anxious to do so.

She heard his truck come up the drive and she met him at the door. They embraced and Lester picked her up and swung her around. "I'm so glad you're finally home," she said.

"And so am I. I missed you, my sweet angel."

The next morning at breakfast was when she would reveal the news. She had painted the words *I'm pregnant* on a plate. She filled the plate with a generous helping of scrambled eggs, bacon, and toast, making sure the words were totally covered, and set it down in front of him. Grinning, she poured them both a cup of coffee and sat down to wait until he finished his plate of food. Her heart was pounding. She couldn't wait until he saw the words. She saw a part of the letters showing through his half-eaten scrambled eggs and wondered, *Will he ever notice?* Finally, taking nearly his last bite of eggs, he saw something, moved the food around on his plate, and then read the words.

"You're pregnant?" he gulped.

"Yes, we're going to have a baby, Lester."

"That is wonderful news. Come over here and let me give you and the baby a hug."

The news of the baby was exciting for everyone. Emily received a letter from Amanda telling her how elated she and Sarah were and wished her a healthy pregnancy and an easy delivery. Emily wished that they lived closer and could get together now and then.

---

Christmas was right around the corner. The cold northern winds were finding their way through the poorly insulated walls of their little bungalow. The coal furnace in the basement constantly needed attention.

"I'll need to show you how to start a fire in the furnace and how to keep it going," Lester announced to her one morning at breakfast.

"Oh no, you're doing a fine job. Why would I need to know how to do all of that?"

"Well, because work has slowed down around here with the weather being so cold, I'll have to be taking a job or two down south again for a while."

"Lester, how can I go up and down those rickety steps to the basement and haul coal, in my condition?"

"I won't be taking any jobs until after Christmas, so I'll have time to fix the 'rickety' steps for you, and I'll fill the coal bin. So, you won't have to worry about running out of coal, which will make it easier for you."

Emily grew silent and went about her chores the rest of the day in a solemn mood. *This was not how I imagined things would be,* she thought to herself. *I didn't come all the way here with him to just be left alone. And now with the baby coming, it frightens me. Is this the way it's always going to be?*

She loved Christmas time and busied herself with baking cookies and making decorations for the house. Lester brought in a small Christmas tree, which she wasted no time decorating with her homemade ornaments and strings of cranberries. She was so surprised, when the next day, Lester brought home some electric lights for the tree.

"Lester, I've never seen lights for a Christmas tree before. Show me how to use them."

"Well, actually, Emily, they should have been put on the tree before you put on all the decorations, but since you were so eager to decorate, that won't be happening, so we'll make it work."

After the lights were on the tree, Lester plugged them in, and then turned off all the other lights in the house. The ambiance of the glowing lights coming from the tree created a melancholy moment. A homesickness flowed over Emily, and a tear welled up in her eye. Lester took her in his arms and held her for a long time. He comforted her by reminding her that next Christmas there would be three of them celebrating. When he let her go, Emily went to the kitchen and fixed a tray of cookies, and they sat around the tree enjoying the cookies and each other.

"I wish we could stay like this forever," Emily said. But in her heart, she knew shortly things would be very different. Dismissing that thought, she asked Lester, "Would you care to go to the Christmas Eve service with me? That was something we always did back home, and it would mean a lot to me."

"Well, sure Emily, that would be nice and then we could go into town and have dinner together."

"That sounds wonderful," she said.

## Chapter 38

The time Emily spent with Lester over Christmas and these last few weeks was comforting. Lester was so attentive to her needs. It made her feel loved, cared for, and safe. But her "ideal" life was cut short when he announced, once again, that he was leaving for South Carolina, this time for two months.

"Two months, Lester? That will take us up to right before the baby is due."

"I'll be back by the end of March. I promise."

"But Dr. Spriggs said that because of my age the baby will most likely come early, which could be in March."

"It won't Emily, don't worry so much. I'll be here for the birth of our little one, I promise."

Emily didn't feel as confident as he did, but what could she do?

The next few months, her days were spent trying to keep the house warm and making a bed for their baby. She took a wicker laundry basket, lined it with soft flannel, and made a pillowcase filled with cotton for the baby to sleep on. She relied heavily on Gloria and Esther for advice and help. Oh, how she wished for Amanda.

Emily was totally surprised when Gloria and Esther held a party in her honor. She was gifted with everything she would need for the baby and was so grateful. She met neighbors she had never met before and found out that one of them was a midwife.

"You need to get well acquainted with Ruth, Emily," Gloria told her. "She is the best midwife in the area. She delivered both Esther's and my children many moons ago."

"So glad to meet you, Ruth. I would certainly like to take advantage of your expertise if you would be so inclined."

"It would be my pleasure, Emily. Come to me whenever you need me."

*I'm glad I'll have someone close that knows what to do when the time comes.* The thought brought comfort to Emily.

After the party was over, Gloria and Esther helped Emily gather all the gifts and take them back to her place.

"Aren't you lonely here by yourself?" Gloria asked.

"Yes, I am, but I just try and stay busy."

"Well, I just couldn't do what you do," Esther said. "I always said that I would pity the gal that married Lester, because of all his traveling. It seems like he's never home."

"I know what you're saying but I love him and want to be with him."

"But that's what I mean, you're never with him for long because he's never here much."

That night, Emily thought about what Gloria and Esther had said. She knew what they were saying was true, and their words just fueled the fire that had been burning in her for some time. Her emotions ranged from anger, to being afraid, to feeling sorry for herself. If it weren't for the regular letters from Amanda, she didn't know what she would do. She shared some of her feelings with Amanda, who would write back and always encouraged her to hang in there, saying that things would get better.

Just as she feared, a few days after the party, she went into labor while Lester was hundreds of miles away. It was late at night, and the snow continued to fall as it had all day. She threw her quilt around her shoulders and trudged over to Esther's house because she lived the closest. As soon as Esther saw Emily standing there, she knew it was time.

"Come in here, dear, before you freeze to death," she said. She woke Harvey, her husband, and told him to go get Gloria and tell her to fetch Ruth.

Because of the snow, it took longer than usual for Gloria and Ruth to get there. Esther tried to make Emily as comfortable as possible in the spare bedroom and keep her calm.

When Ruth arrived, she examined Emily and said, "You are definitely having a baby, and it will be soon."

"I want to have my baby in my own bed" she gasped. But she knew that with as much pain as she was in, there would be no way she could walk back to her house.

After what seemed like an eternity to Emily, but was just a few hours, the baby arrived. It was a tiny boy, and she held him to her breast and broke down crying, for several reasons. First and foremost, was for joy, and then because Lester was not there to experience this with her. After cleaning up everything, including the baby, Ruth wrapped the baby in a warm blanket and laid him next to Emily.

"You rest now and we will see that you get home as soon as possible," Ruth assured her.

The next day, Harvey went over to Emily's house to get the furnace stoked to keep the house warm.

Emily stayed with Esther for a few days while she recovered, and Esther helped her with the baby. Eventually, they went back home. She settled into her own warm bed with her baby snuggled in her arms. The girls took turns staying with Emily and tending to her and the baby. She was so grateful to them since Lester was not there. She thought about sending a telegram to him to let him know about the baby but decided against it. *I'm so upset with him. He had no business cutting the timeline so close. He can just wait until he gets home to discover what happened while he was gone.*

Lester arrived home one week later. At first, Emily was a little cool toward him. She wanted him to know that she was upset because he wasn't home for her. But the fact that she was so happy to finally see him and anxious to show him the baby melted her demeanor.

Lester picked up his little boy who was lying in his little wicker bed and held him so tenderly.

"Oh, Emily, I am so sorry I wasn't here for you. I didn't expect him to come so soon."

"I know, Lester, neither did I, but here he is and he's perfect. He has your nose, don't you think? Now we need to decide on a name."

"What about Joseph and calling him Joey? That was my great-grandfather's name, and I always liked it," Lester said.

"Then Joey, it is," Emily agreed.

# Chapter 39

Joey was just three months old when Emily realized she was pregnant again. The same scenario played out with this pregnancy as the first. Lester was home for about three months and then gone for two or three months throughout her whole pregnancy. The exception this time was that he was home for the birth of their second child, another boy whom they named Raymond. Then he was off again.

During this time, she had become a regular at Dublin's Garden and Feed, and had become friends with the owner, Frank. He offered to help her around the house while Lester was gone. She took him up on it, and he helped with yard work and anything else that she needed done.

When Lester found out about him, he wasn't too thrilled. However, having Frank around to help out relieved some of his guilt about not being home to do it himself.

---

Once again, she found herself pregnant with their third child just shortly after Raymond was born.

Emily was becoming worn down. The weekly letters from Amanda, encouraging her, were the only thing that gave her any hope that things would get better. Gloria and Esther helped when they could. They would help hang the diapers on the line, take them down when they were dry, and fold them just to be used again. They watched the babies while she went for groceries and ran the necessary errands. Emily was relying more and more on Frank to help as well.

Gloria and Esther were appalled at what was happening with Emily and Lester. They were totally disgusted with Lester and told Emily as much.

"It's shameful what's happening to poor Emily. She's just a child herself. Lester should be ashamed of how he's treating her," Gloria ranted to Esther. "You can see that she is totally worn out, and it comes as no surprise. Just watching those two babies for a short time while she's gone to town wears me out. I've a good mind to give Lester a piece of my mind the next time he's home, but it seems like he's been gone more lately than usual."

"I've noticed that as well," Esther said. "It's probably because he doesn't want to be bothered by the babies fussing and crying."

"Well, it's just not right, Esther, and I don't know what she's going to do when the third little one gets here.

Emily checked the mailbox daily. She hadn't heard from Amanda for several weeks. She couldn't understand why she hadn't answered her letters. *This isn't like Amanda.* Her thoughts were interrupted when unexpectedly, Lester drove up.

"What are you doing home?" she questioned. "I thought you weren't going to be finished with your job for another month." She was getting to the point where she didn't really care if he was home or not. She was becoming more and more independent, and with the help of the ladies next door and Frank, she was getting along just fine without him.

"Well, isn't that a great welcome home. Why should you worry about how long my jobs last as long as there's money for you to do what you want?"

*Wait, what did he just say? Isn't that what Papa used to tell Mama when she questioned him about anything?* She hadn't thought about Papa for a long time. *Is Lester starting to act like Papa?*

Lester was only home for a week before he was gone again, but during that week the two argued to the point that the neighbor ladies heard their loud voices. This, of course, escalated their concern and anger about what was happening between them. When they questioned Emily about it, all she would say was, "He's not the same Lester I married."

*Shattered*

---

Emily finally received a letter from home. It had been quite a while since she had gotten one. She was so excited to hear from Amanda, but when she looked closely, she realized the letter was from Sarah and not Amanda. *Why is Sarah writing to me? She's never written before.*

Hurrying into the house, she sat down in her rocking chair before ripping open the letter. It was a good thing she was sitting down because she quickly discovered why the letter was from Sarah and not Amanda. She read:

*My Dear Emily,*

*I'm sure you are wondering why I'm writing to you instead of Amanda. It's with great regret, Emily, that I must tell you that Amanda is no longer with us. She miscarried and hemorrhaged badly. By the time we got her to the hospital, it was too late...*

Emily didn't need to read any further. It felt like all the blood drained from her head. She dropped the letter and screamed, "NO! NO! This can't be happening!" She felt her own baby move and, putting her hand to her stomach, she cried out, "Oh, Amanda, no! I can't believe this. Why did you not tell me you were pregnant?"

She walked through the house, continuing to cry out, screeching at times with a gut-wrenching sound that scared the babies. They started crying, and everything became a blur to Emily.

When Esther returned home from shopping, she immediately heard the babies crying uncontrollably. She rushed over to check on them, and found Emily sitting in her rocking chair, staring straight ahead with the babies left unattended.

"Emily!" she yelled. "What's the matter dear? Look at me. What has happened?"

Esther could tell she had been there for a while. The babies' diapers hadn't been changed for some time, and they were crying with hunger. Esther quickly took care of the babies. She wiped their snotty faces and changed their diapers. She fixed a bottle of milk for each and settled them in their little beds before running out the back door to fetch Gloria.

"Come quick! Something has happened to Emily!" she screamed.

Gloria and Esther quickly ran back to Emily. They tried to get her to respond, but she just kept looking straight ahead and rocking back and forth.

"Where is Lester? He should be here. She needs him," Gloria said angrily.

"Where he always is Gloria, many miles from here."

Esther noticed a piece of crumpled paper lying on the floor and picked it up. It was wet and partially torn from the babies having played with it. She very carefully unfolded it, so as not to tear it further, and was able to read enough to know immediately what was wrong. Sharing the letter with Gloria, they both agreed they had to fetch Dr. Spriggs.

---

"She is in shock," the doctor said, after slapping her cheek and calling out her name loudly with no response. "I need to give her some medication to calm her, but I must be careful that it won't put her into early labor. She is barely in her eighth month. Would one of you ladies fetch the midwife so she can be ready in case we need her?"

Ruth got there in just a few minutes. "Let's get her into her bed and see if moving her will help her snap out of this." But it didn't seem to help at all.

"I'm going to give her the mildest sedative," the doctor said. "We'll see if this will be enough to bring her back to us," and he administered the medication. All they could do was wait.

Esther tended to the babies, and with clean diapers and full tummies, they were content once again.

An hour had passed with still no response from Emily. However, she seemed to have fallen asleep.

Dr. Spriggs inquired, "How can we get in touch with Lester?"

"Only Emily knows where he is, as far as I know," Gloria informed him.

"Well, when we get her back with us, let that be the first thing we ask her, because I'm not sure how this all will play out. He needs to be here in case decisions need to be made that only he can make."

It was only a short time later when Emily finally stirred. She opened her eyes and looked around the room. Getting up on one elbow, she said, "What's going on? Where are my boys? What happened?" When she saw Ruth, she quickly put her hand on her stomach and said, "Oh no, did something happen to my baby?"

Ruth explained, "No, the baby is fine. You received some disturbing news today from home. Do you remember, Emily?"

Emily blinked and shook her head. "Oh yes, Amanda." She fell back onto the bed sobbing.

Ruth encouraged her to let it out. "Go ahead, Emily, cry. It will do you good. It's going to be alright, trust me."

Dr. Spriggs sighed with huge relief. "That's a good sign," he said. "I think she will be alright now."

# Chapter

# 40

They were finally able to get the information out of Emily that they needed to get in touch with Lester, and he was able to get home a couple of days later.

Emily, with help from everyone, was able to get back to taking care of herself and the boys. However, she wasn't quite herself. She was very quiet and didn't want to talk. She moved around the house taking care of things as if she were sleepwalking. Lester was supportive in a way that surprised Gloria and Esther. He stepped up and helped more with the boys and allowed Emily to rest. He noticed a difference in Emily, as did others close to her, and he went to Dr. Spriggs' office to talk to him about her behavior.

Dr. Spriggs had a long talk with him. "For starters," he said. "She *cannot* have any more children for a few years, if ever. Her body has not had the proper chance to recover from being pregnant three years in a row. It's no wonder she's not snapping back to her normal self. She is showing signs of mild hysteria, and she's totally exhausted. I would recommend a quiet environment and plenty of rest. Everyone needs to give her some space and be patient with her. She's just a young lady and fragile. Treat her as such Lester."

Lester lowered his head and reluctantly said, "I understand, doctor."

"Do you think it would be helpful if I took her home for her sister's funeral and to be with the family for a while?"

"Well, that would be a good idea if she wasn't eight months pregnant, but with the stress she is experiencing, she could go into labor anytime now. So no, I wouldn't advise that."

"What is your work schedule now, Lester? Would you be able to stay home until the baby is born?"

Lester scratched his head and said, "I guess I could get someone to fill in for me given the circumstances."

"That's what I would advise you to do. You need to be here with her, giving her the best support you can muster."

Lester went home to Emily and adhered to Dr. Spriggs' advice. He actually started seeing Emily as the fragile young lady that the doctor had told him she was and started treating her with more respect.

"I'm so sorry for what you've been through the last few years. I see all the work that the boys make for you and I'm sorry I haven't been home more for you and the boys. But I'm making arrangements with work to be able to stay home now until the baby is born," he told Emily.

Emily responded favorably to the concern, love, and help that Lester began showing her. However, she was quiet most of the time and showed signs of sadness.

Holding her in his arms, he said, "I'm so sorry that Amanda died. I know how close you and she were."

She cried and said, "I just can't believe it, Lester. I haven't even read the whole letter yet. Would you read it with me?"

"Of course, let me get it."

The crumpled letter from Sarah, which Gloria had retrieved from the floor, had been placed in the Bible, on the stand, by Emily's rocking chair, for safekeeping.

They read it together and when they read about the funeral arrangements, Emily said, "Oh, I wish I could be there Lester."

"I know you do, Emily. I've already talked with Dr. Spriggs about the possibility of taking you home, but he advised against it since you are so close to delivery. He also said that because of the stress of finding out about Amanda, you may deliver early."

"I know, Lester, and I've been feeling some minor contractions lately, but nothing develops."

"How long has this been going on?"

"Nearly every day since the letter came."

"Well, I think you should let the doctor know about this."

"I will if they continue."

## Chapter 41

Lester was awakened by Emily moaning in pain. "Emily, what's wrong?"

"It's the baby, oh, it hurts so bad."

"Stay calm, Emily. It's going to be all right. I'm gonna go get Esther to come be with you while I fetch Ruth."

He quickly ran to Esther's house and pounded on the door. Harvey made his way to the door, with Esther not far behind, and answered it. Lester quickly told them what was happening.

"I'll go be with Emily," Esther said. "On your way to fetch Ruth, stop by Gloria's house and tell her to come as quickly as she can."

Esther was sitting with Emily when Gloria came rushing in. They both did their best to help her through the contractions. It wasn't much longer until Lester arrived with Ruth.

After examining Emily, Ruth knew immediately that this was an emergency. The baby's heart rate had slowed to a point of great concern. The baby was in distress and needed to be born right away, but Emily had not dilated. She was experiencing strong contractions but not making any progress.

"Lester, fetch Dr. Spriggs, please, and be quick about it." Ruth said. He quickly ran out the door. Turning to the girls, she continued, "I'm so glad you girls are here. Please help me get Emily up and walk her around the house. We need to get things moving here."

Emily didn't want to get up, but between contractions, they slung her legs over the side of the bed and got her to her feet. Every few steps they would stop until another contraction passed. Emily screamed in pain and begged to go back to bed.

"No, Emily," Ruth insisted, "keep walking, and I'll check you after a few more contractions."

The next examination showed that she had started to dilate but, the baby's heart rate was very faint. Ruth feared the cord was wrapped around the baby's neck, causing distress. She was relieved when Emily was finally dilated enough for her to start pushing. About that time, Lester and Dr. Spriggs arrived, and she apprised them of the situation.

As Lester rushed to Emily's side, he heard Dr Spriggs tell Ruth, "We have to get that baby out now."

With Emily pushing and Ruth working as best she could, the head emerged. It was blue, and as Ruth surmised, the cord was around its little neck. With a few more pushes encouraged by Lester, Emily delivered the baby. It was another boy. They quickly unwrapped the cord and tried to resuscitate him, but it was too late. The room went silent. There was no crying baby, no cheers of joy. When Emily realized what had happened, she let out a wail that came from deep insider her soul.

Emily lay sobbing and clinging to Lester. "Why, Lester, why?"

Ruth wrapped the baby in a blanket and the doctor quickly took him out of the room and out of Emily's sight.

Emily was in a fog. She wouldn't talk and would hardly eat. Esther and Gloria were taking care of the boys for her and were very concerned.

Lester made the necessary arrangements, and they had a small, intimate funeral for the baby. Emily attended, but it was clear that she was just going through the motions. Dr. Spriggs, seeing her condition, told Lester to make sure that she got plenty of quiet and rest. He also suggested some teas and herbal remedies that might help but let him know that ultimately, it was just time that she needed.

The next few weeks were very hard on everyone. Lester stayed home with Emily as long as he could, but he eventually had to go back on the road for work. Esther and Gloria took turns watching the boys and taking care of Emily. With Lester gone, Emily realized that she had to get herself back to normal, if only for the sake of the boys. Esther and Gloria slowly saw the light begin to return to her eyes. She began eating better and would even allow them to take her outside for short walks or to watch the boys play in the yard.

*Marti Jones*

    She eventually began working in the garden again. The warm sun on her face was healing, and soon she was able to bring the boys back home. She was finally starting to feel whole again. She made many trips to the Garden Shop and would hang around a bit and talk with Frank. Those conversations were a lifesaver to her and made her reflect on her life and realize that she needed more.

## Chapter

# 42

Emily, knowing that she needed to make some changes in her life, decided to ask Frank at the garden shop if he was hiring. Since summer was right around the corner and with business picking up, Frank decided to let Emily come on board. He even allowed her to bring the boys as long as they didn't cause any problems, until she could make other arrangements for their care. She was so grateful. It helped her get out of the house and helped with her mood. Dr. Spriggs kept an eye on her by having her come into his office on a regular basis.

Gloria and Esther agreed to take turns watching the boys for her while she worked. She was enjoying her new job and the time she was spending with Frank. She was following the doctors' orders and things were going well for her until one morning just before leaving for work, a knock came at the door. She opened it with two curious little boys right behind her and gasped when she saw a tall, dark-haired policeman standing on the porch. The two little ones, one on each side of her, their little fists holding onto her skirt, peered out from behind her. They were startled by the large man that confronted their mama.

"Is this the residence of Lester Granger?"

"Yes, but he's not here," she answered.

"Are you his wife?" the policeman inquired.

"Yes, I'm his wife," Emily said shaking. "What is it? Why are you here? Is something wrong?"

"Yes, I'm afraid I have some bad news. Your husband was in a bad accident at the construction site where he was working and is in the hospital in North Carolina. I suggest you make your way there as soon as possible."

The blood drained from Emily's face, and she felt like she was going to faint. She held onto the door frame and asked, "Is he alright?"

"I don't know the details, ma'am. I'm just the messenger. This is the name and address of the hospital," he said, handing her a piece of paper. Turning to leave he added, "I wish you the best."

She closed the door and went to her rocking chair. She called the boys to her. "Come here boys, I need a hug."

They came running and crawled up on her lap. She held them close while she let the news sink in and decided what she needed to do next.

It was past time for her to be at work, but she needed to go on in and discuss things with Frank. "He'll know what I should do," she said to herself.

She dropped the children off at Esther's and told her she had received bad news about Lester but was late for work and would talk with her when she got home.

As she walked in the door of the garden shop, she noticed Frank looking at the clock as if to say, "Aren't you a little late?"

"I know, I know, I'm running late, but I received bad news this morning and I need to talk with you."

"What's happened?"

"A policeman came to my door just as I was leaving for work and told me Lester had an accident at work. He didn't know any details but handed me this piece of paper with the name of a hospital and said I should get there as soon as I could. Frank, I don't know how I can get there. I have no transportation. I have to work" — tears welled up in her eyes— "and I have the boys to take care of. I just don't know what to do."

"Well, first of all, calm down. We'll figure out a way to get you to the hospital. Why don't you go back home now and take care of things there? You are in no frame of mind to work. Things will get handled here. Give me the paper with the hospital on it, and I'll find out where it is. I'll see to it that you get there. In the meantime, talk with Esther and Gloria to see if they can watch the boys, then pack a bag for yourself, and we can leave this evening after I close the shop. We can be there sometime tomorrow."

"Oh, Frank, would you really do that for me? I don't know how I can thank you enough. I'll go now, and I'll be ready, waiting for you this evening whenever you're ready to go."

## Chapter

# 43

It was nearly dark when Frank picked Emily up at her house and started toward the hospital in North Carolina. They drove all night and arrived at the hospital around noon the next day. Frank parked the truck and walked Emily into the hospital. They asked where they could find Lester Granger, and waited patiently while the lady checked the roster for his name.

"He's in the East Ward, Bed 11. That's down the hall, through the double doors. You'll find the room on the right," she instructed them.

They thanked her and started down the hall. Emily was shaking. The sterile smell brought back memories of the only time she had ever been in a hospital - when Papa had his accident. She didn't like it then and she didn't like it now. She was so glad Frank was with her. Not knowing what to expect, her steps slowed as she neared his bed. She moved slowly toward the partition and peeked around it. She was afraid of what she was about to see. Her eyes went first to the bottom of the bed and slowly moved up toward the head, processing everything as she went. There was Lester, lying flat on his back. He appeared to be sleeping. Pillows were placed snugly on both sides of his head for support. His one arm with a cast lay across his chest.

She tiptoed quietly toward the bed, softly laid her hand on his arm, and whispered, "Lester it's me, Emily, can you hear me?"

There was no movement. Emily looked at Frank, frightened, and said, "What do you think is wrong with him?"

About that time, a middle-aged man in a knee-length white coat walked up to Lester's bed.

"Good afternoon, I'm Dr. Kemp." Stretching out his hand, he continued, "Are you Mrs. Granger?"

"Yes, I am, and this kind man" — pointing to Frank— "is my friend, Frank who brought me here," she replied. "I got here just as soon as I could. Can you tell me what happened and how he is doing? I'm frightened. He didn't respond to me when I told him that I was here."

"No, he wouldn't right now. He has had a bad concussion and is in a coma due to the trauma to his head, somewhat like a deep sleep."

"Well, is he going to be alright?" Emily asked, on the verge of tears.

"We will know more in a few days but that is only part of his problem." Lifting the sheet, he revealed Lester's bandaged legs, and said, "His legs have been badly injured."

Emily gasped, "Oh, my poor Lester. How long will it take them to heal? He will be able to walk again, right?

"We won't know that for sure until he comes out of the coma. We will then be able to do a more thorough assessment and have more answers for you, but it doesn't look good."

"Oh no," Emily cried out as she grabbed onto Frank's arm with both hands and sobbed.

"I know this looks and sounds scary to you, Mrs. Granger. The unknown is always frightening but rest assured that he is in no pain right now. He just needs to rest. We will do everything we can for his recovery."

Frank explained to the doctor that they did not live close by, had traveled all night to get there, and wondered if there was a place nearby where they could stay for the next couple of days until the assessments are made.

"There's a small, inexpensive little inn down the street about two blocks, where out-of-town families of our patients usually stay. You both look very tired, and I suggest that you get some rest. There is really no reason for you to stay here the rest of the day unless it's just to be close to him. I'm sure, having been on the road all night, you could use some sleep. I can guarantee you, Mrs. Granger, he will not know that you are here, nor respond to you. He will, no doubt, be in this coma through the night, and perhaps longer. You are actually very fortunate to have been here at this time of day and be able to talk with me because this is when I make my rounds. So, if you will be here tomorrow about the same time, I will be able to give you an update and maybe we can make some plans."

"Thank you, doctor, so much. We will make sure to be here," Emily assured him.

As the doctor left, Emily turned to Frank and said, "I want to sit with him for a little while. I just wish he knew I was here."

"Okay, that's fine, Emily. I'll go check on the little inn that he talked about and see if I can get us some rooms. I'll be back in a little while to get you."

"Okay Frank, I appreciate you so much. I don't know what I would do without you."

As Emily stood beside Lester's bedside, she talked to him even though she knew he wasn't hearing her. "Lester, I'm so sorry this has happened to you. I don't know why so many bad things are happening to us and our family, but I want you to know that I love you and I will be praying for you to get well soon."

She bowed her head and prayed to the God that she had been neglecting. As she stood there in silence thoughts went through her head of when Mama read from her Bible and shared encouraging scripture with her. She felt embarrassed to admit that she hadn't picked up Mama's Bible since she placed it on the table by her rocking chair, except to dust it.

She was exhausted, so she pulled a chair up next to the bed and laid her head over Lester. She was sound asleep when Frank came in to take her to get something to eat and then to the inn.

# Chapter 44

The next day, Frank took Emily back to the hospital where she met with the doctor to get an update on Lester. To her amazement, the doctor said that there had been some improvement.

"The nurse told me he roused during the night, which is a good sign, but he is now sleeping again. It will be several days before he will be able to be moved to a hospital close to where you live or possibly go home. You will need to decide whether you are going to stay here long term or go home and wait for him to be well enough to be moved."

She stayed with him the rest of the day. Throughout the day she would call his name and tell him she was there. He would rouse momentarily but gave her no sign that he heard her.

She discussed her options with Frank, and they decided that he would make arrangements for Emily to stay at the inn for a few more days to see what improvements Lester might make. In the meantime, Frank would go back home to check on the boys for her and see how things were going with the garden shop.

"There's a phone in the lobby of the inn, Emily, that you can use to call me at the shop. Depending on how Lester progresses, you can decide what you want to do."

"Thank you so much, Frank. I have a lot to think about. I don't know what I would do without you. You have been such a help."

"I'm glad to help you any way I can."

"I am really concerned about the boys. I've never been away from them, and I don't know how they are handling not being with me."

"Don't worry, I will check on them as soon as I get back."

"Oh, please give them hugs for me and tell them I love them and will be home real soon."

"I will, Emily. Now don't worry. If you are okay with the plans, I will head home. Be sure and leave the hospital in time to walk to the inn before dark. Call me each evening before we close the shop so we can talk and see how things are going on both ends."

Emily was glad that she had decided to stay on with Lester for a few days. He was in and out of consciousness, and she felt sure that he knew she was there. The doctor and nurses were all surprised at his improvements and felt it was somewhat because of her being there with him.

To her amazement, on the third day when she arrived at the hospital, he was sitting up in bed and eating his breakfast.

"Lester," she exclaimed, "I didn't expect to see you awake, let alone sitting up." She quickly went over to him. Lester pulled her down to him and gave her a big hug and a kiss.

"I am so glad you are here, Emily. The nurse told me that you have been here for several days."

"Yes, I've been waiting for you to wake up. How are you feeling?"

"I've got a pretty bad headache and am in quite a bit of pain, but I'm taking medicine that helps. What I'm really worried about, Emily, is that I don't have feeling in my legs. They say I may not be able to walk again if I don't start getting the feeling back."

"Oh Lester, what a horrible thought. Let's not get ahead of ourselves. You are still healing, and things can change."

Even though Lester was showing some improvement, there was no definitive answer as to when he could be moved. Emily was torn. She needed to get back to her boys and back to work, but she also wanted to stay with Lester. She wasn't sure where the money for the bills was going to come from now that Lester couldn't work. Reality started setting in. She felt like everything was against her.

The next day while Emily was visiting Lester, he had a surprise visit from the men who worked with him on the construction site where the accident occurred. They showed up to see how he was doing. They were shocked to see how badly he was injured and hoped that he would get better soon. They informed him that, if there was anything they could do for him or the family, to let them know.

"I appreciate that. It's hard not knowing when I will be going home. Emily has to go back home soon because she needs to be with the boys and get back to work. Her boss brought her here but needed to get back. He's checking on the boys for us and offered to come back to get her when she is ready to go home."

"When are you planning on going home, Emily?" one of the men asked her.

"Just as soon as my boss can come for me."

"Well, Lester, we could take her home. We have all your tools and equipment in our truck and need to get them to your place anyway, so we could take Emily home and drop off the tools at the same time."

"Wow, that would be great," Emily said. "That way Frank, my boss, wouldn't have to come all the way here just to turn around and go back home.

They agreed to pick her up at the inn where she was staying the next morning and said their goodbyes to Lester before leaving Emily alone with him. She had a very hard time leaving Lester that evening.

"I hate to leave you, but I have to get back. Hopefully, it won't be long until you can be moved home.

"I will be fine, Emily. Please don't worry about me. You just take care of things at home. The hospital has the number for the garden shop and said they would call every few days to keep you updated on my progress."

Reluctantly, she kissed him goodbye and went back to her room at the inn. She was anxious to tell Frank that she had a way back home and he wouldn't have to come and pick her up. Even though she was sad to leave Lester, she was excited to get home to her boys and back to her somewhat normal life.

"We will be leaving early in the morning," she told Frank, "so we should be home late tomorrow night or early the next morning. If you could please let the girls know I would appreciate it. I want to see the boys so badly."

"I'll let them know. I'm anxious to see you as well."

It was early morning when she arrived home. She dropped her bag on the front porch and immediately went to Esther's house to find the boys. Gloria and Esther were fixing breakfast for them when she walked in. When they saw her, they nearly knocked her over with their hugs. She was as excited to see them as they were to see her. She sat and talked with the girls while the boys ate their breakfast.

"Oh, I'm so glad to be home, girls, but I hated to leave Lester in the condition he's in. They still don't know if he'll ever walk again."

"That's terrible," Gloria said. "How will you know how he's doing and whether he's improving?"

"I gave them the phone number to the garden shop, and they promised to keep me updated on a regular basis."

The boys finished eating, so Emily helped clear the table. Anxious to get home, she thanked the girls for all their help with the boys and ushered them out the door to their home.

Over time, she felt the pressure of having to handle everything on her own. The thought of her having to be the breadwinner and caregiver weighed heavily on her. She had no time for herself, and the responsibility of everything seemed to crash in on her. She felt herself going down that black hole again.

To make matters worse, she got a call from the doctor, who said, "Mrs. Granger, I'm so sorry to tell you that the feeling in Lester's legs has not returned, and he's not been able to move them. He will need to remain here until the wounds on his legs heal and have no signs of infection."

## Chapter 45

After several weeks, Lester was finally released from the hospital and able to come home. Lester's buddies from the construction firm, the same ones that brought Emily home, graciously offered to get Lester and bring him home. Though happy to see him, things looked very bleak for Emily. Lester, restricted to a wheelchair, made Emily's life more difficult. She told him she was glad he was finally home, but wasn't sure that was true. It wasn't long before the stress of taking care of him, the boys, the house, and having to work, got to be too much for her.

One evening, after working all day, before she went to fetch the boys, she walked into the house and found a mess in the kitchen, beds not made, clothes lying all over the bathroom, and Lester sitting in his wheelchair listening to his radio.

"I can't take this anymore!" she finally broke down and screamed, throwing her hands in the air. "Look at this place. It's one big mess."

"Well, what do you want me to do about it, Emily? I can't help it that I'm an invalid and can't help around here."

"You could do a whole lot more than you do."

"How can I do more, Emily?"

"There is a lot you could help me with if you just looked."

"Like what?"

"You could help keep the kitchen cleaned up, pull the covers up on the beds, and pick up around here. At least try helping yourself a little bit more. You have two good arms that could be used for more than just holding them in your lap and listening to your music. I no longer have two boys to take care of. Now I have three."

"Oh, is that so?" The argument was escalating into a screaming match. "Is that what you think of me? Do you think I like sitting around all day in this stupid chair?"

"Well, then do something," Emily yelled back at him.

"I didn't plan for this to happen to us, Emily."

"You are exactly right, Lester. You are exactly right. You didn't plan. You didn't have the sense about you to make sure we had some kind of savings that would take care of the family if something like this *did* happen. You knew very well that with the type of work you were involved in, this kind of accident was possible. I don't know what we would do if I didn't have the little bit of money that I make from my job at the garden shop. We wouldn't even be able to have food for us to eat."

"Well at least you have a roof over your head."

"Yeah, but for how long? This place needs so many repairs that you're not doing anything about."

"Oh, really, you want me to make house repairs with me sitting in a wheelchair?"

"I know you can't do them, but you have buddies that you could ask to do a few things for you. They told you in the hospital to let them know if there was anything they could do for you or the family."

As she was going out the back door to get the boys from the neighbors, he yelled at her, "Why don't you get your sweet little fellow at the garden shop to come help you."

Furious, she slammed the door and stomped across the yard to Esther's house. The boys came running to her and, stooping down, she gave them a lingering hug. The boys were the only bright spot in her life these days.

"What in the world were you two screaming about over there?" Esther asked Emily. "We could hear you all the way over here."

Emily, not wanting to get into anything, just ignored her and turned her attention to the boys. "Did you have a fun day with Auntie Esther today?"

They ran to fetch the pictures from the kitchen table that they had made for her. "Look Mama," shoving the pictures at her, "These are for you."

"Oh, how lovely! Thank you so much. Now gather up your things, we need to get home."

Esther moved toward the kitchen, and said, "I made a big pot of homemade soup and fixed a big bowl for you to take home for you and Lester for dinner. The boys ate with Harvey and me earlier."

"Oh, that is so sweet of you. Thank you so much. It smells wonderful."

Esther had no idea how much Emily appreciated this kind gesture, especially tonight because it meant that she didn't need to interact with Lester while fixing his dinner. She didn't want to see him tonight, let alone get into another argument.

After Emily and the boys left, Esther told Harvey her fears about Emily. She was afraid that she had too much to worry about and would have another breakdown. "I'm sure she's not taking the remedies that Dr. Spriggs' suggested, because she can barely buy the groceries she needs. I've got to talk to Gloria about all of this."

"Now, now, Esther, don't get yourself all in a tizzy over this. It's really none of your business."

"What do you mean, 'none of my business'? It becomes my business when I see my friend being destroyed and two precious little defenseless boys, who are in my care most of the time, caught in the middle of all of this." She went out the door to go talk to Gloria.

# Chapter

# 46

Emily brought the boys and the soup home from Esther's. The boys ran over and gave their papa a hug as they always did each evening.

Emily set the soup on the kitchen table and very coldly said, "There's some soup that Esther made."

She then herded the boys to the bathroom for their baths and spent the rest of the evening getting them ready for bed.

"What book would you like me to read you tonight before going to sleep?" she asked them.

"The farm animals," Joey piped up.

"No, dinosaurs," Raymond insisted.

Emily, not in the mood for any more arguing, told them to stop. "I'll read them both, now get into bed."

They scampered off to their little bedroom. Emily lay down beside them and began reading. She didn't realize how tired she was until she found herself drifting off.

"Mama," Joey said, "wake up, you are just getting to the good part."

Waking herself up, she fluffed the pillow and began reading again. She had a hard time but was able to stay awake to finish the second book. Afterward, she turned out the light and laid back down to cuddle them until they fell asleep.

The next thing she knew, she was waking with the sun shining through the little window in the boy's bedroom. *Oh my, I can't believe I slept here with the boys all night. I've got to get up and get ready for work before I'm late again.*

She quietly got up and left the room. Thankfully, Lester was still asleep. *If I'm lucky,* she thought, *the boys and I can get out of the house before he gets up and I won't have to deal with him before going to work.*

Work started becoming her safe place, a place away from Lester and the house. She started confiding more and more in Frank about how Lester was treating her. However, Frank was becoming more and more aware of the change in her demeanor at work. Her home life was affecting her work in a negative way. He couldn't depend on her to open the shop because she was late so much of the time. A few customers complained about her attitude, and he knew he had to talk to her about his concerns and possibly replacing her if things didn't change.

This morning didn't help any. Emily came to work late again, which was becoming the norm lately. She appeared a little disheveled and anxious.

"A rough night?" Frank asked.

"Oh, I fell asleep in the boys' bed after reading to them last night so I'm just running a little late."

Thinking that this might be the time for him to talk with her about his concerns, he squared himself to her, put his hands on her shoulders, looked into her eyes, and said, "Emily, what is really going on at home? I can tell you are very stressed. Your attitude here at work hasn't been the best lately, and most mornings you're not here to open. Is there anything I can do to help this situation?"

Emily started laughing hysterically.

Backing away, Frank said, "What's so funny, Emily?"

"The only way anyone could help me is to get rid of Lester."

About that time a customer came into the shop and Frank went back to his office, but he couldn't get that little outburst from Emily out of his mind. *'Get rid of Lester.' What did she mean by that?* he wondered.

That night, after picking up the boys, Emily came home and saw Lester and his buddies on the front porch. Not to do any repairs, she could tell, but to hang out with Lester and drink beer.

"Excuse me! Are you all drinking?"

Lester yelled at her, "Yeah, what's it to ya?" They all laughed. Lester continued, "We're talking about the repairs that are needed around here. Isn't that what you wanted?"

*Shattered*

Emily, steaming with anger, chose to ignore him, took the boys inside, and started the same old chores she did night after night.

Later, when Lester's buddies left, he came into the house. Emily realized he had way too much to drink and expressed her frustrations to him. "Lester, you know how I feel about drinking and how it has affected my life as a child. I know we need help with repairs around here, but this is not going to work if this is the way it's going to be. I will not have you turning into the drunk that my papa was and still is, as far as I know. I won't put up with it."

With slurred speech, Lester said, "Oh, what ya gonna do honey, run to your little gardener friend, Frankie?"

Emily turned toward him, stiffened, and screamed at the top of her lungs until her face turned red and she collapsed to the floor, sobbing.

Esther heard Emily's screams and went running to see what had happened. Upon entering, she saw Joey and Raymond crouched in the corner of the kitchen. She went to Emily to try to comfort her and gave her a handkerchief.

"Emily, sweetie, get up and tell me what's going on. Why are you so distraught?"

Before Emily could respond, Lester yelled, "Oh, she's just having one of her hissy fits about nothing," and rolled himself into the bedroom, slamming the door.

Esther could tell that it wasn't *about nothing*. "Here" —pulling out a kitchen chair— "sit down and talk to me."

Emily, embarrassed, said, "It's just the same old stuff with him. Now he's had his buddies come here *supposedly* to talk about repairs that are needed to the house, but it turned out to just be a social time of drinking. I refuse to have that going on in my house, especially in front of the boys."

Emily turned to the little fellows crouched in the corner, stretched out her arms, and motioned for them to come to her. She nestled them close and assured them she was alright, and everything was going to be okay.

"Do you want to come over to our house for a while until things calm down?" Esther asked Emily.

"No, it will be alright. I need to take care of things myself. I'm going to get something to eat for the boys and we all will be going to bed soon."

"Well, if you need me for anything, let me know, okay sweetie? I'm here for you." She kissed the boys and saw herself out.

The next morning, Emily dropped the boys off at Esther's and went on to work, late as usual. Immediately Frank knew something was seriously wrong. Still angry at Lester, Emily went to the counter, slammed her fist down, and said, "He's nothing but a stinking RAT! That's all I can say about Lester."

"Oh, well, you know how we take care of rats around here, don't you?"

Emily softened, looked up from the counter, and smiled at Frank. Even though he was joking, he immediately thought, *Oh my, I shouldn't have said that especially not knowing where her head is at after talking about getting rid of Lester.* "Just joking Emily," he quickly added, "and Lester is not a rat."

But before she left work that night, she went to the counter where the rat poison was shelved, took a bottle of it, and put it in her pocket. *Just in case I need it,* she thought.

Emily was becoming more and more angry and depressed every day. Frank knew he had to do something. It was hard for Frank to just fire Emily knowing what she was going through at home, but he knew he had to replace her. So, he decided to go ahead and hire a new girl and just start cutting back on Emily's hours.

Things didn't get better, only worse. Lester had his buddies bring beer to him and drinking became an everyday thing. He claimed he didn't have an appetite, so ate very little, but filled up on beer. He developed severe heartburn and would demand Emily, nearly every day, make him a glass of *salts* to relieve the burning in his stomach. It was a mixture of baking soda and Epson salts mixed with water. Whenever she told him to make it himself, he would scream at her, "That's what I got you for. It's your job to take care of me."

"Well then, who's supposed to take care of me?"

"You have your dear Frankie to look after you."

It made Emily so mad when he referred to Frank as Frankie, especially when he inferred that she and Frank were more than friends. *If he only knew how angry I am at Frank right now*, she thought.

The arguing continued, developing into real fights, especially on the days that Emily had off work, which were more than normal lately.

Embarrassed, she told the girls, "Frank seems to not need me as often, since things are slow."

However, Emily knew the real reason her hours were cut was because Frank had hired another girl to replace her, and he didn't need her anymore. This only added to her frustrations and anger.

Esther and Gloria couldn't stop talking about how afraid they were that she was going to have another breakdown. All the neighbors had begun to talk about what they were hearing night after night and what effect it was having on the children. Both Esther and Gloria, not knowing what else to do, stepped up and offered to keep the boys every day instead of only the days she worked.

"That will give you time to get your housework done without the boys under your feet," they told her.

Esther even offered to have the boys sleep over on the days Emily seemed too worn out. She feared for the little fellows. Sometimes, it looked like Emily never combed her hair, or changed her clothes and she barely spoke a word anymore. The boys would probably look the same if Esther didn't wash their clothes and see to it that they were bathed.

# Chapter 47

The house became a total disaster. Emily didn't have the energy, nor did she care, to keep up with the cleaning or laundry. She became so obsessed with Lester sitting around, getting drunk and not doing anything, that it drove her mad. In her deranged mind, she knew that it was time to use the rat poison. She couldn't take it anymore.

A few days later, on one of her days off work, while the boys were at Esther's, she decided that when he came into the kitchen asking for his *salts*, she was going to make a mixture of soda and the rat poison instead of the normal soda and Epson salts. "I'll fix him for good," she said, laughing to herself.

With a bit of a bounce in her step, she decided to fix him his favorite sandwich for lunch — grilled cheese with hot sauce. She knew he loved it but always had to have his *salts* after eating it. She would get rid of the 'rat' once and for all.

"Lester, come eat lunch," she called from the kitchen.

Lester rolled out to the table. "What did I do to deserve this," he asked.

*Oh, if you only knew how you deserve this,* she thought. "Well, I just wanted to do a good deed today, so I fixed you a special sandwich. Your favorite, right?"

"Yes, it is. Even a nice cold glass of milk. How thoughtful."

*Just sit down and eat already,* she thought.

She pulled a chair up across the table from Lester and watched him enjoy his favorite sandwich.

"It has a little kick to it, but that's the way I like it."

*Just keep eating.* He had eaten about half of the sandwich when he started feeling pains in his stomach. *Good, it's working.*

"Do you think some *salts* would help."

"Yes, I believe they would," he said. "As much as I love it, I just can't take that hot sauce anymore."

She got up from the table and moved to the kitchen. "Coming right up," she said. "I figured as much, so I already have it prepared for you."

Lester took the glass and gulped it down just like he always did. After taking a few more bites of his sandwich he realized something was wrong. Pain began to rack his body and he could barely breathe. The pains became so severe that he fell out of his wheelchair onto the floor.

Emily got up from the table and started yelling at him, "You rat! You got what you deserve."

She started laughing so hard she couldn't stop. Lester started screaming at the top of his lungs hoping the neighbors would hear him.

Between labored breaths, he yelled, "I've been poisoned! I've been poisoned! Please help me, she poisoned me!"

Neighbors came running to see what was going on this time. Harvey stayed with the boys while Esther and Gloria rushed along with other neighbors to Emily and Lester's house. They found Lester on the floor writhing in pain, and Emily standing over him, laughing like a banshee.

Gloria looked at Emily in shock and asked, "Did you really poison him?"

Emily shook her head yes, howling with laughter all the while. Esther grabbed Emily by the shoulders, shaking her and screaming loudly at her so she could hear over her ridiculous laughter, "Emily, what is wrong with you? What have you done?"

Some of the neighbors knelt over Lester and realized he was in real trouble. "Send for the doctor, and hurry."

Others looking at Emily said, "And call the police, this lady is crazy."

The police, along with Dr. Spriggs, were summoned. By the time both arrived, Lester lay silent on the floor in excrement from his body trying to rid him of the poison. Emily had calmed down but was acting very strangely. She had unbraided her long hair and was running her fingers through it, pulling it down over her face as if to hide. She paced back and forth and acted oblivious to anything going on around her.

Dr. Spriggs found no pulse and saw no reason to try to resuscitate him. He immediately summoned the coroner and gave him strict orders to have the body examined for poison.

The police, after questioning the neighbors about what had transpired and having assessed the situation, asked Emily to sit down. With that, she plopped herself on the floor.

Looking up at them through strands of hair, she screamed, "Who are you to tell me what to do?"

The doctor finally got Emily to come out of her stupor long enough to somewhat realize where she was and what was going on around her. Enough, at least, for her to answer some questions presented to her by the police detective. She admitted to poisoning her husband, all the while letting out screeching noises from time to time and contorting. She made no effort to escape or conceal her guilt.

Her actions, observed by the doctor and the detective, were discussed between them as to whether she should be taken to the hospital for observation before being taken to jail. She had calmed somewhat but still sat on the floor, legs crossed, arms folded in front of her, looking straight ahead in a daze. It was decided to take her to the hospital guarded by a policeman until released and taken to jail.

An arrest was made, and she was taken by police car to the local hospital.

The neighbors stood around, mostly in shock watching as the detective collected items of interest, one being a bottle with crossbones on it, and watched as Emily and Lester were removed from the premises.

The neighbors were questioned further and offered information about the yelling and arguments that they heard nearly every night coming from the house.

Gloria gave them more details about Emily and Lester. "They have been married about six years," Gloria explained. "Emily is in her early twenties, but Lester is much older, somewhere around mid-forties. They have two little boys." Pointing to Esther, she told him, "Esther and I have been watching the boys for Emily while she worked."

"Where are the children now?" the police inquired.

"They are at my house with my husband," Esther explained.

"Well, would you be able to continue watching them until we find an appropriate foster home for them?"

"Yes sir, of course."

Esther and Gloria looked at each other. It dawned on both of them, that they were going to have to figure out a way to tell the boys why they couldn't go home tonight and that their mama and papa had been taken away.

With the reports finished, the police left the scene. The neighbors talked amongst themselves. They were not surprised that the police were finally summoned concerning the arguments, but they were surprised that the situation had escalated to the point of someone being murdered. They all left, shaking their heads in disbelief except for Esther and Gloria. They stood hugging each other.

"Oh, Gloria, how did this happen? Why didn't we call Dr. Spriggs when we saw Emily acting so stressed and strange?"

"I don't think there was anything we could have done differently, Esther, that would have helped the situation. She probably wouldn't have listened to the doctor if we had called him. But now we must think about the boys. We need to gather a few days' worth of clothes for them until they are taken to their foster home."

"Esther, I don't know how I can watch them being taken away."

"I know, but as hard as it will be, it's the best thing for the boys. Let's just wait until tomorrow to tell them about anything. As far as they are concerned, they just need to think that they are having a sleepover with Harvey and me tonight. After they are put to bed and asleep, why don't you and Ed come over and let's talk about how we are going to handle this."

"That's a good idea. They're usually asleep by eight o'clock so we will come over around nine. I still can't believe what just happened. It seems so surreal."

"I know. I need to get home and let Harvey know what's going on, and I'll see you later tonight."

## Chapter 48

Emily was kept sedated and observed throughout the night. The next morning, she seemed to be of sound mind and was taken to the police station where she was interviewed.

She reiterated her admission of poisoning Lester but added, "My boss was the one who suggested that rat poison could get rid of a rat like Lester. He gave me the bottle of strychnine and told me to go kill my old man."

This piqued the interest of the officers interviewing her. "Who is your boss?"

"Frank Dublin from Dublin's Garden & Feed Store off Main Street," she was quick to tell them. She was then transported to jail.

Immediately, a policeman was dispatched to the garden shop to pick up Frank Dublin.

Frank saw the policeman arrive at the shop and came out of his office, curious as to why he was there. "Good morning, sir, how can I help you?"

"Are you Frank Dublin?"

"Yes, I am."

The policeman took the handcuffs from his belt and told Frank, "Turn around and put your hands behind your back. You are under arrest for the murder of Lester Granger."

"WHAT? Are you kidding me? What are you talking about? There is no way I would ever do a thing like that. Where is all of this coming from?" Frank questioned the police officer, confused.

"You can ask all your questions down at the station. Now get in the car."

At the station, Frank, totally in the dark about what was happening, asked numerous questions about how he was involved with something he knew nothing about.

"Well, we have someone who says differently," the policeman explained.

"Who? Tell me who would say such a lie?"

"You are being charged with accessory before the fact."

"What? There is no way," Frank argued.

Frank was taken to jail to await his arraignment but adamantly claimed his innocence of any participation in Lester's murder.

A few days after the arrests, Emily's and Frank's arraignments were scheduled. The court had decided to hold them together. As soon as Emily was brought into the courtroom and laid eyes on Frank, she started screaming and lunging at him out of the lingering anger she had toward him for hiring another girl to take her place. She yelled at him, "This is all your fault. Look what you have done. I hate you."

The bailiff restrained her, and the judge ordered her removed from the courtroom. He then ordered Emily to be sent to the asylum for evaluation to see if she was mentally fit for trial. Frank's trial was set for June, and he was able to bond himself out of jail.

News traveled fast. The news surrounding Lester's death, the arrest of Emily for allegedly poisoning her husband, and Frank for allegedly being an accomplice made the front page of the local newspaper. It was reported that Frank had given Emily rat poison and told her to go kill *the rat of a man* she was married to. The community was shocked and in disbelief.

Frank noticed the obvious decline in customers. People who normally stopped by just to talk were not coming in at all. It was apparent to Frank that even though he claimed his innocence, many in the town questioned it.

## Chapter

# 49

Esther and Gloria were disturbed by how all of this was affecting the boys. They were asking for their mother. It was hard, but they had to tell them that she had gone away for a while, and they would be staying with some nice people while she was gone.

"How about if we go to your house and collect some toys and clothes that you would like to take with you to your new home? What do you think about that, boys?" Esther asked them.

Not totally understanding everything that was being said to them or what was happening, the boys seemed to just do what they were told, so they nodded and headed for the door.

Esther helped them pick out some of their favorite toys and books and gathered some of their clothes. She saw Emily's Bible on the table next to the rocking chair and quickly crabbed it and added it to their things.

Only a few days had passed when a representative from the Placing-Out department, the agency in charge of foster care, showed up at Esther's door.

Mrs. Bryan introduced herself. "I've come to meet and get acquainted with the Granger children," she announced.

Esther thought she had prepared herself for this moment but quickly realized that she really wasn't prepared at all when a lump rose in her throat and an overwhelming sense of fear came upon her.

"Come in," she said softly. Realizing she needed Gloria for moral support, she said, "Mrs. Bryan, both my friend Gloria and I have been equally involved with the family and especially the children, so I would greatly appreciate you allowing my husband to fetch her to join us if you don't mind."

"Not at all. I'll just chat with the boys while we wait for her." To Esther's surprise, the boys warmed up to her right away and shared a toy with her that they were playing with.

After talking with both Esther and Gloria and collecting the needed information, Mrs. Bryan concluded that the boys seemed well-adjusted and well-taken care of. Getting up to leave, she explained, "I will file the paperwork and be back in a couple of days to collect the boys and take them to their new home. Thank you for cooperating with us during this process."

Turning to the boys she said, "It was so nice meeting you. Thank you for sharing your toy with me. I'll see you in a few days." Patting them on their heads, she looked at Esther and Gloria, and said, "What lovely lads."

The expression on her face resonated with the sadness of the situation that both Gloria and Esther felt.

*Chapter*

# 50

The weekly newspapers always contained updates on what was happening in the "Granger Murder Case". Esther and Gloria meticulously read and re-read every article, still in disbelief.

It was the first week of June when Frank's trial began. The judge ordered the state to call their first witness. When the attorneys said the name Emily Granger, the Judge, surprised, looked over his spectacles at them as if to say, "Are you kidding me?" He sat for a minute remembering the last time she was in court and then called for a recess. He wanted to look over the results of her evaluation. The reports were inconclusive, so he decided to have her brought to his chambers to question her himself to determine if she was fit to testify.

On the way to the judge's chambers, Emily was trying hard to control herself. *Keep it together. Keep it together. This is the only chance I'll have to get revenge on Frank. Act calm and collected so the judge will allow me to testify.*

When the judge questioned her, he found her to be a calm and rational young lady and fit to testify.

Court resumed, and Emily was brought to the stand. She testified that Frank gave her the poison several months prior to her using it and told her to get rid of her old man with it. She seemed indifferent as she told her story as calmly as if she were talking about the day's weather.

When she had finished, the judge asked the state for their next witness. They informed the judge that Emily was their only witness against him. They proceeded to closing arguments and then the jury was sent to deliberate.

*Shattered*

Frank was found guilty and the judge sentenced him to life on the chain gang.

A few days later Emily's trial started. She was brought before the judge and pled guilty. The judge, still not sure if Emily was sane or not, and believing that she had been influenced by Frank, decided to sentence her to fifteen years in the asylum.

Two weeks later, Emily, still in jail waiting to be transferred to the asylum, started thinking about what she had done to Frank. Her conscience started bothering her as she thought of him working every day on a chain gang. *I know he didn't have anything to do with me poisoning Lester. What made me say a thing like that? I was just angry, that's all. I didn't realize he would have such a harsh sentence.* She laid down on her cot, pulled the pillow over her face, and sobbed into it. Her mind wandered back to her childhood days when her mama taught her and her sisters right from wrong.

*Oh, Mama, what has become of me? I have drifted so far from what you taught me as a child, and now I'm suffering the consequences. I just can't live with myself knowing I'm the reason for Frank being inflicted with such a horrible sentence. I've made such a terrible mess of my life. I've been listening to the wrong voice. You told me that God's voice brings peace. I have no peace. Yes, I've definitely been listening to the wrong voice and now, I've lost everything — my boys, my husband, my family, my home, my friends, my freedom, and the person I used to be. I wonder, can I ever be redeemed?*

She cried herself to sleep. When she awoke, she knew what she had to do. She had to get word to the judge and recant her story. She reached out and was able to write a letter to him explaining how she had lied.

When Emily's letter reached the judge, he offered the information to Frank's attorney. Immediately, his attorney filed an appeal in court on his behalf. The appeal was granted, and because there was no one to accuse him of any wrongdoing, he was released.

## Chapter 51

Asylum life was different for Emily than her time spent in the county jail. Life was rigid and very tough in jail, but she felt safer there than in the asylum. At least the jail cells had see-through bars. Even though it didn't allow for any privacy, at least people could see what was always going on around them. But in the asylum, except for daytime activities, the women were pretty much isolated. The guards were unfeeling, sadistic, and drunk with power. They would often abuse the girls, simply because they could. The women were made to endure different treatments, often experimental, and take various drugs, which would often leave them feeling intoxicated, disoriented, and pliable.

At night, most of the women were able to sleep in a large dorm-style room. However, the women considered more dangerous, such as Emily, were locked down solitarily in tiny rooms with no windows and only a cot. They were often secured to the bed with restraints. The only people who had keys to the locked doors were the doctors and the guards who roamed the halls. The four walls seemed to close in on Emily and with sleep eluding her, she would lie on her cot frightened by the sounds she would hear.

Emily felt very isolated even during the daily routines. She knew she wasn't the only one who felt that way. Even though they had activities such as dance therapy and music therapy, the girls were not allowed to talk with each other for any length of time, or they would be quickly separated. They had perfected a secret language of looks and small gestures to communicate with each other, and it didn't take Emily long to learn it. They all lived in fear of saying or doing something that would cause them or someone else to be punished.

At night, she would hear footsteps coming down the hall, opening and closing doors. She heard muffled noises and didn't know exactly what was happening but knew it wasn't good. It was something that no one dared speak of. Every night that they didn't stop at her door, she would breathe a sigh of relief, and would pray that they never would.

She settled into the routine and made it through the first few years without suffering too much at the hands of the doctors and guards. She kept her head down and kept to herself. However, she still prayed every night as she heard the doors opening and closing, that they would pass her by, and felt lucky every time they did.

One night, her luck finally ran out. She heard the boots coming down the hall as usual, but this time, they stopped at her door. She held her breath and slid down into her blankets. The key went into the lock and the door slid open. That was the night she found out exactly what had been happening. She heard the boots coming close to her cot, and she squeezed her eyes shut tightly, pretending to be asleep. Covers were thrown off her and the guard quickly stuffed a rag in her mouth, put her wrists in the restraints that were attached to the bed, and proceeded to rape her. Trembling, she kept her eyes shut tight with tears rolling down the side of her face. When he finished, he removed the rag, released her hands, and left without as much as a word.

She lay shivering, too afraid to move, until she heard him leave the room. As soon as she heard the door close and the key turn in the lock, she quickly grabbed the covers and pulled them up all the way over her head, curled up into a fetal position, and cried. *Oh, God what have I done with my life? How did I sink so low as to get myself in such a place. Mama if only you hadn't died.* She felt as though her mama was there, with her arms around her, holding her tight. Remembering all the things her mama had taught her, she sobbed even harder and prayed to God for comfort.

The next day, Emily was in a daze. She spent as much time as she was allowed in the shower, trying to wash herself clean. She felt violated and dirty. As the days passed, she just went through the motions, not really paying attention to anything around her. Before long, she realized that she had missed her period and became worried that she might be pregnant. She didn't know who to tell. She was afraid of what might happen to her if anyone found out. So, she kept quiet and prayed that it wasn't true. After a few months, she couldn't deny it anymore. She was definitely pregnant. She had to tell the doctor. To her surprise, he didn't even ask how it had happened, and as the pregnancy progressed, she had regular checkups with him.

Emily thought about what was going to happen when the baby was born. Would they take the baby away from her right away? Would they let her keep it? If so, how would that work? At times, she wished that she could just stay pregnant, that way her baby would always be with her. The guards seemed to leave her alone while she was pregnant too, another reason she didn't want to give birth.

The day finally came, and the baby was born. It was a relatively easy birth compared to her other ones. They cleaned the baby up and put him in her arms. It was a little boy. Her heart swelled with joy and love. She held him tight, afraid that if she let go, they would take him from her and never give him back. As happy as she was in this moment, her heart also ached as the memories of the two precious boys she left behind flooded her thoughts. Oh, how she longed to be able to hold them in her arms again and introduce them to their baby brother.

The baby was given a number instead of a name – number 0076. Secretly, she gave him the name Moses because out of all the Bible stories her mama had told her, that one was her favorite. She prayed her little one would one day be rescued from this horrible place.

At least now, she had a baby that needed to be taken care of. It gave her a purpose, a reason to go on. She was able to move out of her tiny room and into the children's wing. She was surprised to find several more women there with infants. It dawned on her that these were the women and children that she had seen in the dining hall. The mothers of the children were responsible for taking care of their own babies and the other children who had been placed into the asylum for various reasons. She had more freedom here and was able to talk freely with the other women. She found that most of them were victims just as she had been.

The children's ward was different from what Emily was used to. She and the baby slept in a large room with the other mothers and their babies. There was another large sleeping room for the older children, and she expected that Moses would be placed there when he was older. There was a large playroom, which also doubled as a schoolroom for the older children. Off of that area was a small chapel where they were required to attend services. For meals, they shared the main dining hall with the adult women. Emily remembered seeing the group of children and women come in to eat but never really thought about where they came from. Parts of it scared her. She saw some children in chairs with restraints and others in straitjackets. She wondered what a child could have done to deserve such treatment and prayed that Moses would never have to endure such things.

Emily became friends with one woman in particular named Anna, who had a baby around the same age as Moses, and they spent a lot of time together.

"This is no place for children," Emily stated one day.

"No, it certainly is not," Anna agreed. "But you know, from time-to-time children are removed from the asylum. I'm not sure where they go. Some say they are adopted, but the mothers have no say in the matter. Also, several of the mothers seem to have just vanished after their child is taken."

"Oh my," Emily sighed, "As much as I would love my baby to be rescued from this horrible place, it would rip at my heart to let go of him."

# Chapter 52

Several years had passed since Emily and Moses had been assigned to the children's wing of the asylum. She had settled into a comfortable daily routine, making the time there bearable. The mothers who were capable would have classes for children of similar ages. They would teach them based on their age and ability to learn. Moses was almost seven now. He was a good reader and seemed very smart. Among the collection of books the children had was the Bible. When she could, Emily would have Moses read different stories from it, just like she had as a child. Of course, one of his favorite stories was about his namesake, the little baby boy named Moses. She wanted him to know about the Bible and the things her mama taught her as a child. She would spend as much time as possible telling him stories about herself growing up, and her family. He loved hearing those stories.

One day, a small group of men came into the children's wing. They walked all around the children sizing them up from head to toe. Emily had watched this scenario before and knew that one or more of the children were going to be taken. Her heart sank when they walked by Moses a second time, lingering while talking among themselves. As they slowly moved on through the children, Emily drew Moses close to her and in a low voice told him to listen to her very closely.

"Do you remember reading in the Bible about baby Moses?"

"Yes, of course, that's my favorite."

"Do you remember how he was taken away from his mother and was rescued from bad things happening to him and how God took care of him in a great way?"

"Yes."

"Well, the men who are here are looking for a child to rescue and take to a place where they can be taken care of in a great way. That child might be you, Moses."

"But I don't want to go away."

"Of course you don't, my child. But remember the rest of the story? How it was best that Moses was rescued because he grew to be a great man and God took care of him?"

Emily was trying her best to prepare him for the possibility that he might be taken because she truly sensed in her heart that the men were considering him.

She continued, "If they decide to 'rescue' you, you must be brave and know it will be for your own good. Do you think you can do that Moses?"

Moses was silent for a moment and then looked at her and said, "Will God really take care of me like he did the other Moses?"

"Oh, I know he will."

The men started walking back towards Emily and Moses. She gripped his hand a little tighter and waiting for them to approach, whispered to him, "Remember Moses, be brave, and don't ever forget, I love you and always will."

One of the men came close. He stooped down, totally ignoring Emily, looked at Moses, and said, "How would you like to come with me?"

Without waiting for a reply, he took Moses by the hand and started to walk away with him. Moses looked back at his mother longingly and held onto her hand until his little hand slipped out of hers. She watched him until he was out of sight and then turned and ran to a bench in the yard. Curling herself nearly into a ball, she wept. The other mothers came to comfort her, but she was inconsolable until she finally realized that she was going to have to be brave just as she instructed Moses to be. *There is nothing I can do about the situation now but pray*, she thought. However, Emily realized she hadn't made prayer a priority since she left home and had gotten married. *Maybe if I had kept praying and reading my Bible like Mama taught me to do, things would be different.*

It was just a few days after Moses was taken from her that another little boy showed up in the children's wing, about the same age as

Moses. He was a very wild little fellow and would not listen to what anyone told him. He would hit and kick the women who would try to take care of him and was totally unruly. It took several weeks of working with him and talking with him before he calmed down, at least to the point of being manageable some of the time.

Emily learned later that he came from the local orphanage. The teachers there could not handle him, classifying him as crazy and unteachable. Arrangements had been made between the orphanage and the asylum. The asylum agreed to take the "crazy" little boy from the orphanage, in exchange, they would take one of the children from the asylum. She at least knew where Moses was, which made her somewhat relieved.

Emily was very good with the children, especially the unruly ones, so she was kept in the Children's wing to help. She missed Moses tremendously and longed to know how he was doing. She channeled her love for Moses into the other children and it showed. They responded to her in a way they didn't to anyone else.

Time went by more slowly now, but she was as happy as she could be under the circumstances. Before she knew it, three years had passed since Moses had been taken away.

*He's about ten now,* she thought to herself. *I've only got two more years here, then I get out of this miserable place and can go to him. There's finally a light at the end of the tunnel.*

She was biding her time and trying to make the best of the situation. She and the other women had become close over the years. They would share with each other the circumstances that brought them to the asylum, and to the children's ward. They came to the realization, that each of them who had been assaulted and had children as a result, were women who had no one who cared about them, and for one reason or another, never had visitors or anyone who inquired about them. They knew it wasn't a coincidence. It was done on purpose so no one would find out about what was going on in there.

*I'm getting out of here in just a few years and I guarantee you that I will make sure that people know about what is happening here,* she thought to herself.

# Chapter

# 53

The last two years seemed to drag on, but Emily held on and made it through. She only had three months left until her release date, so she was surprised when she was informed that she wasn't needed in the children's wing anymore. She was taken back to the general ward and was assigned to a tiny room again. She hated it because it brought back memories that she had tried to forget. *I only have three more months. I can do this,* she convinced herself.

The first night she was back, the guards brought her some Jello before she went to bed. They told her that this was the new procedure and that she had to eat it all. She settled into the new routine and reminded herself every night that it was only for three more months. She kept to herself and tried to stay out of trouble. It wasn't long before she started feeling ill. She thought it was something that would go away after a few days, but it only worsened. She became very weak and lethargic but couldn't understand why. She asked to see the doctor, but the guards ignored her. When she could no longer go to the cafeteria to eat, they assigned an inmate to watch over her and bring her food. It wasn't unusual for inmates to act as caretakers for others. These inmates, however, were very carefully selected. They too were the ones that didn't have outside visitors for one reason or another. There were those who, like Emily, had lost contact with family, or those who were left there, abandoned by their family, and unable to take care of themselves outside of the institution.

In addition to the food her caretaker would bring from the cafeteria, a guard would still bring Jello to her room before bed. He would wait and watch her until she had eaten it all. She continued to get worse day by day. An inmate named Hannah, who was young and new to the asylum, was assigned to her room and ordered to take complete care of her, replacing the other caretaker. Hannah acted as her nurse, taking care of her every need, including hygiene and bathroom needs. In a short time, the two became very close.

Emily requested again and again to see a doctor, but one never came and no medicine was administered. She was eventually only allowed water and the Jello that the guards would bring.

Emily and Hannah both realized something wasn't right. Emily knew by now that she was never going to get out of the asylum alive, even though she only had a couple of months left until her release date. Her hopes of going to the orphanage to see Moses were dashed. She had longed for the day when she would be free and could tell her story and expose the atrocities that she experienced and knew were taking place there.

The only thing Emily knew to do was to relay what she knew was going on in this horrible place to Hannah and hope that she could do something about it.

"Please pull a chair up close. I have something I need to tell you." Emily said in a weak voice.

Hannah did as she asked and leaned in to hear what she had to say.

"Listen carefully to me," Emily told her. "I was placed in here for fifteen years for poisoning my husband, Lester Granger. I had two little boys named Joey and Raymond who were taken away from me when I was arrested. I have no idea where they are. I assume that they went into foster care. They would be about eighteen and nineteen now. One night not too long after I came here, a guard came into my room in the middle of the night and raped me. I had a little boy as a result and they assigned him a number – 0076, but I called him Moses. We were sent to the children's wing where I cared for him and other children. He was with me until he was almost seven years old, then they came and took him to a local orphanage. I don't know which one, but he would be about twelve now. In the children's wing, I found other women taking care of their babies who had the same thing happen to them. I know I'll never get out of here to tell my story. I'll be one of those women who just come up missing. You and I both know that I am being poisoned. I'm

*Shattered*

begging you, when you get out of here, please expose the operation of this asylum. Tell people about the inmates who have no family and no visitors disappearing, and about the rapes. Also, could you please try to find all three of my children and tell them that I'm sorry for what I did to them? I am sorry that I shattered all of our lives. Tell them I went to my grave loving them with all my heart. Please, I'm begging you."

Hannah was shocked at what she had heard. "I promise Emily I will do everything in my power to do what you have requested."

Emily thanked her and turned over, realizing she had some unfinished business to take care of with God. She knew her time was short, so she closed her eyes and prayed. When she had finished, she let out a huge sigh of relief and was gone.

Hannah, sitting by the bedside, noticed the expression on Emily's face slowly soften and become peaceful. Leaning in closer, she realized Emily had passed. Before informing the guard of Emily's passing, Hannah took her hand, held it tenderly, bent down to her ear and whispered, "I'll never forget my promise to you, my sweet Emily."

Upon notifying the guard, she immediately started planning a way to fulfill her promise.

---

*A week later, Emily's obituary appeared in the local newspaper. It read:*
*Emily Granger of Clinton, New York passed away Monday, July 25, 1932, while an inmate in the local state asylum; Cause of death: Cervical Cancer.*

## THE END

## *Author's Notes*

Thank you for reading my book. I hope you enjoyed it. If you did, I would appreciate it if you would leave a review.

Although this story is a work of fiction, the idea was born out of some of the details from my mother's life and my husband's grandmother's life. In the first part of the book, Emily depicts my mother, who lost her mother at a young age. Her father became involved with a girl who was close to her own age, which was very disturbing to my mother and resulted in her marrying young to remove herself from the situation.

The second part of the book beginning with Emily moving to New York, depicts my husband's grandmother. She was found guilty of murdering her husband and was sent to an asylum. I used newspaper articles written about the murder trial to help fill in some details. She did become pregnant while she was incarcerated, but the circumstances of how it happened are unknown. My husband's father was the little boy who was born in the asylum and moved to an orphanage at the age of seven.

If you enjoyed my book, be on the lookout for my future books, continuing the story.

Printed in the USA
CPSIA information can be obtained
at www.ICGtesting.com
CBHW021538300624
10899CB00012B/166